## *"Allie, stop. I don't want your pity."*

"Tough!" she yelled. "I feel sorry for you. There's no great sin in that. What kind of person would I be if I didn't ache for you and all you've lost?"

Jake pivoted to face her. He was a heartless bastard, and he knew it. Time for her to find out, as well. He had to do something to wipe away the expectations in her eyes. Given the least encouragement or any more of his maudlin revelations, she would box him up to take home like a pathetic pound foundling.

"What do you want from me?"

Her tilted chin brought her lips a whisper away from his. "I want you to stop confusing me. Let me in or slam the door shut."

Wavering forward, she pressed her lips to his. A surge of desire flooded him, an impulsive rage against the thought of losing anything more. Everything he'd suppressed since meeting Allison St. James slammed through him with a body-tightening ache.

"Jake," she whispered, her breath caressing his cheek, "if I'm the one we have to count on for self-control, we're in big trouble."

Jake gave up the fight. "Then we're in trouble."

Dear Reader,

The warm weather is upon us, and things are heating up to match here at Silhouette Intimate Moments. Candace Camp returns to A LITTLE TOWN IN TEXAS with *Smooth-Talking Texan*, featuring another of her fabulous Western heroes. Town sheriff Quinn Sutton is one irresistible guy—as attorney Lisa Mendoza is about to learn.

We're now halfway through ROMANCING THE CROWN, our suspenseful royal continuity. In Valerie Parv's *Royal Spy*, a courtship of convenience quickly becomes the real thing— but is either the commoner or the princess what they seem? Marie Ferrarella begins THE BACHELORS OF BLAIR MEMORIAL with *In Graywolf's Hands*, featuring a Native American doctor and the FBI agent who ends up falling for him. Linda Winstead Jones is back with *In Bed With Boone,* a thrillingly romantic kidnapping story—of course with a happy ending. Then go *Beneath the Silk* with author Wendy Rosnau, whose newest is sensuous and suspenseful, and completely enthralling. Finally, welcome brand-new author Catherine Mann. *Wedding at White Sands* is her first book, but we've already got more—including an exciting trilogy—lined up from this talented newcomer.

Enjoy all six of this month's offerings, then come back next month for even more excitement as Intimate Moments continues to present some of the best romance reading you'll find anywhere.

Leslie J. Wainger
Executive Senior Editor

Please address questions and book requests to:
Silhouette Reader Service
U.S.: 3010 Walden Ave., P.O. Box 1325, Buffalo, NY 14269
Canadian: P.O. Box 609, Fort Erie, Ont. L2A 5X3

# Wedding at White Sands
## CATHERINE MANN

*To Ann,*

*Happy Reading*

*Catherine Mann*

**Silhouette**®

I N T I M A T E   M O M E N T S™

Published by Silhouette Books

**America's Publisher of Contemporary Romance**

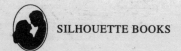 SILHOUETTE BOOKS

ISBN 0-373-27228-6

WEDDING AT WHITE SANDS

Copyright © 2002 by Catherine Mann

All rights reserved. Except for use in any review, the reproduction
or utilization of this work in whole or in part in any form by any
electronic, mechanical or other means, now known or hereafter
invented, including xerography, photocopying and recording, or in
any information storage or retrieval system, is forbidden without
the written permission of the editorial office, Silhouette Books,
300 East 42nd Street, New York, NY 10017 U.S.A.

All characters in this book have no existence outside the imagination of
the author and have no relation whatsoever to anyone bearing the same
name or names. They are not even distantly inspired by any individual
known or unknown to the author, and all incidents are pure invention.

This edition published by arrangement with Harlequin Books S.A.

® and TM are trademarks of Harlequin Books S.A., used under license.
Trademarks indicated with ® are registered in the United States Patent
and Trademark Office, the Canadian Trade Marks Office and in other
countries.

Visit Silhouette at www.eHarlequin.com

**Printed in U.S.A.**

**CATHERINE MANN**

began her romance-writing career at twelve and recently uncovered that first effort while cleaning out her grandmother's garage. After working for a small-town newspaper, teaching at the university level and serving as a theater school director, she has returned to her original dream of writing romance. Now an award-winning author, Catherine is especially pleased to add a nomination for the prestigious Maggie to her contest credits. Following her air-force-aviator husband around the United States with four children and a beagle in tow gives Catherine a wealth of experience from which to draw her plots.

To Rob, my own hero and inspiration.
Thanks for your love and unwavering faith in me.

And to our four wonderful children. Thanks for learning
to work the microwave while Mom's writing.

# Chapter 1

"How much do you cost?"

"Pardon me?" Allie St. James, Private Investigator, glanced from the open file to the scruffy male silhouetted in her office doorway.

Great. Another client who couldn't pay. More than her services, he looked like he needed an ice pack and a new pair of jeans. He also lacked a few front teeth, but then what elementary school kid didn't?

"What am I gonna have to pay you?" The gap-toothed boy shuffled into her cluttered workspace, the glass door smacking him on the bottom as it closed.

"Well, that depends." Her boardwalk mall agency attracted an odd assortment of wander-in clientele, but this one took the prize. For safety's sake, she would play it through, discover who his parents were, then chew them out for allowing their son to roam the streets of Fort Walton Beach unsupervised.

Allie tossed aside the file, just missing the lopsided pile

of unfinished billing. Palms flat against the edge of her desk, she pushed to her feet. "I'll need some information first, like your name."

"Oh, uhm." He inched further inside, his tennis shoes squeaking against cracked tiles. "Robbie. Uhm, I mean Robert. Robert Larson."

"Hello, Robert. I'm Allie St. James."

He chewed his bottom lip indecisively while tracing the grouting with his toe. Rush hour traffic honked and roared past as she sized up her prospective client. He must be around seven or eight, like her youngest nephew. Robbie's white blond hair shone, the chili-bowl style cut glistening with health. New Air Jordans. GameBoy sticking out of his backpack.

The little guy came from money in spite of the busted knee on his jeans. Possibly a neglected rich kid? Plenty of parents substituted toys for attention. She could identify with that. After all, she'd lived it with her own father. Her old man may have been prompt with his child support payments, but his time had been in short supply.

The boy looked ready to bolt out the door. She had to get him talking, fast. Allie snagged a note pad from her middle drawer. "Why do you need to hire me, Robbie, uh, Robert?"

Prepared for his pitiful saga of a missing Spot, she perched a hip on the corner of her gunmetal gray desk. Maybe a playground bully had stolen his book-order money. That would explain the black eye and torn jeans. Her foot swung a lazy dance above the overflowing trash can while she waited.

"Somebody's trying to kill my dad."

Her tennis shoe stopped midswing. Now that wasn't what she'd expected.

Robbie scrunched his forehead, then pivoted away. "Never mind."

"Hang on a second!" Allie sprinted forward. Who knew what would happen to the kid on his way home? She wasn't going to risk seeing his face on the six o'clock news. "Not so fast, cowboy."

He stared back over his shoulder, cobalt-blue eyes warily hopeful. "Yeah?"

While almost certainly exaggerating, he must have some reason for his assumption. Curiosity could be an asset for a P.I., and a real pain in the butt. Paperwork would have to wait another hour, no great sacrifice since she despised mundane tasks. "Let's hear your story. Come on. Park yourself for a minute."

Worry wrinkles smoothed from his brow. "Okay. Thanks."

Allie hauled two metal-frame chairs to face each other. She flattened the split vinyl over protruding puffs of stuffing and gestured for Robbie to sit.

Given her packed client roster, she should have been able to afford better furniture. She'd developed quite a reputation for tracking deadbeat dads, a personal crusade she embraced with a passion. Too often, once the mother received child-support payments for her overstretched budget, Allie couldn't bring herself to charge more than a nominal fee, enough to cover her phone and light bills.

Who needed heat anyway? She lived in north Florida, not North Dakota. Her air conditioner had long ago died a dramatic, spluttering death, but a perfectly good fan whirred an ocean breeze through the open window.

Allie ruffled Robbie's corn-silk hair as he flopped into the chair. Good heavens, the kid was cute. "Would you like something to drink? A Coke maybe?"

"Sure."

"How did you find out about me?" She reached into her compact refrigerator on the filing cabinet. For a blessed minute, she let frosty air refresh her heat-flushed face.

"My friend, Shelley Phillips, told me. She used to live next door, before her folks split. You worked for her mom, and they said you didn't cost a whole bunch."

Allie winced. Her stepbrothers vowed her impulsive generosity would land her in bankruptcy court. They were probably right. "Well—"

"Maybe I could help you clean up around here." Robbie leaned forward. "I don't wanna hurt your feelings or nothing, but it doesn't look like you can pay a maid."

Super. Even the kid had better financial sense than she did.

"We can discuss my fee later, if I decide to take your case." She huffed a curl off her forehead, closing the refrigerator door on the only cooling relief in the muggy room. Allie turned to Robbie and pressed the chilled can to the purplish green bruise staining his cheekbone. "What happened here, cowboy?"

"Nothing much." He flinched away from the makeshift, aluminum ice pack.

She popped the top on his drink and passed it to him. "If I'm going to work for you, you have got to be straight with me."

Robbie tossed his knobby shoulders back. "Jerk at school called my dad a name. So, I punched him, hard. He punched me back, kinda hard." His bottom lip quivered as he rested the can on his knee. "No big deal."

Did the kid have to tug her every heartstring? Already, Allie envisioned typing the file header with Robbie Larson's name on it. At least her trash cans would get emptied.

"That's really brave, sticking up for your dad." She

paused, feeling compelled to add, "Uh, but you shouldn't fight."

Robbie shrugged. Allie winked. She'd given a decent stab at saying the responsible thing. "Tell me about your parents."

"I only have a dad. My mom's dead."

"Oh, Robbie, I'm sorry." If he plucked any more heartstrings, he could apply for the harpist's position in the local symphony.

Robbie slurped his Coke. "It was a really long time ago, when I was little."

Like he was Methuselah now?

Yet in spite of his age, there seemed to be a mature air to him that defied years. Could his concerns, even his defense of his father against playground thugs, stem from a fear of losing his only remaining parent? She'd gotten lucky, ending up with the perfect family after her father had left. All the same, Allie felt a connection with the abandoned wives and children she helped. "That's pretty tough, Robert. You and your dad are close?"

"Sure we are, but he's been really busy lately. He's got a lot to do, running his business and stuff."

Strike two against Mr. Larson. He'd already racked up one on a foul ball for not keeping track of his son. "Who is he? Maybe I've heard of him."

"Jake Larson. He's an entrep—uh, invest—uh. He makes money."

Strike three. She lived to make guys like that squirm.

Allie wrote his name, underlining it with a vengeful slash. "Why do you think someone wants to hurt your dad?"

"We've gotten lots of funny phone calls from mean-sounding people. Dad makes me leave the room." Robbie sipped the excess Coke from around the rim of the can, his hand trembling. "Then there's this really creepy guy who keeps coming by, and he's got a gun under his coat."

"Hmmm." She stared at Robbie's fist as he clutched the drink, his knuckles bruised, fingernails grimy. Secret phone calls and a "creepy guy" didn't offer much evidence. All the same, how much trouble would it be to check out the boy's story while talking to Mr. Larson about his son's wandering ways?

A restless curl twisted free from her banana clip. Even her hair couldn't honor practical restraints. She'd given up trying to contain her natural waves and impulsive temperament. Some people were born to think. Some were born to act.

Allie thrust her hand forward for a shake. "Okay, Robert. You've officially hired a first-rate detective with a really messy office."

The signature gap-toothed grin crinkled Robbie's face, a smile more valuable than any retainer fee.

The next day, Allie pushed in through the back entrance to the small, but luxurious, building housing Larson Investments. There had to be a shorter route to Jake Larson's office, but the parking spaces out front were full. She never rushed anyway. The indirect path usually provided more details, not to mention excitement.

"Not bad." The place smelled rich, felt rich. Plush, green carpet cushioned her feet, like walking on a stack of money. No real surprise. Fort Walton Beach wasn't a large community, so she'd heard of Larson's clout, even though they didn't run with the same crowd. Further digging had indicated the business to be a successful, privately owned overseas investment company.

She would take her mom's old kitchen and her stepdad's

police station cubicle over a place full of triple-matted artwork.

Hitching her backpack onto her shoulder, Allie followed the echo of clanging metal down the deserted hall. Her feet adopted the melodic rhythm until her voice followed suit.

"La-da-da, cha-cha-cha." She broke into an impromptu serenade in her off-key tones she loosely labeled as alto. Her collection of slogan buttons pinned to her backpack rattled in time with each step.

The clanking from down the corridor increased as she rounded a corner. Slim windows at the end of the hall looked in on a weight room.

"Cha-cha-cha…" Her voice dwindling to a hum, Allie glanced around the workout area. The athlete within her inhaled the familiar smell of sweat and exertion. She'd haunted more than a few gyms, attempting to gain acceptance from her new family after her mother had remarried. Allie had kept pace, except when it counted most. Her stepfather and stepbrothers were police officers.

Her dream, an abandoned goal.

She'd passed academy entrance exams and physicals with ease, but her free-spirited nature balked at thoughts of rigid departmental structure. Surely her investigations business provided a good compromise, didn't it?

Allie shrugged off depressing regrets, a waste of energy. What she lacked in self-control, she made up for with ingenuity. If she planned to meet her rent, she needed to close the case with Robbie Larson and move forward with paying clients.

Meanwhile, she needed directions. The place wasn't exactly hopping with activity. A single clank sounded from the back corner, followed by a muffled conversation as workout partners exchanged lifting and spotting.

Allie twined around the free weights and Nautilus, stopping a few feet shy of a bench press in action.

*Oh, my!* She had seen more than her fair share of bare chests with a houseful of brothers and their friends. But never had she seen a pair of pecs like the muscles rippling across the guy working two hundred pounds. She would bet good money he didn't need the spotter standing in wait.

She'd never had much use for pretty boys, but this fellow was potent eye candy. Thick hair, no doubt coarse to the touch, clung to his scalp with perspiration. Sun-highlighted streaks of blond shone through. While not as long as she preferred, his hair still begged her fingers for a threading touch.

Eyes closed, he displayed no signs of strain or fatigue, just efficient movement. His square jaw seemed more pronounced with his intense concentration. No metal music blared like in other gyms she'd frequented, just the soft whoosh of his breath as he exhaled the count of his reps.

A simmering awareness burned along her skin as she glanced down the considerable length of his body. His gray shorts and gym shoes covered as much as any beachwear. Still the elemental force of his strength seemed raw, intimate.

Somewhere around his mid-thirties, the guy was in prime condition. His tanned, washboard stomach glistened with the sheen of sweat. Taut skin stretched over solid muscle delineating every sinew, chest and arms defined, but not overly so like some steroid junkie.

Allie needed directions, and she'd just found her tour guide. Maybe she could wrangle some information about Larson from the mindless jock. Of course, the weight-lifting hunk had to be a moron. Right? Otherwise there was no justice in the world.

*Please, Lord, let him be dumb as a rock.*

Not that she would spend time with some shallow stud muffin. Her brothers would have a field day teasing her, if they lifted their vigilance long enough for a man to land within ten feet of her.

The spotter bent to tie his shoe, and Allie started to call a warning. Didn't he know it was dangerous to leave a partner with no backup?

Slowly, she closed her mouth. What a perfect in with someone at Larson's corporation since she hadn't bothered to make an appointment with Robbie's dad. Or was she just making up excuses to get closer to the guy pumping iron? Either way, Allie shrugged her backpack into place and sidled between the man tying his Adidas and her weight-lifter tour guide.

"Two. Three. Four." Jake Larson breathed through his second set of reps. Eyes closed, he focused, routine over-riding pain. "Five. Six. Seven."

He enjoyed these quiet moments free of distracting emotions, like the old days when he'd been an Air Force officer, Special Investigator…and whole.

"Eight. Nine. Ten." He flexed his ankle, almost managing to ignore the familiar ache that stabbed up his calf, and began another set without hesitation. "One. Two."

His nose itched. Jake fought the urge to scratch. The annoying tickle persisted.

*Ignore it.* "Three. Four."

Wafting down, he smelled—roses? He would have to talk to Tom about switching deodorants.

"Five. Six."

A tingle crept through his sinuses until his eyes burned worse than the muscles in his arms. His concentration was shot to hell. He had to sneeze.

"Damn. Here, Tom." Jake reached for his business partner. Instead, he found a woman's face framed by dark, spiraling curls.

His arms threatened to buckle. The sneeze gathered force like a tidal wave ready to roll free. Two hundred pounds of metal could soon come screaming down on his chest. All that stood between him and crushing pain was a hundred and twenty pound female spotter with ten pounds of hair.

She grinned, her face faintly visible through the cinnamon brown curtain. "Hi! Need some help?"

Her husky tones did nothing to improve his concentration.

"Tom!" Jake locked his elbows and sniffed through the itch.

"Let me have that." Ms. Hair grasped beside his clenched hands and with surprising strength helped lower the weights to the rack. Only a scant second to spare, he slid his head from beneath the bar.

*"Achoo!"* Jake shot up, the force of his sneeze doubling him over. He pressed the heel of his hand to his nose and blinked fast, clearing his vision.

His substitute spotter tunneled through her backpack, shoulder-length masses of hair shielding her expression. Tom stood to the side with a bemused gawk plastered across his face, never having been one for self-control when it came to women. Tom's ogling had nearly cost Jake a couple of broken ribs.

Jake scowled. Tom shrugged and beat a hasty retreat to the showers.

"Thanks, pal," Jake grumbled.

A second look at the woman convinced him that perhaps he would forgive Tom's lapse in attention. Not more than five feet and a couple of inches tall, Ms. Hair had a compact body that could stop a train. Faded jeans cupped trim hips, sliding over a curvaceous bottom. If she climbed any further into her backpack, the vee of her purple T-shirt would gap open, unveiling more than he was comfortable viewing while wearing nothing but a pair of shorts.

She straightened and thrust the wadded Kleenex toward him. "Bless you."

Her gaze slammed into his with a power that could rival the press of weights against his chest. Violet eyes sparkled with light and energy. She shuffled from foot to foot, curls dancing around her face.

The woman was pure motion. Jake preferred peace.

"Here." She waggled the tissue.

"No thanks." He shook his head. "Do you need help with something?"

"Oh, yeah. I'm trying to find one of the offices, and I took a wrong turn a couple of corners ago." Allie stuffed the tissue into her backpack. "It's not completely my fault, though. There really aren't enough parking spaces out front. The signs aren't at all clear when you come in the other way. Anyone could get lost traveling that maze."

Did she ever come up for air?

No question, the woman was hot. But he recognized a hurricane when one hit.

Jake pulled in calming breaths. He didn't like the rush of awareness he couldn't quite control. He prided himself on his discipline, an essential trait for rebuilding his life after the car accident that had stolen his wife and his career as an Air Force investigator.

Swiping the back of his wrist over his forehead, he willed away thoughts about things he couldn't change. "And?"

She hooked the sack over her arm. "I need to get moving because I have to be across town in an hour so I can snap some pictures of two-timing Harold—"

"Excuse me?" Jake paused midswipe. "Two-timing Howard?"

"Harold. That's my job." She scrambled through her bag again, coming up with a business card. "I'm Allie, Allison St. James, Private Investigator."

"Private Investigator?" The sweat chilled on his skin. What the hell was going on? "Which office are you looking for, Ms. St. James?"

"Call me Allie."

"All right, Allie. Which office?"

The clench of his stomach predicted her answer.

"Jake Larson."

"Larson's." He stalled, scratching his shoulder. A long exhale cleared his fogged senses. Old professional instincts kicked into overdrive. "And you're searching for more two-timing Harveys?"

"Harold. But no." Leaning forward, she placed the card beside him on the bench. Her attention lingered on his chest for a second beyond polite, then skittered away as she straightened. "Can't tell you about Larson, though. Client confidentiality and all that."

"Of course, uh, Ms. St. James." He tapped her card and made a mental note to call his contact with the state police.

Could she be a plant from White Sands Resort? If so, they should have used a more subtle approach.

Could be coincidence. But he didn't think so. The timing was too odd for that, her stopping in shortly after he'd been recruited to help the state police.

The whole White Sands sting lured him. He hungered for the opportunity to recapture his lost past as an investigator, not that his current role came close to the intricate operations he'd handled then. He told himself to be grateful for his understated part. His days with the Air Force Office of Special Investigations, OSI, were over. He couldn't afford to risk his life. Robbie had already lost his mother.

Jake didn't allow himself to think of what he'd lost.

He could never repay his parents for their sacrifices in helping with his recovery and caring for Robbie after the accident. But, bringing down the crooked owner of White Sands Resort who'd tried to scam his folks would make a good start.

Allie perched a hand on her hip, her eyes sparkling like sunlight glinting on a pool. "So, can you help me?"

"Huh?" With more effort than he liked to acknowledge, Jake reined in his libido. He attributed the power of his reaction to his near monkish existence since Lydia had died.

*Lydia.* His jaw clenched, teeth pressed tight. With practiced precision, he slammed the door on the memories and his needs. "Help you what?"

"With directions," she said slowly, as if to a child. "I need directions to Larson Investments."

"Oh." He frowned at her condescension and considered introducing himself, then decided against it. Patience being his forte, he opted to finish their meeting in the office, his turf, where he could control the situation. And where he would be wearing a suit instead of workout shorts. "Out that door, two lefts, and you'll run into the elevator. Second floor, you can't miss the sign."

"Thanks." She hitched the backpack over her shoulder, pins clanking into place. "I hope I won't have to fight for an appointment."

The sooner he checked out Private Investigator St. James's agenda, the better. "Oh, I'm sure he'll have time for you."

## Chapter 2

Waiting in Jake Larson's office, Allie sighed a mental farewell to the blond weight lifter. "Think about the kid and his father instead."

She rubbed her hands along her bare arms, but couldn't quite manage to banish the goose bumps, goose bumps that were surely just a by-product of the place's near sub-Arctic temperature. The air in Larson's building swirled far cooler than any chill from her defunct air conditioner.

Allie meandered around the room, tapping books along the shelves, eyeing a row of non-alcoholic drinks lining the wet bar shelves. "Mineral water. Orange juice. Not a Coke in sight."

What was keeping Larson?

The day before, she had walked Robbie home rather than offering a ride, since she didn't want to encourage climbing into cars with strangers. Their mile stroll had provided ample time to interview her pint-sized client.

Someone had done a good job with the boy. As the only

sister in a house full of stepbrothers, Allie understood men. The little guy was top-notch. Would he stay that way without an active father figure?

Robbie's house had confirmed her assumption. Rich kid. The sprawling two-story, brown stucco had screamed upper middle class. It had even sported a three-car garage and a pool.

She'd waited at the end of the drive while Robbie had sprinted up the path to meet an elderly lady at the front door. Grandparent? Sitter?

Allie had faded into the background, planning to confront the father later, when Robbie wasn't around. Jake Larson had a lot to answer for, and she intended to manage the accounting. If only she could meet the man.

Her thoughts wandered back to a pair of outstanding pecs. The poor guy in the weight room had barely been able to string three words together. She'd soon realized he couldn't offer much in the way of reliable information. She would be better off cutting her losses and finding Larson herself. Conning her way past the secretary hadn't even been a challenge.

An overpowering mahogany desk beckoned with the promise of secrets about creepy men with guns. How much longer until Larson returned from lunch? She wouldn't be so unscrupulous as to check his filing cabinet, just a glimpse or two at any common domain.

Allie strolled past the wall packed with diplomas, each frame complimented by no less than three mats, and stopped beside the desk.

What a neat freak, not even a Cross pen out of place.

"Wait a second." Her gaze settled on airline tickets dated for the following morning, with a return flight five days later. His itinerary listed a rental car. "Miami? Then driving where?"

Craning her neck, she checked his humming computer. The screen saver scrolled the company logo. A bump of her hip against the desk nudged the mouse, reactivating a monitor crammed full of information just waiting for her to speed read. "Hmmm. The Keys."

"Find what you're looking for?" a familiar masculine voice inquired.

Allie would've swallowed her gum, if she'd been chewing any. The blond hunk lounged against the door frame, arms crossed over his magnificent chest. A double-breasted gray suit stretched across his shoulders. His freshly washed hair was brushed straight back, revealing a scowling brow. He pinned her with a boardroom stare, his amber eyes darkening to almost black with intensity.

He unfolded his arms, extending a strong, broad hand. "Jake Larson."

"Uh-oh." She masked her surprise with a grin. "I expected someone older."

He quirked a golden brow and stayed silent.

Apparently blond hunk had an I.Q., but no sense of humor. Bravado in place, she charged forward and clasped his hand. "Allison St. James, Private Investigator."

Her hand disappeared in his, his warm grasp closing around her with a searing heat that burned the moisture from her mouth.

"So you told me earlier."

Allie pulled free, the air whispering chills over her skin after his touch. "Sorry about the mix-up downstairs, but you should have introduced yourself."

"You didn't give me much of a chance." His eyes narrowed with his half smile.

Perfect teeth. Perfect body. Perfectly wrong for her.

He pushed away from the door frame, towering over her

by a full foot. "Do you always snoop through personal files?"

She bristled, spurred by frustration at being attracted to someone so totally unsuitable. "If you didn't want something seen, you shouldn't have left it out. I didn't look at anything that wasn't in plain sight."

"Thanks for explaining the finer points of investigative work, but my clients expect privacy." He glanced at his watch. "Ms. St. James, on second thought, you're going to need to make an appointment. Check with my secretary."

He brushed past Allie to turn off his computer without sparing a glance in her direction. Allie's retort stuck in her throat.

Not a perfect body, after all. He had a limp, a decided sway to the right. He didn't wince in pain or sport a bulky bandage under his pants hem. His ambling stride had a natural flow, indicating a long-term compensation.

Of course she'd had no way of knowing downstairs since he'd never left the bench. She'd just assumed from his performance in the weight room that he was like her brothers, ready to tackle any sporting event. Jake Larson couldn't plow through a grudge match of football at her family picnics. He didn't shoot hoops at the local park with the guys. But the power in his body, in his mere presence, was without question. She didn't want him to be intriguing, multidimensional—tougher to resist.

He glanced across the desk and caught her staring. Embarrassment flamed from her stomach, warming her cheeks. She tried to think of something, anything to cover her rudeness. Inspiration seemed in short supply, for once. Allie fidgeted with a button on her backpack.

"Well, Ms. St. James, you appear determined to stay. I'll give you an *A* for persistence, certainly an asset in your line of work. Have a seat, but make it brief."

"Thanks," she said, grateful he seemed willing to ignore her gaffe. Allie settled into the overstuffed leather chair, a far cry from her cracked vinyl seats. How could she have forgotten about Robbie, her whole reason for the visit? This man still deserved a good chastising. "I've never been particularly subtle—"

"Oh, really?"

Maybe the rock had a sense of humor after all. Damn. The attraction had been easier to ignore in the weight room when he was half-naked. "I'm here about your son."

Jake straightened. "My son?"

His ruthless gaze pinned her, giving her momentary pause. Allie tossed her hair over her shoulder and gathered her confidence. "Do you know where Robbie is right now?"

Jake tipped back, the chair issuing a long, slow squeak. "At school."

"Where does he go after school?"

"Listen, Ms. St. James, you've come into my office without an appointment, invaded my personal files and now you want to talk about my child." Impatience dripped from his words like the beads of water from his freshly washed hair. "I don't know what you're driving at, but you'd better spit it out now or you can leave."

"Yesterday afternoon, your son came to my office, alone." For Robbie, she hoped Jake would be outraged, concerned, all the reactions of a good father. What did she want for herself?

He eased forward, his face devoid of expression. He tapped a pencil against the edge of his desk. "All right, I'll take care of it."

Abruptly, he stood and sauntered across the room. This time his limp didn't surprise her. She found an innate grace in his gliding swagger.

He swung the door wide and nodded. "Thank you for coming by to tell me personally."

His dismissal snapped her from her sophomoric day-dreaming. "That's it? Thanks?" Allie bolted to her feet, slinging the backpack over her shoulder as she closed in on Mr. Ice Block Executive. Did the guy have any emotions buried beneath all those muscles? "Don't you even care about why he came? Or how he got home?"

"Robbie will fill me in when we talk. Thank you for bringing this to my attention." His jaw clenched. "It won't happen again."

"This is your kid we're talking about, not some business acquaintance!" She paused an inch away from him, rising on her toes to close the distance between them. Her finger jabbed the air like a weapon. "You should be kissing my feet in gratitude."

She made the mistake of punctuating her last remark with a poke to his chest. Lord have mercy, the man was a rock.

He closed a fist around her finger and lowered her hand. "Ms. St. James—"

"Allie."

He smelled so good, fresh soap and musky male mingling.

"Allie, I care about my son. If you spent even five minutes with Robbie, you know he's a great kid. He's just a handful, especially since his mother died."

She would have thought him unfeeling, with his flat tone and cold eyes. Except, he didn't let go of her hand. At the mention of his wife, his grip had clenched, a small twitch that belied much coming from such a reserved man. Somehow she knew losing his wife had hit him—hard.

She curved her other fingers around his wrist and squeezed lightly. "I'm sorry, about your wife, about Robbie."

Her heart thudded in the silence. She'd always had a weakness for strays, and for a moment, she wondered if this man might be wandering lost through a fathomless maze.

His throat convulsed with a heavy swallow. "Don't be. That's the reality life gave us, and we deal with it." He released her hand. "I'll keep a closer watch on Robbie."

She believed him. With no logical reason to call upon, she knew he cared about his son. His son also had some worries too large for such little shoulders.

"There's more." Allie glanced at the secretary and lowered her voice. "Robbie thinks you're in some kind of danger from a 'creepy guy' with a gun. That's why he came to my office. He wanted to hire me to check up on you." A grin pulled at her face just as the child had tugged at her heart. "He even offered cleaning services in trade."

Jake smiled, a full, magnificent smile that shaved away five years and endless cares. An irrational surge of joy pulsed through her at having been the one to bring it to his face.

He pressed two fingers to his eyes. His hand fell away as a chuckle slid free. "The kid certainly has a sense of the dramatic."

"Inherited from his father, I'm sure." Allie flinched. When would she learn to keep her mouth shut?

His smile widened. "No doubt."

*Oh, my.* This man was dangerous. Where were her overprotective brothers when she needed them? "There's no creepy guy?"

"Absolutely not. I'm putting in a new security system. The contractor will be amused to know my son thinks he's 'creepy.'"

Allie studied Jake's even features, his long straight nose so unlike her brothers who had speed bumps down theirs from all the breaks. "Okay, I guess I've done my Good Samaritan bit."

"Admirably so." Jake opened and closed his hand that had held hers.

"Bye, then." Gracious, he smelled really good.

"Thank you." He nodded brusquely. Then as if regretting his abrupt dismissal, he barred the doorway with his arm to stop her, almost brushing her breasts. "My son is very important to me."

The sincerity of his words called to her more than a lengthy speech. The heat of his corded arm called to her more than any touch. A heady combination. She needed to leave. Fast. "If I didn't believe that, you would have a lot more trouble prying me out of your office."

"Good point." Jake nodded, before the cool executive slid into place as he gestured through the door. "Follow the signs, and you shouldn't get lost."

"I'll let you know if Robbie comes by again." Allie backed away, then pivoted on the heel of her tennis shoes.

Strangely, she did believe Jake Larson. He seemed the restrained type, but he hadn't lied about caring for his son.

The alleged security system was another matter altogether. Instinct told her he'd lied through his perfect white teeth about that.

Jake waited for Allie St. James to bustle through the reception area, a wake of silence settling behind her. Robbie's wanderings frustrated him, but at least he could rule out any ulterior motives for Ms. St. James' appearance on his doorstep. Compared with the hidden agendas in his past and calculated business dealings of his present, Allie was refreshingly without artifice.

Now to take care of his son. He'd been so certain he'd protected Robbie from Officer Morgan's visits. There'd al-

ready been too much Jake couldn't shield his child from
experiencing, like losing his mother when a drunk driver
had swerved over the yellow line.

Lydia had finally convinced him to take leave. He'd sure
as hell accumulated more than enough vacation days. Robbie had needed time with his grandparents, Lydia had insisted, and she'd wanted them to sneak away for a weekend
alone. It had been a simple plan, a few hours drive to his
folks' house to leave Robbie.

Biting off a curse, Jake pivoted away from the door. Pain
stabbed up his ankle like a bolt of white-hot heat. He caught
the edge of his desk for balance and gripped the corner
until his knuckles turned bloodless.

Lydia had only unbuckled her seat belt for one damned
minute to find Robbie's pacifier. That single lapse, a momentary loss of control, had cost them the world.

No matter what people told him, Jake couldn't stop
blaming himself. Why hadn't he pulled over for a minute?
Or stopped for the night? He'd let her down, let his family
down, by not being enough somehow, even before the accident. Had he ever been there for them when they needed
him?

Jake screeched the distracting thoughts to a stop, a huge
waste of time and energy he didn't have to spare. He loosened his grip on the desk, counting until his breathing
steadied and his world narrowed back to a steady focal
point. His ankle still throbbed, but he could handle it.

Shrugging through the kinks in his shoulders, he pushed
back a step. Jake cancelled his appointments for the afternoon and catalogued all he would have to reorganize before
his morning trip to White Sands. First on the agenda included firing an apparently incompetent sitter. His mother
had already volunteered to watch Robbie during the week-

long "business trip." As much as he disliked asking for help, he would have to accept her offer.

How did other single fathers manage? He had money and family to help with Robbie. What about people without those luxuries?

Dancing brown curls and sparkling violet eyes crept into his memory. God, he was tired and too damned lonely. Jake shoved aside the tempting invitation to mayhem, a dangerous threat to his painstaking control.

He was lonely, not crazy.

Allie plowed out the back entrance of Larson Investments into the parking lot.

"What an afternoon." She puffed a curl off her damp forehead. Allie adored surprises, but not the kind like Jake Larson.

Her quick glance at his computer screen had revealed more than enough to link him to the White Sands Resort located just past Key Largo. Local and state papers had plenty to say about White Sands and its slimy owner Neil Phillips, deadbeat dad of the month on her hit list. Not that the courts or police seemed able to do anything about Phillips, king of the invisible paper trail and marshland sales. What business did Jake Larson have with that loser?

Something niggled at Allie. Hadn't Robbie mentioned hearing about her from his little friend Shelley Phillips? If the Phillips and Larson families were connected, that explained a lot about why Jake might be hanging out with money moguls and dangerous types.

Why was she disappointed to discover his connection to the infamous lowlife? She told herself to be grateful for another reminder that Jake Larson was no different from her father, an uptight businessman, a man stingy with his emotions if not his money. She may have misjudged Jake as a parent, but overall, his chilly reserve rivaled his air conditioner.

Not the kind of man she could ever be interested in.

Okay, so he interested her. Her mother had even managed to fall in love with someone like Jake Larson. But the marriage had only lasted long enough for Allie to be born and abandoned.

Allie wanted a man like her stepfather and stepbrothers. She wanted a houseful of rowdy children and a husband with enough love to wrap them all in more security than any bank balance. At twenty-six, she wondered if her time might be slipping past. That didn't mean she was willing to risk repeating her mother's mistake.

Weaving around parked cars, Allie managed to forget the Larson males for two minutes before she began worrying about Robbie. Would Jake be understanding, or chew the kid out? Would Robbie buy that lame story about a security system? What was Jake up to with White Sands and creepy gunmen?

"Not my problem," she mumbled. Time to put Mr. Larson, the stone-hearted guy with a Midas touch, out of her mind. She would give Robbie a couple of follow-up calls and enjoy a clear conscience.

Allie rounded the cab of a Mack truck and stopped short. Her poor little Prism tilted to the right with a flat tire.

"So much for an easy end to a tough day." Allie twisted her hair in a loose knot, preparing for the ordeal ahead. "Might as well get to it or two-timing Harold will be long gone."

She popped the trunk and dug through surveillance equipment for a jack. Tools in hand, she crouched low by the back tire to inspect the damage. A telling hiss also seeped from the front.

"Two flats?" She circled her car.

All four tires leaked from small puncture marks.

Fear slithered down her spine as a curl slipped loose.

A white piece of paper glistened from the driver's seat. Inching forward, she reached through the open window and pulled out the note.

*Nosy private eyes get more than their tires slashed.*

Panic prickled over her scalp at her third warning in a week. Disgruntled Harolds were a by-product of her business. Right? Certainly her stepfather and stepbrothers had received threats. She needed to toughen up, consider it a compliment to her high success rate.

She still had one problem. Her brothers. Sam in particular would flip when he found out.

Resigned to the inevitable, Allie tugged free her cell phone, a Christmas present from her brothers. Many more days like this and she would never be able to convince them she could take care of herself.

Allie paused halfway through punching in the number. Who said Sam had to know about the note? She could attribute the tires to vandals and simply go undercover until she discovered who was sending the threatening letters. Snapping through a roll of incriminating evidence on Harold at the Sleep E-Z Motel would free her of local commitments.

Confrontational by nature, she balked at seeming to run from the note-writing scum. But the thought of dealing with her four brothers in full overprotective mode was beyond daunting. Undercover work would be impossible with her hulking, uniformed siblings tagging along.

A low profile until the heat died down would be best. She had plenty of out-of-town work she could pursue, such as the White Sands deal.

White Sands? Why had she chosen that case?

Mr. Uptight Larson had nothing to do with her decision,

or so she tried to reassure herself. So what if he would be there, too? She owed Robbie. The kid had insisted on emptying every trash can in her office in exchange for checking up on his father. And Jake Larson *had* lied to her.

Never one to concern herself with insignificant details, she wouldn't worry about financing an investigative trip while still making her rent payment. Inspiration would strike as it always did, like an exploding rainbow.

Mentally packing her suitcase, Allie finished dialing Sam's number.

Jake parked his Lexus in the driveway. He didn't bother checking in the house since Robbie usually stayed outside. His son thrived on open air spaces.

Rounding the corner of the garage, he scooped two Hot Wheels cars from the lawn so they wouldn't catch on the gardener's mower blade. Gardeners. What a shift from days in Air Force housing when he'd maintained his own postage-stamp lawn to military inspection standards.

He found Robbie in the backyard, pouring over a workbook under the umbrella shade of the poolside table. Jake tossed the toy cars on the table. "Hi, son."

"Dad, you're home early!" Robbie shot to his feet and locked his father in a hug, almost tipping the wrought-iron chair in his enthusiasm.

"I wanted to spend some time with you before I go." Jake held him close for an extra second, grateful nothing had happened to Robbie during his downtown jaunt to visit Allie St. James. "Missed you today."

"Me, too." Robbie reclaimed his seat, sitting on one knee. "Check this, Dad."

Jake sat in the other chair and slid the math workbook across the table. Pennies and quarters had been colored and calculated. Almost illegible, but correct. Pride swelled within his chest. "Good job, son."

He passed the homework back to Robbie, enjoying their daily ritual. This he could do for his son, even if he'd dropped the ball according to Ms. St. James. Parenting was tough, the toughest job he'd ever tackled, but he'd done his best. Why did he feel the need to defend himself to a woman he barely knew?

Jake stretched his legs in front of him, flexing his feet, working through the ache shooting from his ankle up his right calf. "What do you say when I finish with this business trip we go camping, get in some swimming and fishing?"

"All right!" Robbie's fist punched the air.

*Now for the hard part.* "But first, we need to talk about something before I go."

"Okay." Robbie settled back into his seat. His clenched fist opened as he nudged a Hot Wheels Camero around the table.

"I had a visitor at work today." Jake laced his fingers over his chest. "I think you may know her."

Robbie gulped, a fearful glimmer staining his eyes, a glint seen too frequently of late. "Who?"

"A private investigator, Allison St. James."

"Allie came to see you?" Robbie's eyes widened. He was in deep trouble and apparently he knew it.

"Yeah, pal."

His little shoulders slumped. "Did she tell you why I was there?"

"She sure did." For some reason, he hated selling out Allie when she'd done the right thing in coming to him. She could have called and saved herself trouble, but instead had put forth the extra effort for his son. Not many would have done the same. "Robbie, everything's okay with me."

"Really?"

"Yes, really." He paused to align reason over the emotion that seemed closer to the surface than normal since Allie had burst into the weight room and into his concentration. "I know not having a mom is tough for you. I'm going to do my best to stick around as long as I can."

He hoped he was being honest. In all fairness, he didn't expect his end of the investigation into White Sands to lead to anything dangerous. His contacts with the Florida State Police had carefully orchestrated the plan. His mouth watered with a hunger for what he'd lost, something he had to accept he couldn't have back.

Jake leaned toward his son. "I'm careful, because I know you need me. But you know what? I need you, too." Any thoughts of losing his son threatened every ounce of Jake's considerable control. "Robbie, you can't wander around like that after school. It's not safe."

"But Allie's really nice. I already checked her out with Shelley. Allie walked me home, told me she couldn't give me a ride because it wouldn't be smart for me to get in cars with strangers."

"That's not the point." Jake pressed a thumb and finger to his brows just above the headache that had started right about the time Allie St. James had shaken her hair in his face. "What about your walk to her office?"

Robbie stared at the top of his shoes. Silently, he chewed the collar of his T-shirt, a habit he'd abandoned when he'd started school.

*Damn.* Jake scrambled for what he should say next. He could have used help with something as important as this. He found himself wondering what Allie would say if a child of hers had tried such a stunt. What kind of a mother would she make?

A fun one.

Yet, given her vehement defense of Robbie, she would also be a fierce mama bear protector. The twofold image rattled him. He needed to quit thinking about Allie St. James, a woman he wouldn't be seeing again anyway.

"Pal, I wish the world was safer and we didn't have to worry about things like this, but we do. You know better." He paused, waiting. "Robert?"

Robbie spit out his shirt, a wet ring staining the neck. "Yeah, I know better." With an overplayed sigh of resignation, he flopped back in his chair. "You're gonna punish me, aren't you?"

"What do you think I should do?" Bottom line, he felt guilty as hell raking Robbie over the coals for being concerned about his father. But safety was too important. He couldn't lose his son, too.

"I guess you could make me weed Gramma's flower garden." Robbie shuddered, gagging dramatically.

"That and a promise not to wander off again should cover it." Jake gripped Robbie's shoulder and squeezed. "You scared me, pal."

"Sorry," Robbie whispered.

Jake nodded, squeezing once more before reclining in his chair. "We're still on for camping."

"Okay." A gap-toothed grin split his face.

"Want to go for a quick swim before Gramma and Gramps get here for supper?"

"Yeah!"

Relieved to have survived another day on the parental obstacle course, he cupped the back of Robbie's neck as they went inside to change. A week was too long apart, but necessary. Jake would take care of the White Sands boss. His folks would have their justice. Robbie wouldn't have to worry about "creepy" Officer Morgan.

Life was settling nicely. He'd even managed to divert Allison St. James's suspicions.

## Chapter 3

After landing in Miami, Jake picked up the keys to his rental car. Each step focused him on the task at hand, distancing him from Fort Walton Beach and the distracting presence of a certain private eye.

The perky Hertz agent behind the counter chirped, "Enjoy your stay, Mr. Larson."

"Thank you." While not a superstitious man, he decided to accept the cheerful grin as a good omen.

A quick call from a pay phone to Officer Morgan took care of checking in with the state police. He would enjoy his momentary step into the past, then life could return to normal. No more White Sands. No more police.

No more Allie St. James?

He gripped the keys until they dug into his palm. Did she have to plague his thoughts even from hundreds of miles away? The scent of her shampoo itched along his memory, his nose twitching in response. Garment bag slung over his shoulder, he walked to the parking lot, clearing his senses with a breath of sticky, saltwater air.

Jake peered through his sunglasses to check the rental tag. *Green Bonneville*. He jingled the keys with a toss and a catch while he searched the line of cars.

Two cars in, he heard a woman singing softly. The hair on the back of his neck prickled. A sense of foreboding gripped him by the throat. Even lilting along the breeze, the voice held a too-familiar quality.

Three cars later, he spotted a flash of brown hair bobbing in time with the off-key crooner.

Up a row and one car over, he found Allie St. James sitting on the hood of a sedan. His green Bonneville. Why wasn't he surprised?

She tipped her face to catch the late-afternoon rays, knees clasped to her chest, eyes closed. Her singing dwindled to a hum, drawing his attention to the graceful arch of her neck. A rogue wave of desire surged through him, almost knocking him back a step. Where the hell had that come from? Allie wasn't his type, her elfin quality so different from Lydia's smooth beauty.

Allison St. James intrigued him nonetheless.

He studied her, trying to determine what elusive quality had so tilted his world. Khaki shorts and an aqua T-shirt left her arms and legs bare, lightly tanned and too damned alluring. Strands of hair battled to escape the loose bundle gathered on her head.

She rocked almost imperceptibly, her feet arching and relaxing within leather sandals. A stray curl caressed her shoulder. The ever-present backpack dangled from her elbow, a small suitcase resting beside her on the hood. Apparently she planned to stay a while.

Practical concerns edged away his desire. He'd opted not to tell Officer Morgan about her visit to his office. Had that been a mistake? This time, her arrival couldn't be coincidental. Physically, she looked as dangerous as a butterfly. His mental health, however, could be in serious peril.

"Afternoon, Ms. St. James. Lost again?" Jake draped his hang-up bag over the roof of the car. Her lashes fluttered, and she directed the power of her near-purple eyes toward him, rattling his already shaky restraint.

"I guess I should have turned left instead of right at the Florida panhandle." Allie unfolded her legs, stretching her arms overhead and yawning with the lazy reach of a kitten warming in the sun. She presented a dangerous mix of innocence and sensuality.

Since Lydia's death, more than a few women had made overtures, his bank balance undoubtedly a hefty enticement. He could recognize a come-on in a flash, and Allie didn't seem aware of her appeal. Still, he couldn't trust her. Too many people depended on his visit proceeding without a hitch. "And you're here because?"

"I have a case in the area." She slid off the hood, landing with a hop beside him. Her hair threatened to spill loose before settling off-center.

"Oh, really?"

Her gaze scurried away from his. What was she hiding?

Allie plucked at her shirt. "Whew, the sun was really starting to heat up that metal. Anyhow, I've had this trip planned for a long time. And yeah, when I was, uh, browsing around your office yesterday I noticed you had a ticket to the same place. Is that bizarre or what?"

"Or what."

"Well, I think it's closer to divine providence." She shrugged her backpack into place. "Some creep stole my wallet while I was buying lunch which leaves me officially stranded. I cried all the way through my burrito, mind you. Then I remembered that little ticket sitting on your desk and figured you could help me until I can get some money wired. Isn't that too perfect?''

This was almost fun, wondering how her mind would twist around the next convoluted story. He leaned against the driver-side door, instinctively favoring his right ankle. Her gaze dropped to his foot, and she winced with a sympathy that seemed genuine, looking nothing like the pity he'd seen on other faces.

Even so, Jake wanted to tell her that the emotion was misplaced. He didn't care about the limp, to do so implied a vanity he would disdain. He cared about what his shattered ankle and calf had cost him, and he didn't plan to risk losing anything more. Somehow he knew sharing such thoughts with Allie St. James could be a substantial risk. "So it's just another coincidence that brought you to the hood of my rental car?"

"Don't be silly. What kind of rock head would believe a story like that?"

"Only an idiot." Jake pulled a tight smile.

"Absolutely." She nodded, another lock of hair sliding free from the lopsided topknot.

"How did you find out which car is mine?"

"I told the lady at the rental desk that I'm your wife."

"What?" A headache began throbbing just behind his eyebrows.

"Your wife. I swapped a ring from my right hand to my left." She waved her fingers in his face, silver band glinting in the sun. "She thinks I'm surprising you by tagging along on this business trip because we needed some time alone together since we'd been having problems lately, you know, in the bedroom."

Jake choked on a cough. "In the—"

"Sorry, buckaroo, I was improvising, and that's the first thing that came to mind." Allie tipped her head to the side and crinkled her nose. "Don't worry. I assured her once we get to our suite, I can entice my stud muffin back."

"No doubt." The hotel image was one he could have lived without.

Allie turned to retrieve her suitcase from the hood of the car, her shorts hitching up. Another step to the side and she would brush against him. She had great legs, trim muscles defining as she reached. His body wouldn't have any trouble functioning around her.

She pivoted to face him, her luggage dangling from one hand. "The dear lady, having five kids of her own, understood our dilemma."

Maybe he should have let the weights pin him to the bench press when he'd had the chance. "Dare I ask why she understood?"

"Baby blues." Allie patted her concave belly. "I told you, we need some time alone together. Weren't you listening? When Mom offered to watch the twins, well, I couldn't let a windfall like that pass. We have a marriage to save!" She paused, gasping. "You're not smiling."

"I'm homesick for the twins."

Allie grinned, her sparkle rivaling the Florida sun glinting off the windshield. Squinting one eye, she slid his sunglasses from his face and nudged them into his shirt pocket.

"Not bad, Larson. You're pretty funny outside the office." She hooked a finger in his lapel and slid it down his jacket. Through his shirt, her knuckle scorched a trail over his chest. "Get you out of that suit and I bet you're actually fun."

His muscles flexed in response. She halted midstroke, her head tucked from view. "I didn't mean—"

"I know what you meant." Sadly, he did and she didn't intend what his body wanted, no doubt for the best.

The bundle of hair tickled his chin. Her intoxicating

scent teased his senses, like the blast of an opened flower shop refrigerator, so many incredible fragrances mingling together, but without the chill.

A car spluttered by, breaking the spell. Allie jerked her hand free and stepped back. She clutched her overnight bag with two hands. "Will you help me or not?"

Jake cleared his throat more easily than he managed to clear his muddled brain. She'd said something about having a client in the area. What kind of case would she have so far from home? Could she be as artless as she appeared? He couldn't spare the time to find out. "Why don't I loan you some money, or better yet, buy you a ticket home?"

"I don't need your money. And you came in on the last flight."

"Of course, you just happen to know that." Suspicion crept in, making him almost grateful for the distraction. If she threatened his restraint in two brief meetings, what could she accomplish with a more prolonged exposure?

She tapped her temple and winked, her smile only at half-wattage. "Mind like a steel trap for useless facts. Besides, I'm here on a case, remember?"

"Really?" he asked, knowing he wouldn't believe her even if she agreed. He'd done a little checking of his own on Allison St. James, P.I. Her operation wasn't large, her clients mostly as flat broke as she appeared to be. Someone must have financed her trip. "All the way down here?"

"I do have a job and clients. I own a business, too." Her pointy jaw thrust forward. "My office might not be on your grand scale, but I take my work seriously."

"Okay. No offense meant." Allie might not approach her profession in the same manner he did, but he recognized the fervent glimmer in her eyes. This woman considered her work more than a means of meeting the bills. That, he could understand. His company was important, certainly a challenge, but being an agent had been a part of him, a calling.

Jake looked into her eyes so full of reminders of things he'd lost. He needed to get her on the first plane back to Fort Walton Beach for more reasons than he'd originally thought. He reached for his wallet. ''How about a loan to tide you over until you can get some money wired?''

''Put that away.'' She straightened, glaring at his billfold as if it were a snake. ''All I need is a ride, not a handout.''

''Sorry I offered.'' Jake eased away, hands raised in surrender. He should hit the road and forget about her. If genuinely stranded, someone as resourceful as Allie could haggle for a car rental of her own given two minutes and half an inspiration.

Her whole story about a stolen wallet was paper-thin. She probably had Fort Knox stashed in that backpack, or at least a couple of credit cards.

But what if she didn't?

How could he win an argument with anyone so totally devoid of logic? Rules? Like it or not, he felt responsible for her. His sense of honor wouldn't allow him to leave her stranded in a parking lot.

Consoling himself, he decided if she were somehow involved with the ongoing investigation, then he needed to keep her in sight until he could confirm her story. Being seen with her didn't interfere with his cover story for coming to the Keys, and he would be safeguarding the integrity of his case. ''I imagine you're staying at White Sands Resort, just past Key Largo.''

''Is that where you're heading?''

''Yes.'' He braced his shoulders, the inevitability of her answer already charging him with frustration—and an anticipation he hadn't felt in years.

''Then that's where I'm going, too.''

* * *

During the hour and a half drive from Miami through Key Largo, Allie savored the butter-soft upholstery of Jake's rental car. Exhaustion rarely conquered her, but the day had been a kicker. Staying a step ahead of Jake Larson had taxed even her creative powers, leaving scant energy for resisting his raw appeal.

She hadn't intended to bombard him the minute he'd stepped off the plane, but financing new tires and rent had left her with limited cash to waste on a rental. She could squeak a room reservation onto one of her credit cards, with a bit of luck and an off-season special.

Once she wrangled enough evidence for the courts to *persuade* Neil Phillips, owner of White Sands, to catch up on his child support, she could bill her client and return to financial solvency. Phillips was a genuine high-profile snake. If only someone could nail him with solid evidence.

Why was Jake mixed up with him? Robbie had mentioned the neighborhood connection. But Jake's business was squeaky clean, just like the man.

He hadn't spoken to her since stowing her luggage in the trunk. His forbidding scowl had lasted past Key Largo, making it abundantly clear he wanted to toss her in the trunk with his hang-up bag.

How could he not be awed by the magnificence of skimming along A1A, the Overseas Highway? Atlantic Ocean on the left. Gulf of Mexico on the right. Was there no time for appreciating the moment?

At least Jake wasn't frowning anymore. Sunglasses again shielded his eyes as he drove. He sat cool as marble, not a crease out of place. She smoothed her travel-wrinkled shorts. Did the guy own anything other than suits?

Unbidden, an image emerged of him in his workout shorts. She swallowed, battling the swell of claustrophobia.

She shouldn't even consider throwing herself in his path. His flashes of humor didn't change the basic man. The suit reminded Allie of her priorities.

Her work. Her independence. Not letting herself replay her mother's mistake. Sure her mom had found love the second time around, but Allie saw less pleasant endings too often in her line of work.

She had a job to accomplish with two clients counting on her, the resort owner's daughter and little Robbie Larson. She would do well to remember them and collect information rather than wasting her last few minutes alone with Jake. "I've told you why I'm here. What about you?"

Jake didn't answer for a moment, instead slowing to turn off the main road into the parking lot. He eased under the latticed portico of the White Sands main building, a sprawling wooden resort the color of Key lime pie topped with cream trim. His ankle popped in the silence as he flexed. Was he in pain?

"Business." He turned off the car and pocketed the keys.

"Hmmm." Allie watched him rotate his foot. "Big investment deal?"

"Something like that." He reached for his door handle.

"Wait!" She couldn't let him get away so easily. How could she investigate Robbie's story if Jake ditched her in the hotel parking lot? Snatching her backpack from the floor, she leapt out of the car. She skidded to a stop beside him just as he lifted their luggage from the trunk. "Thanks for the ride."

"No problem." He peered over the rims of his sunglasses, his eyes shifting from onyx to a shade more like warm chocolate. "You'll be okay now? Sure you don't need any cash?"

Pride bit her in her vulnerable bank balance, and Allie tugged her case from Jake. "Thanks, but no. I don't need your money. You've done the gallant thing and delivered me safely to my door. I'm a big girl. I can take care of myself.''

''Good.'' Jake turned away, retrieving his garment bag.

Allie's shoulders slumped. She'd let her emotions do the talking, yet again, taking away her options for appealing to his chivalrous nature. Probably for the best since she wouldn't have been able to scare up much enthusiasm for playing the helpless female. The wallet-stealing excuse had been a stretch for her to bat her eyelashes through.

''So this is it.'' How would she tag along without being more obvious?

''Yes, it is.'' He made no move to leave.

''Tell Robbie I asked about him.'' She'd expected it to be harder to trail him. Didn't he want to get rid of her?

''I will.''

*What is he waiting for?* Suddenly, she realized he wanted her to go first. So used to her brothers charging ahead of her, she'd never considered going through the door before him. The nearly antiquated notion felt strange. She decided to go with the flow. After all, he couldn't desert her if he was busy opening doors.

The lobby of White Sands sprawled before her, steel, chrome, towering palms and overstated opulence. The air conditioner's arctic chill sent a shiver of premonition down her spine. She thought of Neil Phillips hoarding such wealth while his daughter and ex-wife struggled to pay rent on a two-bedroom apartment. Resentment churned. She and her mother had lived too many lonely days, back before the time when courts could force fathers to act like parents.

Getting the better of Neil Phillips would score one for her side and impress her brothers. Checking on Jake for Robbie would simply be a bonus.

Reassured she'd restored her focus, Allie felt the dance

return to her step. Calypso music filtered from the sound system, adding an extra spring to her walk. She didn't bother with a low profile. She'd never been one for a dark glasses undercover persona, having found people responded more openly to a wide-eyed act.

She hummed in time with the music. A quick, censorious glance from Jake fired the wicked voice inside her. He didn't like scenes? Hmmm.

She couldn't resist a challenge.

Allie added a bit of a shoulder bob to her erratic stroll. Perhaps she might be going a bit far, but his by-the-rules attitude stirred old resentments. Geez, that canned music had a nice beat. Her feet found the rhythm as she hummed along.

Jake stood straighter, glancing at the people milling past them. He whipped his sunglasses off. "Do you mind?"

"Aw, come on! We're in the Keys. You have to enjoy the music. It's all a part of the culture, the ambiance." She shrugged her slipping backpack up, button collection chiming its own percussion with her walk.

She hummed louder.

He walked faster.

How far could she push him? And why did she need to win this small victory?

Allie scanned the crowded lobby, smiling and waving at each passerby. Jake's jaw worked. After the churning emotions he had evoked in her, she reveled at unsettling him for a change.

"Hold on a second." She grabbed his wrist. "Excuse me," Allie called to a young family of four. Stopping, she knelt beside a toddler with pigtails. "Your shoe's untied, sugar."

Jake halted just before stepping on her. He stuffed a hand in his pocket and shuffled restlessly, adjusted his hang-up bag, shifted again. Apparently, Mr. Chivalry wasn't going to bolt after all.

The little girl's mother brushed a hand over her daughter's auburn hair. "Thank you. We keep meaning to get some of those new shoelaces, the curly kind that don't need tying."

Allie double knotted the bows. "Good idea. I swear by them, personally. I'd be forever tying the twins' shoes otherwise."

Jake growled low in his throat.

The young mother smiled at Allie. "You have twins? Oh, how cute."

Allie stood, hooking an arm through Jake's. She had him on the run, and she knew it. "We promised ourselves we wouldn't discuss the children while we're away, right muffin?"

Jake stared at his watch, his gorgeous, strong jaw clenching again. "Time to go."

"Isn't he precious?" Allie rested her cheek against his arm, tensing muscles rippling under her cheek. "Impatient for me already. Bye now."

With a terse nod to the strangers, Jake pressed a warm hand to the small of her back and charged forward. "Allie, enough." His voice rumbled low in her ear. "You're drawing a crowd."

"Is that bad?"

He gripped her arm and tugged her to a standstill. Her latest dance step tangled her feet, slamming her against his granite wall chest. He smelled of the most wonderful combination of soap, tinged with musky perspiration. She wanted to climb inside his suit jacket and burrow into the sheer sensation of him. Her edge evaporated. She was in over her head, and she didn't even remember jumping into the water.

Allie tipped her chin defiantly. "Why don't you like calypso music?"

"I don't like scenes. Especially not when I'm on business. This trip is—important. You're not helping."

"Well, I'm sorry," she answered without an ounce of
contrition. Defensiveness roared like an underfed lioness.
She'd been pushed aside for years by her father, an unwanted, embarrassing reminder of his failed marriage. "I'm
just not a low-profile kind of girl."

"Fine. I've had enough. You're on your own." He let
go and turned to the front desk. "Jake Larson. I have a
reservation for the week."

*Good riddance.* She'd had enough of Jake Larson and
his restrained attitude. She liked open, boisterous personalities. Why waste her energy plumbing the depths of some
guy who was probably as shallow as a puddle in a desert?

*Fine,* she thought while checking room rates. Allie studied the little blackboard with the posted prices and gulped.
She could pay if they let her use two credit cards. Once the
Phillips case was concluded, she would be able to collect
her fees from the ex-Mrs. Phillips and make a decent dent
in her Visa.

And her obligation to Robbie? She would do her best to
check up on Mr. No Scene, though it would be difficult if
she couldn't finesse her way into a room at White Sands.

The receptionist stopped drooling over Jake long enough
to spare a second for Allie. "What can I do for you,
ma'am?"

Inspiration struck, as it always did, fast and full force.
Allie bit her bottom lip, twisting the silver ring still in place
on her left hand. She owed it to Robbie for all those emptied trash cans.

She stepped closer to Jake. He paused from signing in
and peered over his shoulder. Frowning, he glanced down

at her fingers. His eyes widened with a deer-in-the-headlights horror.

He twitched his head. "No."

Allie shrugged her insincere apology and turned to the concierge, passing her case and backpack. "Take these up to my husband's room, Mr. Jake Larson." She winked. "I didn't bring much."

Pivoting back to Jake, Allie wrapped her arms around his neck and planted a big kiss on Mr. No Scene's lips.

## Chapter 4

Allie's scent might remind him of an assorted bouquet, but the taste of her kiss was like a straight shot of brandy, nothing diluting the flavor. Only through sheer determination did Jake resist opening his mouth over hers and creating a scene that would have rivaled anything she could concoct.

He stepped back, regret and relief jockeying for dominance in his throbbing body. Allie's arms slid from around his neck, dragging down his chest before falling to her sides. Sighing, she swayed, eyes purple and wide.

He wanted to rejoice in rocking her balance for once, but he was too busy remembering how to breathe. He had definitely been too long without a woman if one near innocent kiss from Allison St. James could stun his honed instincts.

The receptionist shoved two room cards across the counter, her glasses chain clinking. ''Hope you enjoy your stay.''

Their stay? Allie's announcement just prior to the kiss blasted through his muddled senses. How the hell could he extract himself from this one without attracting more attention than Allie had already showered upon them?

Shower? The woman was more like a torrential downpour.

Anger wiped away passion. What right did she have to play games with his life? He knew he'd made her angry with his warnings to quit causing a scene, but her form of payback was more than a little radical.

He would simply tell the receptionist the truth, or enough to diffuse this mess of Allie's making. She couldn't actually plan to carry out the charade.

Jake narrowed his gaze on the private eye who had too much nerve to go with her wild hair. Allie straightened, her chin tilting. She'd better prepare herself for the fact he planned to plant her on the first return flight to Fort Walton Beach.

As Jake opened his mouth to oust her, three men and a woman rounded the corner, jostling Allie from behind. Jake gripped her shoulders to steady her. His fingers curved into her soft flesh.

Over her shoulder, Jake found Neil Phillips. Damn. Allie attracted more than her share of hits from Murphy's Law.

Phillips broke away from the two men in Bermuda shorts, his lady friend glued to his side. "Jake, my man! Welcome to White Sands."

Jake pushed free from Allie's too distracting scent and crossed to his old neighbor. Of course, Phillips had played on that loose connection to scam Jake's parents into one of his land deals. Not for the first time, Jake thanked heaven that his parents had brought him the paperwork to review so he could keep them from signing.

One meeting with Officer Morgan had set things in motion for putting a stop to Phillips's questionable real estate dealings. The lure of Jake's high-powered clients had been too tempting for Phillips to ignore.

Phillips extended a hand, his loose silver suit rippling over a magenta T-shirt. "Good to see you again."

"You too." Jake returned the man's grip, aware of Allie shuffling a few steps away while raking Phillips and his girlfriend with her gaze.

Although as tall as Jake, Phillips lacked forty pounds of bulk. A graying ponytail trailed from his balding head to the middle of his shoulder blades. "Hope you packed something besides a coat and tie. Feel free to make this a working holiday. Soak up the sun. Drop in at the bar, check out the ladies."

The receptionist tapped her glasses against her teeth and frowned, looking from Allie to Jake. "But I thought you were here with your wife?"

Phillips frowned. "Wife? I didn't realize you'd remarried."

Jake clenched his jaw and weighed his options. He could explain to Phillips about the crazy woman who'd followed him from Fort Walton Beach, and the guy might just believe him. But could he risk Allie telling Phillips her supposed reason for coming? One mention of her private eye profession and Phillips wouldn't be quite so forthcoming.

At least Allie looked contrite. Having her around might even divert attention from him since she had a way of snagging plenty for herself. Jake decided to cut his losses and turn the situation to his advantage, not that Allie had left any other viable alternative. "Of course you didn't know since we just eloped. We're on our honeymoon."

Allie's eyes widened. So she hadn't expected him to play along. Good. Let her worry for a minute.

Jake slung an arm around her shoulders and anchored

her to his side. Soft curves fit against him. The charade had definite advantages. "It was a spur of the moment thing. She finally said 'yes,' and I didn't want to give her a chance to change her mind." He found himself sinking into the cover story with an ease from days of old as an Air Force agent. "Since it was too late to cancel our plans, I just brought the little wife along."

"Little wife?" Allie slid her arm around his waist and pinched his side.

Apparently Ms. St. James wasn't pleased with being on the receiving end of her games. Excellent.

Jake quirked a brow.

Her shoulders slumped, and she gave Phillips a half smile. "Isn't he romantic?"

Phillips extended a hand. "Neil Phillips."

Jake felt her stiffen against him. She tipped her head to the side, her hair begging to escape the topknot. What was she planning?

Allie slowly held out her hand. "Allie Larson."

She'd made a quick recovery, no doubt. What would it be like to battle wits with this woman and win? He enjoyed a good challenge, whether from untwining a case, or even outwitting the odds of the investment market. He liked to win, and Allie definitely had one up on him.

The owner clasped her fingers. "Congratulations. Pleased to meet you, Mrs. Larson."

Mrs. Larson. The words blindsided him. That was a name he'd never planned to hear again except in reference to his mother. The game wasn't fun anymore.

Jake swallowed, shoving aside the past. He needed to focus on the woman beside him before she launched them both into something more complicated.

Her smile widened. "Call me, 'Allie.'"

"Allie it is then." Phillips nodded. "Jake here must be

quite a thrifty guy combining business with a vacation. Now don't let him cheat you out of a proper honeymoon." He nodded to the receptionist. "Book them in the Honeymoon Cove and all the extras that come with it. No additional charge."

"Thanks." Allie snuggled closer to Jake. "What a generous offer. Right, sweetie?"

Honeymoon Cove? The charade had taken a gut twisting turn. Control was fast becoming an elusive commodity. He needed to get Allie away from Phillips before she said something he couldn't repair. "That's not necessary."

Phillips stopped further protests with a raised hand. "Please, I insist."

"Jake?" Allie grinned as if daring him.

He didn't want to notice her long lashes sweeping with each overly innocent blink. He didn't want to think about palming the middle of her back and flattening her against his chest for a silencing kiss. Most of all, he absolutely did not want to discover how full her breasts were, hidden under her baggy T-shirt.

He needed to get her away from Phillips, not to mention himself. At least a suite would be larger than a standard room. "Absolutely. Very generous. Thank you."

She turned the power of her eye-crinkling smile on Phillips. "This will be a real treat since our wedding was such a rush job."

Irritability added an edge to Jake's already peaked frustration. "Yeah, I decided it was time to give the twins my name."

"Give the twins your name?" Allie walked backward down the hall toward their room. She still cringed at his announcement, followed by the crowd's censuring focus on her supposedly post-partum stomach.

Over the years, she'd kept her brothers in line through mentally outwitting them. She wasn't used to being on the receiving end. Her stupid kiss had backfired, leaving her unable to think.

She needed time to regroup. Jake's humorless expression didn't give her much hope of a pleasant reckoning when they reached the Honeymoon Cove.

He swiped the card through the door lock and shoved it open, gesturing her inside. "After you."

The suite gaped before her like a prison cell. Her great inspiration wasn't so brilliant after all. She hadn't expected Jake would be happy. What had she thought?

As usual, she hadn't thought, just acted.

"Come on, Allie. You wanted a room. We have a room. Let's go."

Allie twisted her fingers around the strap of her backpack, shuffling from foot to foot as she stalled to wait for the next flash of inspiration.

"No over-the-threshold into Lovers' Lagoon?" Allie prodded, then glanced at his foot and winced. How did her mouth always manage to lead her astray?

She didn't really expect he would sweep her up, but what if he didn't have the option because his ankle couldn't support her weight? Had she ventured into some sacred territory of his masculine ego? Men could get rather touchy about such things. She'd vowed more than once her brothers must eat toasted testosterone flakes for breakfast.

Allie might be mad as spit at Jake for his highhanded attitude, but she didn't want to hurt his feelings. "I mean, shouldn't we eat first? That burrito from lunch is long gone, and I'm absolutely starved."

Very slowly, Jake eased his garment bag to the ground. *Uh-oh.* She should definitely shut up, but of course she couldn't. "I really could go for a hoagie, or maybe we could hit a buffet."

He reached for her suitcase and backpack. Her fingers instinctively clenched. He tugged once, pulling the bags free, and with a flick of his wrist, he tossed them on top of his.

God, he was tall. And gorgeous. And her roommate.

She backed a step. "I was only joking."

"Which time?" Jake hooked his hands on his hips. "Twins, stolen wallets, waning stud muffins, coincidental meetings? I'm beginning to lose count."

"Jake, I'm sorry. I just—"

He ducked, cutting her reply short by tucking his left shoulder into her stomach and hefting her into a fireman's carry. The air whooshed from her lungs, surely due to the shoulder in her stomach and not the sight of Jake's long legs inches away.

She stared at the carpet instead. Allie watched her luggage bob past her line of sight as he carted her over the threshold.

"Jake," Allie squeaked as he bounced a gasping breath from her. "Wait! I know you're mad, but I said I was sorry. Impulsive isn't always great, right, so learn from me. Stop! Please put me down."

Four strides later, he flung her on an overstuffed sofa filled with lacey pillows. Her topknot gave up the fight, and her hair fell over her face in a whipping curtain. She tossed her head to clear her vision. Jake stood looming over her, but surprisingly not in the least intimidating. He was mad, but he wouldn't hurt her. Already she recognized his incredible self-control.

What kind of lover would he make with that superhuman patience?

Her body suddenly felt languid, bathed in a pool of delicious longing. His eyes turned from onyx to a warmer shade of honey-brown. His chest rose and fell faster under his jacket, and she knew it wasn't from exertion. The luxurious suite shrunk to a closet-sized space with a big bed.

Allie blinked, swallowed hard and studied her toes that had somehow curled until circulation seemed a thing of the past. Jake pivoted toward the open doorway to grab their luggage.

Sighing, Allie sagged against the smothering pillows. She'd gotten her way. She'd even wrangled them a better room in the process. Why then did she feel like a first-class loser?

The Honeymoon Cove unfolded with blinding clarity, like an entire room dipped in bleach. Neil Phillips had created the ultimate newlywed getaway, stocked with a virginal white sofa, wet bar, hot tub and a bed with a heart-shaped headboard. Her eyes widened as she surveyed the whole romantic setup.

What had she done?

Jake dropped their bags on the floor by the couch. His jaw flexed, and she remembered the rasp of his late-day beard over her face when she'd kissed him.

Shaking off distracting thoughts, Allie propped on her elbows. They needed to reach a truce before he yelled at her, or before she did something stupid like kiss him again. "Jake, listen, I'm really sor—"

"Hush…dear."

Allie shot up straight, legs swinging off the edge of the sofa. Already she regretted her apology. She hated condescending orders more than just about anything. "Wait just a—"

Jake waved a silencing hand over his shoulder as he ambled to the CD player, grabbed a disk, and shoved it in. Classical guitar, digitally enhanced by ocean sounds and squawks of mating whales, eased from the speakers. He raised the volume another notch before turning back to her.

"Jake?"

"Hold on," he whispered the words over her as he settled into a chair beside the couch, popped his ankle once, and angled toward her. "We don't want anyone to overhear us shouting and boot us out."

Respect for his quick thinking trickled through her. She should have thought of the same. Of course, he probably wouldn't let one simple kiss rattle his unwavering control. A stab of resentment edged into her kinder inclinations.

He pinned her with his boardroom stare. "Why are you here?"

"I told you." Why didn't he trust her? Allie sighed. Dumb question. "Business."

"Try again," he said with a lazy blink. "And don't lie to me."

She resented his inquisition, but recognized it as necessary. "I'm sorry for embarrassing you out there. But you made me mad, telling me to cool it, and when I'm mad, I do impulsive things. I would have straightened it all out." She stifled a wince at her fib. "Then you jumped in, so—"

"I said don't lie to me."

Allie draped her elbows on her knees and met him nearly nose to nose. She resisted the urge to close her eyes, float forward and steal another sample of what she'd experienced in their too-brief kiss. He wasn't her type, all uptight and brooding. "I'm not lying. I'm here for a client."

"My son? Come on, Allie. You can dream up something better than that."

She thought of her long list of clientele, abandoned wives and neglected offspring. Who was keeping little Robbie while his dad went off on business? Who held Robbie and kissed his owies? Men like Neil Phillips didn't dispense bandages and Popsicles. "Someone else."

"And?"

"Why don't you just worry about increasing your bank balance. My clients aren't any of your business."

"Lady, we're sharing the Honeymoon Cove at your instigation. I think that entitles me to some explanations."

She could see he wasn't going to give up. What should she tell him? Inspiration seemed to be in short supply. No doubt, she'd already used her quota for the week.

"Well…" Allie glanced at the hot tub as if for a fresh batch of ideas.

Jake tucked a knuckle under her chin and tilted her face toward him. "Don't you know people look away when they're lying?"

She did, and cringed that some suit-wearing executive had to remind her of basic interrogation techniques.

He slowly rubbed the soft underside of her chin, his callused finger scratching against the vulnerable spot. "This deal is important. You really put me in a bind down there. How was I supposed to explain away your convoluted story and still sound competent? Your stunt could have cost me, big."

Regardless of her thoughts about Phillips, she couldn't help but feel twinges of guilt. Jake was right. She had landed him in an awkward position because of her impulsiveness. She owed him something.

"I'm here checking out a father behind on his child support. The courts haven't had much luck garnisheeing his wages." Allie squelched the rising tide of frustration. Even her brother hadn't listened when she'd tipped him off to what a creep Phillips was. Why should she expect Jake to be any different? "The sleaze is a master at hiding his assets."

"And?" Jake quirked a brow.

Time to pull out the big guns and feed him another piece of the truth, any part but the bit she feared most, that she'd chosen the White Sands deal to investigate because she wanted more time with Jake Larson. She needed there to be something more to this man than a great pair of shoulders encased in a suit that cost enough to meet her rent payment.

She focused hard on not looking away, tough when she needed to pace, jog, run a marathon. She couldn't remember ever feeling so restless. "I've been getting some, uh, threatening letters."

Jake tensed, gaze narrowing. "What kind of threats?"

Allie recognized the protective look in a flash, having seen it more then once stamped across her brothers' faces. At least it would work to her advantage for once. "Nothing specific, and definitely nothing the cops are going to be able to do anything about. Happens in my line of work. I usually lay low for a while."

God, it hurt admitting to running from her problems and appearing weak in front of such a competent man. But if she didn't convince him of her legitimate need to stay at White Sands, she would be back in the lobby with her maxed credit cards and nowhere to sleep.

And she might never see Jake Larson again.

He rubbed a thumb and forefinger to his brows, pressing. "So you just hopped the first plane to the Keys?"

"Sort of." No doubt, Jake hadn't done anything spontaneous since first donning argyle socks with a pinstriped suit. "I decided maybe some time out of town might be— prudent. I thought of the tickets on your desk and my case here, and it just seemed providential. And yeah, maybe I planned to report back to Robbie about his old man's relaxing vacation. The kid was worried."

"Damn." Jake's eyes flashed with concern before he scrubbed a hand across his brow.

"I'll pay you for my half of the room, as soon as I collect on this case."

Jake gripped her chin and stared straight into her eyes. "How many threatening letters?"

"Three." Allie met his piercing gaze, for once allowing the instinctive fear of those notes to roll free within her until she knew it would be visible to Jake.

"Okay. You can stay." Jake dropped his hand and eased back in his chair. "Just keep out of my way."

Relief tingled through her, almost as strong as the lingering heat from his touch. "What about the whole newlywed thing?"

"We'll eat meals together, make a few obligatory appearances at the pool, the basics."

"Be still my heart."

"Tell everyone I'm not the romantic type." He linked his hands over his chest. "Make it convincing. That shouldn't be too difficult for someone with your fine improvisational skills. You owe me for jeopardizing this deal. All right?"

"Sure. I'll play the neglected Mrs. Larson role with great style."

Jake's brows drew together, as if he wanted to add something. His thumb rubbed over his bare ring finger. He didn't even seem aware of the small but telling action so like the near imperceptible clench of his hand back at his office. A cold knot swelled in Allie's stomach, a wad of something that felt remarkably like sympathy.

Why hadn't she considered the memories their roles might stir? Because she hadn't thought, and her impulsiveness might very well have hurt him more than any reckless caveman carry.

Allie leaned forward, touching a hand to his thigh. "Jake, I'm sor—"

Abruptly, he pushed to his feet. "I've got some business to take care of. You can use the time to settle in, unpack, whatever."

"Jake!" Allie called as his hand gripped the doorknob.

"What?"

"Thanks." She clasped her knees to her chest. "You won't be sorry."

He shot a glance behind him, a wry smile creasing over his face. "I thought I asked you not to lie."

The door eased shut after him with a gentle snap.

More than ready for the release of sleep, Jake padded through the moonlit room toward the damned heart-shaped headboard. His foot, ankle and calf throbbed, and he had no one to blame but himself and his ridiculous ego. What had made him fling Allie over his shoulder? Not his style at all and plain stupid.

Her hesitant flash of sympathy when she'd realized his almost certain inability to carry even a lightweight had spurred an irrational need to prove himself. And Jake wasn't an impulsive man.

Through the dim light streaming between the part in the curtains, Jake could discern Allie curled asleep on the sofa. He should have known she'd be too stubborn to take the bed. But he couldn't carry her again, and if she woke up...

They could settle the sleeping arrangements tomorrow.

Jake picked at his T-shirt, an old Air Force regulation brand. The worn cotton clung to skin still damp after his tepid shower. *Hell, Larson, be honest. It was a cold shower.*

After his check-in call with his parents and Morgan, Jake had bought two conch salads and a loaf of French bread, figuring if Allie had her mouth full she wouldn't be able to talk. He had plowed through a briefcase full of paper-work and done a halfway decent job at pretending to ignore her while she watched an old Katherine Hepburn movie. Apparently, Allie had seen it more than once since she mouthed all the lines with her full, pouty lips.

He had to admit she tugged his interest. Even wearing sweatpants and an oversized jersey, she had a unique appeal he couldn't deny.

Jake limped past Allie and stopped by the bed. He tossed the comforter aside, lowering himself to the edge. He slapped a pillow at the end of the mattress and swung his aching foot to rest propped on top.

Lifting his dog tags, he tucked them inside the shirt, his ID clinking against the two wedding bands. During the day, the chain lived in his pocket. Only at night did he allow himself to wear it.

He stared at his damaged ankle, something he couldn't tuck away. It seemed absurd to bemoan the loss of a job and his mobility when Lydia had lost her life in the same accident. He would have given anything to trade places with her, still would.

He'd had five years to resolve the changes life had thrust upon him. He'd moved forward. Why the sudden ripples of discontent?

His gaze scanned back to Allie, the moonlight from the parted curtains streaming across her face. She'd fallen asleep hard and fast, as if her body understood the incredible demands her energetic nature placed upon it.

Her curls were draped over the pillow and blanket, no more contained than usual. A single spiral caressed her cheek, floating and resting with each breath whispering through.

No question, she enticed him. A simple sexual attraction he could have handled, but her threat to his self-control was a temptation he wouldn't allow. He wasn't interested in a relationship. He couldn't afford to risk the hard won peace he'd found in restructuring his life.

An annoying voice taunted, reminding him he would trade the whole investment business for his first, more challenging, profession, a calling rather than a job. How much money did he have to pile over his disappointment before he buried it?

Damn, but he hated darkened, quiet moments with too much time to think.

Jake sagged against the pillow and regulated his breathing as if starting another round of reps in the gym. With a determination born from experience, he squashed the disquieting emotions. He mentally counted his way through the ache and past the dissatisfaction, until he settled into a pinpoint of focus, recapturing a time when he'd been an OSI agent, part of a family…and whole.

# Chapter 5

Allie blinked once and woke, clearheaded and refreshed, as she did every morning. Not one to loll around and waste a minute of sunlight, she sat upright, eager for new adventures.

And the day promised to be memorable.

She would nail Neil Phillips, and even manage to work Jake Larson out of her system in the process.

A tremor of excitement quivered low in her stomach. How much time would she need to spend with Jake to maintain their cover? How much did she want to spend with him?

Kicking free of the blanket, she perched on the edge of the sofa, taking advantage of the opportunity to study Jake.

*He's a bed hog.* The notion surprised her. He slept sprawled on his back, arms splayed with the covers tangled around him as if he'd tossed aside his restraint in sleep.

Jake was a puzzle, and she enjoyed mysteries, always had, being the type to scour the neighborhood with her

Nancy Drew decoder ring even as a child. Something about Jake Larson tugged at her, making her long to understand him. While she wasn't sure she would like what she found, she couldn't turn away without knowing.

His shoulders strained against his T-shirt. Whisper-thin with age, the fabric looked ready to give way against his breadth. She knew there was a clue to be found from that worn shirt, but couldn't pinpoint what.

Allie trailed her gaze down his body wrapped in the spread. A pillow peeked from beneath the covers. His foot rested on it with his toes uncovered. Looking at those toes, bare and tanned, seemed more intimate than when she'd seen his gleaming chest in the weight room.

Snapping her focus back up to his broad shoulders, she thought of the raw power he'd displayed pumping iron, his strength when he'd flipped her onto his shoulder—a power and strength betrayed by a leg propped on a pillow.

She needed to jump in the shower and forget about the complex man dominating the room. She might be a top-notch detective, but her experience in the romance department was sadly lacking. Jake could probably hurt her, bad, if she let him.

Allie had always managed to bluster her way through challenges with sheer bravado and a fly-by-the-seat-of-the-pants improvisation. Resisting Jake would take a more studied approach. For the first time, Allie doubted her ability to succeed.

"Well, Jake, my man!" Silhouetted by the picture window in his office, Neil Phillips thumped Jake on the back. "You've certainly given me plenty to consider. Those Internet stocks seem especially promising."

"Keep in mind, I can't promise anything, but it looks good." Jake gathered the printouts scattered across the conference table, more than ready to end a meeting that was going nowhere fast.

"I'll have my number crunchers run those figures and get back to you within a couple of days."

Phillips was cagey, his unwillingness to commit making Jake edgy. The man knew how to skirt the law, and the line between proof and entrapment was too damned thin.

The guy was laundering money through his slippery land deals. That much the feds and state police knew, but couldn't yet prove. They only needed an ounce of evidence, even the name of his bank to trace the trail to the Caymans or some other offshore account where the stringent privacy laws offered havens for crooks.

Phillips stuffed his hands in his pockets and rocked back on his heels. "Too bad we couldn't work a condo deal for your parents."

"Uh-huh." Jake kept his face set, calm.

"What a shame their loan fell through. Maybe we can bring the whole family down and look at some alternatives."

"I'll mention it to them."

"No more business for now, though. Go enjoy your honeymoon."

"Thanks." He'd had hoped for a quick wrap-up. Apparently he and Allie would be spending another night in the Honeymoon Cove.

"Aren't you anxious to join your bride?" Phillips slapped him on the back—again.

Jake shrugged through the irritation. The pseudolocker room bonding games were getting old. Where was the thrill he'd expected from bringing down Phillips?

"Allie's fine by the pool." Jake peered through the glass wall. He couldn't see her, just her bundle of hair peeking over a lounger. Her curls bobbed, and her hands periodically flayed as she gestured. A genuine smile creased his face. He did that a lot around Allie. Smile.

"I wouldn't leave a pretty little thing like that alone if I were you." Phillips eyes glinted with unmistakable lust.

Jake's smile faded.

Had he placed Allie in danger? During his call to Morgan, he'd mentioned running into a female friend, and although Morgan hadn't been pleased, he'd acquiesced in the end since Jake would be leaving before anything major shook down.

Jake thought through those crucial moments when he'd decided to go along with Allie's charade. Had he made a mistake? Even if he'd explained the whole Phillips deal to her, or exposed her plans, he knew she wouldn't have gone home, which would have left her unprotected.

He didn't have any indication that Phillips was more than a white-collar criminal. But the man still had a less than savory reputation with women, all the more reason for Jake to stay near Allie. "You know, I think I will join her after all."

"Wise move." Phillips led him to the door. "Bring Allie along and be my guests for dinner."

"Thanks, but I'm not sure what she has planned—"

"You have to come up for air sometime, old man."

Jake's smile hurt. "Sure."

"Seven o'clock on the veranda. Tonya will love the company."

"See you then." Jake clasped Phillips's hand in the required handshake, exerting more grip than needed.

After a quick change into his swimming trunks, Jake headed for the pool. Certainly the speed with which he'd left Phillips's office had nothing to do with the fact he hungered for one of Allie's unrestrained smiles.

One minute she tossed his world into chaos, then looked

at him with surprising innocence. Definitely the kind of lady he needed to stay away from. His few relationships since Lydia's death had been with women who were no more interested in commitment than he.

So why had his first thought that morning been of Allie?

Surely it was merely a by-product of enforced closeness and a natural physical reaction to an undeniably attractive woman. Which, of course, was a damned technical explanation he'd concocted to distance himself from his near constant state of arousal.

Jake cleared the gate into the pool area.

"Over here, Jake!" Allie waved enthusiastically.

Her no-holds-barred grin sucker punched him. Then he looked at the rest of her and lost any remaining air in his lungs. His sunglasses did nothing to dilute the power of her voluptuous appeal.

He had wondered more than once about the shape beneath Allie's loose T-shirts. His answer mounded snugly beneath the top of her two-piece purple bathing suit. Although Jake considered himself well beyond adolescent oglings, other men at the pool weren't near as concerned with hiding their approval.

A surge of protectiveness urged him to stake his claim, fast.

Jake ambled past the row of loungers toward Allie, pausing beside her to drop a kiss on her forehead. "Hi, babe."

"Hi, Jake." Her voice wobbled a note before steadying into breathier tones. "How was your morning?"

"Productive." He wanted to touch her, put his mouth on places that would make those near-purple eyes slide closed. "How about yours?"

"Tonya has been filling me in on the local gossip." Allie patted the arm of the sun-baked woman beside her. "She's really been a fountain of information. I could write a soap opera off her tales. Right, Tonya?''

"What can I say? All this steamy sun inspires me.''

Jake spared a quick half smile for the woman, before turning his attention to Allie as she launched into another gab session with Tammy? Terry? The scent of coconut radiating from the woman's suntan oil was nearly nauseating.

The woman flicked her belly-button ring, smoldering a look through her eyelashes at Jake. He wasn't interested. How could he be when Allie's laugh glided over the water and along his already ragged nerves?

He studied Allie's pink tinged nose, the first touches of sun kissing her skin. Slowly, her words penetrated his fogged senses. Jake could have handled the wayward attraction with a gulp and jump in the pool, but Allie's next shocker took him back a step.

She wasn't lounging by the pool after all, but gathering information. Her ditzy act had the tanned-to-a-crisp beach bunny spilling her life story. Allie might be a bit more disorganized with her approach to life than Jake preferred, but he'd couldn't deny her innate intelligence.

Her willingness to don a dizzy façade for the betterment of her case stirred an odd, and unwelcome, respect.

Had he also fallen victim to her act? The insight bothered him more than her bathing suit.

Jake cupped the back of Allie's neck. ''I'll leave you two to talk while I swim.''

His mouth rested against hers before he knew he'd leaned, just a quick brush that made him want to toss her over his shoulder for real and carry her back to their room.

He opted for the swim instead—unsatisfying, but wiser. ''See you later.''

Jake tossed his towel and sunglasses onto a lounger,

kicked off his deck shoes and walked away from the lure of Allie's scent mingling with suntan lotion.

Allie sagged against her lounger. Jake's kisses had scrambled her concentration. She knew it was a part of the cover. He'd done little more than whisper his lips over hers. But the tantalizing swipe had left her with a residual humming sensation that distracted her from business.

She needed to focus on work, rather than drool over Jake. Through the morning, she'd accumulated more than a few leads for tracing Phillips's hidden assets, not to mention some interesting stories about his extra-marital exploits before his divorce had been finalized. His current paramour, Tonya, had been quite forthcoming about Phillips's romantic trips out of the country.

Allie turned back to Tonya and promptly sensed a loss of attention from the woman she'd been grilling. All she could see was the back of Tonya's head, the short, black hair slicked and shining wet.

"Hello?" Allie snapped her fingers in Tonya's line of sight, hoping to recapture her attention. Tonya stretched her bronzed legs the full length of the recliner, wriggling her red toenails as she leaned to the side, ignoring Allie.

Allie followed the direction of the woman's heavily mascared gaze straight back to her weight-lifting hunk.

Jake sauntered along the pool's edge toward the deep end. The collective gaze of Tonya clones sunning in a line of beach loungers followed Jake's progress.

Tonya let loose a sigh. "Not bad at all. Can't help but wonder what happened to his foot. Must have been something pretty awful."

Allie frowned, realizing she'd never seen his bare feet or his scars, just those sexy toes peeking from under his covers as he'd slept.

Faded incisions climbed both sides of his right ankle.

Other smaller, jagged lines, less surgically precise, threaded over his foot and leg. Just thinking about the pain he must have undergone made her piddly little appendectomy scar itch.

How many times had she noticed him flexing his foot? Her brothers whined over a bee sting, yet she'd never heard Jake complain. Did his leg still hurt? She wouldn't know from his attitude.

Unbidden, the memory of his slight wince at the mention of his wife's death came to mind. He masked pain well.

How should she deal with such an emotionally reserved man? She preferred the openness of her family, certainly considered it a healthier approach to life.

After a quick stretch of his arms overhead, Jake executed a clean dive into the water. She had to admit, his limp didn't impede his athleticism. He sliced through the water with powerful strokes, lapping the pool.

Tonya fanned a hand in front of her face. "Well, girlfriend, the foot doesn't detract from the man."

"Jake doesn't let anything slow him down." Allie thought of his weight lifting. Jake had done an admirable job at channeling his life to fit his limitations. She couldn't help but admire his focus, given the opportunities her scattergun approach to life had cost her. She should be wearing a police uniform, bringing down crooks face-to-face rather than concocting schemes on a shoestring budget.

She stifled the old resentment. What a waste of energy to wish for something that couldn't be changed. Jake hadn't let his disappointments stop him.

Tonya slicked back her hair. "Well, the ankle thingie doesn't matter anyway since he won't need his feet in bed."

Allie wanted to spring from her lounger and demand that Tonya stop gobbling her husband with those lascivious eyes. Even if he wasn't really hers, Tonya didn't know that, and she wouldn't know if Allie had anything to say about it. "You'd better not let Neil hear you talk like that."

Tonya smiled. "Neil and I have an understanding."

Allie flopped back in her recliner and glared at Tonya. Jealousy was a really ugly emotion.

But if she didn't act the green-eyed wife to this woman's obvious panting, wouldn't that appear suspicious? Allie latched onto the logical explanation for pouncing on her very illogical impulse to erase the woman's leering look.

Jake broke the water's surface and shook excess water from his hair. Tonya preened.

For the integrity of her case and not because she desperately wanted to paint a wart on Tonya, Allie snapped, "Well, Jake and I don't have any such 'agreement.'"

Jake rolled onto his back, his arms sweeping broad strokes. Droplets of water glistened along the golden hair on his chest. Allie forgot about cases and investigations and cover stories.

"Lucky lady," Tonya whispered.

"Yeah." Allie waggled her ring finger, still bearing the wide band. "And he's all mine."

"Then what are you doing sitting here with me?"

"Good question." She launched to her feet, kicking aside her sandals. "Enjoyed visiting with you, Tonya. Maybe we can chat more later."

Allie sprinted along the pavement, her feet hugging the ground at a fast pace like a kid told not run by the pool. A quick spring off the diving board landed her in the pool with plenty of splash, if not finesse. Parting the underwater haze with wide strokes, she kicked toward Jake's lazily treading legs.

She propelled herself to the surface, sliding free just inches in front of him. "Hi."

Jake stared without speaking. Slowly he raised a hand from the water. Allie stiffened, ready to protect herself from a dunking as she'd done countless times over the years. She didn't mind a quick dive off the board when she could see bottom, but she didn't like the helpless feeling of vertigo when the surface and bottom became confused.

Instead of dunking her, Jake grazed his knuckles over her cheek before he lifted a curl off her shoulder, his finger skimming the top of her breast. "So you decided to swim after all."

"Uh-huh." She shivered, and it wasn't from the chilly pool.

His legs scissored below with even, efficient kicks. The backs of his fingers stroked a lazy path along her neck, smoothing her hair. The water suddenly seemed deeper, the cement floor too far to see, much less hope to touch.

Allie bobbed, her arms extended and sweeping by her sides.

"I missed you," she said the practiced cover lines, yet found them oddly true.

Jake frowned, and she nodded toward the gawking women. He sighed, pulling his hand away. "Missed you, too."

"What are we going to do for the rest of the day since you neglected me all morning?" She tapped his aristocratic nose. "Not very romantic, dear."

"You knew this would be a working vacation. Not much I can do about that now." His gaze narrowed, his long lashes spiked with water. "We have the rest of our lives for me to pay you back."

"Touché," she whispered.

Jake swirled water behind her with his arms almost encircling her. "Actually, I thought we might take in some sight-seeing tomorrow. The shopping and tour are a part of the honeymoon package.''

Her heart tripped at the thought of spending all day with him. ''Maybe we can pick up T-shirts for the twins.''

He rewarded her efforts with a low chuckle. ''Good idea.''

Why did she feel the need to test her wiles on him when he was clearly not the kind of man who usually snagged her interest? It couldn't be because she was miffed he hadn't noticed her the night before.

They'd spent a whole evening stuck in a room together, and he hadn't even hit on her. Heaven knew, her brothers had drummed into her head often enough what a guy would do if given half an opportunity. Her ego had taken a pretty harsh blow when Jake had spent hours shuffling papers and clicking away on his laptop computer.

She accepted she wasn't the sex-kitten type, more like everyone's pal. She'd worn ball caps and jerseys, rather than barrettes and prom dresses.

A few of her brothers' friends had expressed interest, only to be squashed by an overprotective glare from one of her hulking siblings. Even when she'd reached an age to skirt their vigilance and pursue relationships, she'd either found the guy lacking when compared to her brothers or too like her father.

''I expect you to sleep in the bed tonight.''

Allie spluttered on a gulp of water. ''What?''

''The bed,'' he whispered. ''You should sleep there. I'll take the couch.''

''That's ridiculous!'' She glanced at the sunbathers and lowered her voice. ''It's your room.''

''Call it stupid male pride, whatever you want.'' He shrugged. ''Besides, my mother would chew me out for bad manners if she knew I took the bed.''

Gracious, he had a great smile.

"Jake, we can talk about it later."

He smiled again.

*Ohmigosh.*

Her brothers' protection and advice had saved her from suffering a broken heart, like her mother. But she'd also never experienced the full extent of passion. Why did the thought bother her more than usual? "I guess you'll have to spend the evening working to justify time off tomorrow."

"Most likely. But we'll eat dinner out tonight, rather than in the room."

The light rolling waves inched her closer to Jake. Her feet tangled with his legs. Sighing, she sunk an inch and gulped another mouthful of water. She grabbed his arms, coughing.

He braced a palm on her back, his other hand trailing forward to palm between her shoulder blades. "Easy there. Relax. I've got you."

The insistent pressure nudged her nearer. Her breasts brushed his bare chest in a tingling swipe that rivaled the burn of that first plunge into the chilling water.

"Thanks." She stared straight into his eyes and instead, plunged into the warm depth of his gaze. "Dinner sounds nice."

Instincts she hadn't realized she possessed took control. Her arms felt heavy and languorous as she lifted them. She hooked her wrists around his neck and slowed her tread until their legs worked a synchronized pace, not touching. Swirling ripples of water caressed along her skin, teasing her with hints of what waited a simple breath away.

What would it matter if she played along with the charade a little? Her heart was safe from a man like Jake.

"Supper is forever away. Are you gonna feed me any time soon? All this honeymooning has me weak-kneed."

Jake laughed, his deep bass rumbling over the water and down Allie's spine. She felt a greater sense of accomplishment over evoking that laugh than when she'd discovered the locale of Phillips's Caribbean bank.

"Can't have it said I've starved you." Jake's fingers started a gentle massage along her back.

She stared at his mouth and remembered the feel of it from the day before, moments ago. She wanted to kiss him more than she wanted lunch, and Allie was fond of her food.

Jake urged her the last inch until their bodies met. Would he actually kiss her? She wanted to yank him forward and shove him away all at the same time. Of course that was the story of her life, too many conflicting impulses leading her places she wasn't ready to go.

Her lips parted. Jake closed the last millimeter between them and rested his cheek on her forehead. She wasn't sure whether to be relieved or disappointed.

Allie picked at the hair along his nape. "Do you think all this acting will convince them we're newlyweds?"

"Yeah, Allie. I think they're pretty damned convinced we'd like nothing more than to lock ourselves in our suite for the rest of the week."

Was it only her wishful imagination, or could there be a hint of genuine longing in Jake's voice?

# Chapter 6

*C*runch. Allie popped another chocolate-covered pretzel in her mouth as she sat cross-legged on the sofa. Dinner had been a bust, and she was starving. She munched another pretzel, knowing full well she wasn't hungry for food.

Jake studied the computer screen in front of him as he took a swig from his bottled water. His strong columned neck rippled with each gulp.

Allie rattled her bag. "Want one?"

"No thanks," he said without looking up.

He still wore the khakis and the cream colored polo he'd chosen for supper with Neil and Tonya. Against the pale fabric, his tanned arms glowed warmly, begging her fingers to test the heat.

If Allie could just stare at Jake's hunkish body without wanting to touch, they wouldn't have any problems. His shoulders rolled under the fabric as he shuffled papers with single-minded focus.

Too bad he had to ruin the effect with his money-grubbing ways. Ten minutes with Neil, and Jake had been Mr. Big Bucks. He knew the act, the networking lingo of a man well versed in such transactions. He'd obviously orchestrated deals like that before.

She reached for the remote control and paused. "Do you mind if I turn on the TV?"

Jake shook his head without speaking. Allie flopped back on the sofa with a sigh, not even bothering to increase the volume on an Audrey Hepburn movie, the second in a marathon night. She knew all the words anyway.

The evening had started off promisingly enough. Jake's eyes had lit with appreciation at her dress, the only one she'd brought, a light-cotton black sleeveless that stopped just above her knees. Sandals, a swipe of lipstick, and a loose topknot finished her typically casual ensemble. She'd wondered if he might prefer a more elegant look, but she couldn't change herself, and certainly didn't plan to do so for Jake Larson.

They'd shared an outside table, talked, laughed, leading her to slip into fantasizing it might be a real date. Then Neil Phillips and Tonya had joined them and Jake had changed back into the calculating business-guru type. How could he shut down his emotions so quickly?

Unfortunately, she found it difficult to recall why she didn't like him now when he drummed his long fingers across the white-topped table.

Allie tossed the empty pretzel bag on the end of the sofa. She had the munchies something fierce, and she'd already scrounged every bit of change out of the bottom of her backpack for the vending machine.

What would Jake think if he caught her scavenging under the couch cushions for quarters? Would he even notice with his head buried in his laptop? She really hated being ignored.

Maybe there was something left in the minirefrigerator. She launched to her feet and headed for the wet bar, trying not to breathe in Jake's tangy scent as she passed. She grabbed the last soda and guzzled a much-needed gulp.

Allie placed another bottle of water beside him.

He glanced up. ''Thanks.''

''Sure.'' She padded to the sofa, her skirt swirling around her knees. Feeling Jake's eyes follow her gave her a thrilling rush of feminine power.

She knew enough to realize he wasn't as unaffected by her as he liked to pretend. So why didn't she simply jump him and get it over with?

Because while she might be impulsive, she wasn't in any great rush to get her heart stomped. In spite of her sweatpants and jerseys, weight lifting and bravado, a small corner of Allie's heart yearned for romantic dreams and cool customer Jake Larson simply wasn't the type to offer tender promises.

She would be better off hunting down a bag of sour cream-and-chives potato chips before she ended butt-in-the-air flung over Jake's shoulder again.

Allie grabbed her sandals. ''I'm going for a walk.''

''Great idea.'' Jake extended his arms overhead in a muscle rippling stretch.

She struggled to slip into her shoes faster, jumping on one foot toward the door. ''Good luck with your work. Don't bother waiting up. I'll try not to wake you when I come back.''

''Hold on. I could use a break.''

Allie wrestled her other shoe on as she hopped to face him. ''What?''

''Do you mind if I join you?''

At least he looked as shocked by his words as she felt.

They both seemed victim to the irresistible pull that led them into doing exactly what they didn't want to.

Chemistry stunk.

"Don't neglect your work on my account."

"I've finished for the day." Jake raked a restless hand through his hair. "And a dark beach probably isn't the best place for you to walk alone."

She should have known he would have a logical reason.

While she could protect herself against would-be muggers, she couldn't resist the chance to talk to Jake. Maybe a conversation would lead her one step closer to solving the mystery of what attracted her to him, beyond the simple physical tug. "Sure. Come on."

Jake grabbed his wallet and stuffed it in his back pocket. He gestured Allie into the hall, pulling the door shut behind them.

On the beach, Allie slid her sandals off and savored the squishy sand between her toes. She nodded to Jake's Italian leather loafers. "Sure would hate for those to get wet."

Jake hesitated for a beat, before reaching to slip off his shoes and socks. He tucked his socks inside the loafers and precisely cuffed his khakis.

Side by side, their bare feet looked a little too cozy and intimate for Allie's peace of mind.

She charged ahead and waded into the swirling surf, staying free of the deeper undertows that led out to murky depths where she couldn't see bottom. Since racing after her brothers into the waves and over her head years ago, she'd always opted for shallow breakers and crystal clear pools.

Jake pulled up beside her without talking. Couples strolled past chatting or simply leaning into each other. Humid salt air swirled around them, binding Allie to Jake with a musky breeze.

Maybe the room had been less tempting after all. The beach scenario made her long for things far more dangerous than could be found in the honeymoon suite.

Allie circled around a half-eroded sand castle. "Who's watching Robbie?"

Jake shoved his hands in his pockets, his shoulder brushing hers with each limping stride. "My parents."

"That's good. My brother's boys enjoy their time with my mom and dad. Grandparents are special people for kids."

"I just don't want to take advantage. They've already raised their own kid." He glanced down at her. "I fired his sitter after you came to my office."

"That's even better." She stared up into his face, the features a hardened, matured version of his son. No one would mistake the relationship. The eyes, though, were different—Robbie's a cobalt blue, Jake's more of a warm whiskey amber. Had Robbie inherited his mother's eyes? Allie gulped past the uncomfortable lump at thoughts of the real Mrs. Larson. "The timing couldn't have been worse though, I bet, with your trip here."

He shrugged.

"It must be tough for you, juggling the schedule by yourself." She waited, wondering if he would tell her about his wife. Did she even want to travel that path of confidences?

"My parents pinch-hit for me. We manage."

She couldn't decide whether or not to be grateful Jake had dodged her hint. "Why didn't you just bring them along? Robbie would have had a blast tearing into the waves and playing in the sand."

Jake's eyes glinted in the starlight with a glow of paternal pride. "Yeah, he would have built a maze of underground sand tunnels for his race cars that could have rivaled any engineering plan."

"So why didn't you bring him?"

"Questioning my parenting again?"

"Not intentionally."

The light in Jake's eyes dimmed. "It's not a matter of simply tossing him in the car to go. He has school, routines, not to mention needing someone to watch him while I'm in meetings. I can't just pick up and go whenever the mood strikes."

"Guess not." What different lives they led. Her decision to skip down to the Keys hadn't involved much more than pulling clean clothes out of the dryer. Jake, as a single parent, had concerns and commitments she couldn't begin to comprehend. And he managed them alone.

The nurturer within urged her to hold out her hand. Waves crashed in the pause that followed as Jake stared at her, frowning. She nodded toward the other couples. "All a part of the cover."

She laced her fingers with his, his callused warmth enclosing her. "I wish you could have seen Robbie shuffle into my office. What a kid."

"That he is." Pride blanketed his words.

Any fool could see Jake loved his child. What did that do to her image of him? Would further sharing give her answers or leave her more confused than before? "I grew up in a houseful of boys, older brothers. Now they've added my nephews into the mix."

"So that explains your outstanding skiils spotting me in the weight room."

His thumb drew lazy circles over her palm, making it difficult for Allie to string words together. "I had to keep up if I wanted to tag along."

"So it was important to you, keeping up?"

"Important? Yeah, I guess you could say so."

"I'm an only child, so the sibling rivalry thing is pretty

much a mystery to me. But I can understand the drive of competition.''

''I'm an only, too, sort of. They're actually my step-brothers. Mom remarried when I was in elementary school.'' Blending into the new family had become essential to her then, so scared of being abandoned again. ''Keeping up meant I fit in.''

''Seems like you've done well.'' Their arms swung between them. ''I imagine you were a real princess in that house full of guys.''

Allie flashed him a smile. ''A scruffy princess, but yeah, they petted me like crazy. I have to admit, I adored all the attention.''

''Lady, you do have a way of stopping the show.''

''Hey, now.'' She tugged a step away. ''I'm not that bad.''

He pulled her back in step. ''Tell me more about your brothers.''

''The teenage years were a little tough. They outweighed me, outran me. They were buying athletic cups, and I was filling 'C' cups.'' Allie grimaced, thumping herself on the forehead. Jake's rumbling laughter wafted down over her embarrassment. ''When will I ever learn to control my mouth?''

He slung an arm around her shoulders. ''I don't know. It's got advantages.''

Allie gave up the fight and decided to simply enjoy the moment of closeness. What would it hurt? She looped her arm around his waist, a shiver skittering a trail from her fingers to her shoulder.

Each rolling stride of his limp brushed his leg against hers as they walked. ''I talked to Robbie after supper.''

She gestured him on. ''Tell me about Robbie and I'll give you Mom's latest update on the twins' first words.''

His fingers smoothed over her collarbone. "Nothing quite so monumental as that. He lost another tooth."

Allie answered with a shaky laugh, her breath hitching a skip faster at his light touch. Jake was the master of small gestures that related much. "The poor kid isn't going to be able to chew."

"But he's rich."

*Money.* A twinge of irritation threatened to steal the moment from her. She nudged his shoulder. "All right Mr. Big Bucks. There's more to life than a bulging bank balance."

Jake's face sobered, his arm weighting heavy on her shoulder. "Yeah. I know."

She'd lost something with her mouth again, a thread between them that she desperately wanted back. "You're lucky to have your folks close. I don't know what I would do without my family."

"Yes, I am." Jake stared straight ahead. "They were there for me after the accident."

"Accident?" she prodded.

Jake gave a quick nod toward his foot. "You've been unusually restrained in not asking about it."

"Some things aren't my business."

His brows rose into his hairline. "Since when?"

She shrugged. "It wasn't important for what I need to know about Robbie's safety, so I figured if you wanted to tell me, you would."

They walked without speaking for the duration of a half dozen foaming waves before Jake broke the silence. "We were in a car accident five years ago."

She knew she shouldn't ask, had even just reassured Jake she didn't need to know. She didn't even really want the answer and all its emotional implications. But she couldn't have stopped the question if she'd tried. "Is that when your wife died?"

His steps faltered, before he resumed his pace, his breaths flowing in a regulated rhythm with the rolling tide, each exhalation reminding her of his routine in the gym. "I'm sorry. I shouldn't have—"

Jake walked, his chest rising and falling heavily. "My parents were a big help with Robbie while I was recovering from surgery."

Apparently Jake had slammed the door closed on confidences. Her joy in the moist sand, the moon, in Jake, palled.

How ridiculous to be jealous of a few gawking women by the pool. It seemed Jake was the faithful type and his heart was firmly committed to his wife, the real Mrs. Larson.


Jake dropped a pillow on the arm of the sofa and swung his foot to rest on top. Sagging back, he wished for an extra six inches on the couch's length. He'd claimed the sofa while she'd been in the shower. A shallow victory, but at least he'd managed to control something in the crazy, mixed-up day.

Damn it, he'd gotten over losing Lydia. When people asked about his wife, he unrolled his practiced answer: "She died in a car accident five years ago."

He would then grit his teeth through the condolences and move on. No big deal.

Until Allie.

She had a way of picking at his protective armor that left his emotions closer to the surface than he preferred. He'd never been good with demonstrative displays, part of why he and Lydia had been so well suited for each other with their matching conservative personalities.

Nothing like the canyon of differences between he and Allie.

Why then did he want her so much that no amount of breathing exercises could work past the rock-hard ache? He could still feel the brushes of their underwater tangling, the gentle nudge of her leg between his.

He had almost decided to give in and enjoy mind-numbing sex with her, until she'd slipped her hand in his and talked about family. The way her eyes had shimmered when she'd discussed her brothers, her affectionate smile when Robbie's name had been mentioned, all warned him to stay away. Any woman who blushed over the mention of her bra cup size was definitely too innocent for him.

The rustle of blankets sounded from the bed. "Jake, are you awake?"

But God have mercy, she had the husky voice of a siren, urging him to lose himself inside her warmth.

"What?" Damn it, he hadn't meant to snap. It wasn't her fault he couldn't control himself. Well, it was partially her fault for landing them in the Honeymoon Cove, but he expected better from himself. Jake cleared his throat to gentle his tones. "Yeah, Allie, I'm awake."

"I'm sorry about my nosy questions."

"Forget it."

"No really." Blankets rustled again from across the dimly moonlit room. She sat up, arms wrapped around her legs in the middle of that inviting bed. "I shouldn't have pried, about, well, things that might hurt." Her head fell forward to rest on her knees. "Seems like I'm always apologizing to you."

She looked so pitiful and gorgeous and appealing. He scrounged for words to make her feel better so she would lay down and go to sleep.

Jake adjusted his foot on the pillow. "You didn't say

anything wrong. I'm just not the chatty type. So don't take
it personally if I don't spill my guts. Okay?''

''Okay.''

He waited for her to sink back onto her pillows. Instead
she eased off the bed and padded on bare feet to the wet
bar. She opened the refrigerator, the slim light knifing
through the darkness.

Ice clinked as she dug through the bucket. Midnight food
raid. Typical Allie. A few minutes more and they could call
the day over.

Allie's light tread closed in on the sofa. The muscles in
his stomach tensed. Allie stood beside him, something cradled in her hands.

Jake elbowed to his forearms. What was she up to now?
He never knew for certain with Allie.

She lifted her hands. ''I thought maybe you could use
this.''

She held an ice pack, or rather a plastic laundry bag with
ice inside. He knew he needed it, but he hated to ask.

He wasn't used to taking help, only accepting it when
Robbie's needs left him with no other option. He'd done
what the doctors had advised for recovery and gritted
through the pain so he could care for his son sooner.

Allie looked so earnest, holding the dripping bag that
would leave the sofa a soggy mess.

Jake extended a hand. ''Yeah, I could probably use
that.''

Instead of passing it to him, she knelt beside the couch
at his feet. Her flowery scent flowed up his body to catch
him square in the libido. He would be better off with the
ice on his lap.

Allie's cool fingers brushed his heated skin as she draped
a hand towel over his ankle, then wrapped the bag so it

rested over both sides of his foot. "I've iced down more bum knees and ankles for my brothers than I can count."

Her attempt to salvage his pride was misdirected and too damned sweet. Laying in a darkened room with Allie's scent twining around him, her fingers gliding over his skin, he couldn't think of anything except burying his face in her hair and regulating his erratic pulse with deep breaths of her. "Allison."

"What, Jake?"

"Do you know what you're doing?"

"I told you. I've done this in gyms a hundred times."

"That's not what I meant."

"I know."

When had her hands slipped beneath the towel? She continued with a gentle massage against his ankle, not anything medical, more of a therapeutic healing touch.

Jake rasped in a ragged breath. "Allison, you're a beautiful woman, and I'm hanging on by a thread here. So if you don't want to finish this, you need to walk away, now."

She continued her slow kneading for at least another minute, the longest minute of Jake's life, before sliding her hand away. Allie stood, her features a blur in the dark. Her outline, shapely even in the oversized shirt, backed toward the bed. "Sorry, Jake."

"Me, too."

*You're a beautiful woman.*

Memories of Jake's deep voice resounded in her mind throughout the night, nudging into her first thought of the morning. She'd been called attractive, athletic and worst of all, cute.

No one had told her she was beautiful.

It shouldn't matter. But it did. Not because she cared

about her looks, but because "beautiful" was a term men used for women, not cutesy pals or buffed workout buddies.

Which Jake was real? The contemplative, powerful man she shared a room with, the man who unveiled that magnificent smile at the mere mention of his son and winced at thoughts of his wife? Or was he the cold, driven man too like her father?

With her hormones begging for relief, how could she trust her judgment?

Allie scrubbed a hand over her gritty eyes, blinking against the harsh light. The room was quiet, no rhythms of Jake's even breaths or sounds from the shower.

A tentative peek at the sofa showed her Jake had already left. A glance at the clock confirmed she'd overslept. Another way Jake Larson had upset her body chemistry. She slept deeply, but she never snoozed in.

She kicked the covers free from around her ankles. Irritability being such a rare emotion for her, Allie almost didn't recognize it swirling inside her. But she felt downright cranky, experiencing none of her usual joy in facing a day. She balanced a hand on the end table to steady herself as she rose.

Halfway up, she paused, frozen by the sight of her personalized room service resting by the lamp. A bag of chocolate-covered pretzels waited with a Coke. Beside them, Jake had left a note telling her he was meeting with Neil Phillips.

Which Jake was real? The cool investment broker? Or the thoughtful dispenser of chocolate pretzels? She feared he might be both.

## Chapter 7

Allie stretched the length of the cabana hammock by the ocean and studied her toes. There wasn't much else to do. God, she hated boredom.

She hated being forgotten even more. Of course Jake wouldn't remember he'd promised to go sight-seeing with her. He probably didn't bother with such frivolous pursuits.

So why didn't she simply pack her bags and go home?

After another stint by the pool, she'd stumbled onto more than enough information from Tonya to annihilate Neil Phillips in family court. Jake could tell everyone the twins had come down with some dreaded childhood illness, and she'd rushed home to administer Tylenol and hold their little hands.

Sure, the threatening letters were worrisome, but Allie knew better than to lie to herself. A few daunting notes hadn't sent her jetting to the Keys. She'd come because she'd wanted to see Jake, the same reason she hadn't left. She refused to consider he might actually be a crook like

Phillips. Jake had simply exercised a bit of bad judgment, right?

Lord have mercy, she'd landed in a big mess this time.

She'd parked herself on the beach, as if to recapture that special moment from the night before. Palm trees rustled a serenade to shared secrets that echoed along the roaring surf.

Silly. It wasn't the same in the daylight.

The groomed beach sported clusters of sweat-sheened men hitting on women with big earrings. A jogger sprinted past with his dog on a leash.

What could she possibly hope to gain by exploring her tenacious attraction to Jake? Initially, his brooding moodiness might be intriguing for a woman enticed by mysteries. But over the long haul of a relationship, such reserve would frustrate her.

She had to admit, she probably wasn't Jake's type either. The thought of not measuring up stung more than a little. She knew he was attracted to her, but she wasn't the elegant executive-girlfriend type. Never again would she be found lacking, not by her father or any other man.

Time to pack.

Allie sprung to her feet, grabbing her towel on the way up. Pivoting, she smacked into a hulking chest, a rock-solid torso with a spicy scent she recognized well since she'd buried her nose in Jake's bottle of aftershave just that morning. "Oh, hi. Sorry, Jake."

"No problem." He cupped her shoulders, his grip steadying her, the feel of his strong, broad hands on her bare skin rocking her mental equilibrium. "What's your hurry? Relax. We're in the Keys, remember?"

Relax? What alien spacecraft had snatched the real Jake while she'd been sleeping in the sun? "I'm heading back to the room."

"Good idea. You'll want to change before we go."

"Go?" How did he know she planned to leave? Not that it mattered. Judging from the smile on his face, he was probably ready to escort her all the way to the plane's boarding stairs. "You don't have to come with me."

"Of course I do. Sight-seeing isn't fun alone. Sorry it took me so long, but I thought you would be by the pool."

He hadn't forgotten his promise from the day before.

He hadn't forgotten *her*.

Desperately, she tried to loosen temptation's grip. Ten minutes to pack and she'd be on the next shuttle to the airport.

*Yeah, right.* Allie never had been one to lie to herself. "Where're we going for lunch? I'm starving."

Having finished his report to the Florida State Police, Jake replaced the pay phone receiver. He wanted Allie safely out of the Keys before they implemented phase two of dropping the net on Phillips. Sight-seeing provided a benign method of watching her.

He pulled the folded tourist agenda from his back pocket and wondered if Morgan could look into those threatening letters Allie had been receiving. Only then could he send her home with a clear conscience. Jake made a mental note to mention Allie and the notes when Morgan arrived in the morning.

Slowly, Jake tucked the brochure back in his pocket and watched Allie haggle with a barefoot vendor for a "pet" conch shell decorated to resemble a pig. Neither Allie nor the lounging artisan seemed in any rush to close the deal.

The free-spirited air of the Keys complemented her unique appeal. She sparkled with a candid quality Jake had forgotten existed. Her lopsided topknot beckoned him to set it free. Her casual clothes, a jean shirt left open over a red tank top and khaki shorts, complemented curves that seemed to defy her slight figure. Allie was nothing if not a mass of contradictions.

But her candor was about to cost her five dollars more than she should be paying for a shell-encrusted souvenir. Jake sidestepped a cyclist pedaling along the sandy sidewalk and wove his way toward Allie.

The vendor hitched his Bermuda shorts up his hips as he settled into the canvas chair beside his display. "Fifteen dollars apiece, lady. Not a penny less. I'm an *artiste,* after all."

Jake peered over Allie's shoulder. He didn't even fight the urge to inhale her scent. "What have you got there?"

"Pet shells." She shifted her feet in a restless dance, placing a conch cow and horse beside her pig. "I'm buying three of these suckers, so I'd think he could cut me a deal, even given his creative investment."

What the hell was Allie going to do, start a seaside farm? But if Allie wanted them, Jake intended to make sure she got a bargain. He pinned the middle-aged beach bum with his best corporate stare. "Twenty-five for all three."

"Okay." The vendor grabbed a bag from the hook on his display cart. Apparently haggling with Jake, as opposed to the more scenic Allie, involved more energy than the vendor wanted to expend.

"Okay?" Allie stilled. "Okay!" Straightening, she dug into her backpack, her slogan pins jingling. She tugged out a crumpled twenty and tucked her hand back inside to rummage for the difference.

Jake passed the vendor a five just as Allie pulled her hand free from the depths of her sack, cupping wadded ones. "Thanks, Jake, but I've got it."

"Save those to make change for the vending machine. We can settle up later."

She opened her mouth, to argue no doubt, then charged toward the vendor. "Pack them in extra newspaper so they don't break on the plane, please."

Allie hovered with vigilance as he wrapped her barnyard purchases, then looped her bag of treasures over her arm. Jake palmed the small of her back and guided her toward the other newlywed couples from White Sands as they returned to the tour trolley. His fingers seemed to posses a will of their own, massaging her slim waist. Spending the day with Allie wasn't a hardship.

They climbed into the trolley, the flattened stuffing on the steel-backed chairs having long ago lost any cushioning relief. Normally he wasn't much for canned tourist agendas. His OSI days had channeled him to places like Dhahran and Cypress. He'd been to the Keys more times than he could count.

Yet seeing the same scenery through Allie's eyes cast a new light on his jaded perspective. Hell, Allie's enthusiasm even made the conch pig seem endearing. "Where are you going to put those?"

She clutched her souvenirs to her chest as the trolley rattled along the rutted seaside road. "These? You actually thought I bought these for myself? I think maybe I've been insulted."

Jake slid his sunglasses off and hooked them in neck of his shirt. "I'm sorr—"

She placed her fingers on his mouth. Her touch jolted through him, her widening pupils issuing a second punt to his shaky control.

Allie eased her hand away and twisted it around the handle of the sack until her fingers turned white from lack of circulation. "They're for my nephews."

He slung an arm along the back of the seat and let her relax into the crook of his arm. "Your brother's kids?"

"Yeah." Her eyes creased with a half-bemused smile. "You're a good listener."

He remembered everything she'd told him, a holdover from his OSI days combined with an uncontrollable need to know more about her. "Do they live close?"

"My oldest brother Sam and his wife Carly live a couple of blocks away from my apartment. They're great. I baby-sit, and Sam fixes things around the office. It's a good trade since I would've watched the boys anyway."

He could envision her with her nephews, dispensing noo-gies and even sassy reprimands. Then Robbie eased into his mental picture, unsettling Jake with the sense that his son would want to belong in that kind of environment.

He'd tried to provide for Robbie's needs, needs so very different from his own as a child. Jake had been content with his quieter upbringing, more of a loner anyway. Even his early athletic choices of wrestling and swimming had been solo activities, no team sports for the reticent only child.

Allie patted her bag. "Dustin and Eric will get a kick out of these."

"Dustin and Eric? Ahhh, your secret is out. You bought one for yourself after all. Which one lands in your kitchen window? The pig, cow, or horse?"

Allie blushed, pink creeping up her cheeks to match her sun-kissed nose. She shrugged from under his arm. She averted her face, studying the palm trees and telephone poles whizzing by as if they were of monumental interest.

He didn't like the way she wouldn't meet his eyes, the self-conscious wariness so unlike her. Had he hurt her feelings? Who would have thought someone of fearless as Allie would be so sensitive?

Jake leaned to snag her gaze. "Allison." When she didn't look, he tucked a knuckle under her chin and guided her face toward him. "Allie. I was only joking. The thing's kind of cute."

"Cute. Yeah, it's real *cute.*"

"Hey, what did I do?" What was wrong with "cute"?

She smiled with overplayed enthusiasm. "No offense taken. Of course you would think I'd picked one for myself."

Her defensive stance broadcast embarrassment more than anger. He felt like a first-class heel and knew there wasn't a chance of being able to find the right words to fix it. He could haggle for a lifetime supply of chocolate pretzels, but soothing wounded feminine emotions left him bewildered. There wasn't a manual or proven plan to follow.

And Allie had a way of changing any rules he might have unwittingly stumbled upon anyway.

He opted for an impromptu solution, although improvisation wasn't his forte. "Want to get something to eat?"

"Feed me again?" Allie looked at him as if he'd sprouted an extra nose, then laughed, musical chimes that tripped over themselves. "No thanks. I'm not hungry."

"Okay." He hooked his elbows along the back of the seat and let his hands dangle. Damn. Women were tougher to understand than any case he'd worked.

She smoothed her fingers over the furrows ridging his brow. "Relax. I'm not going to dissolve into tears because you accidentally stepped on my feelings. I have four older brothers who pick on me with far worse than that. As long as you don't stuff me in a laundry bag and suspend me off the banister, I'll get over it."

He wanted to pull her into the crook of his shoulder again, but she still kept her chin tilted with that wary thrust. "Banister?"

"Yeah. The bag was Sam's. He'd just come home from college with a sackful of dirty socks and stuff." She shuddered. "Once they set me free, I realized it was only a foot off the ground."

"So what did your parents do when you ratted on your brothers?"

"Not a thing, because I didn't tell them. The banister was payback for my telling Carly Barnes that Sam had the hots for her."

Her grin almost covered the residual uneasiness. Why hadn't he realized she entertained to distract others from looking too deep? Her story was merely a diversionary tactic.

The trolley jolted over a pothole, and her hip brushed his. Their gazes locked and held and yearned. She was so close he could see her nose had already begun peeling. It was going to be a long ride back to the hotel.

Allie inched away. "The pig is for Robbie."

"For Robbie?" He went from feeling like a heel to feeling like a complete ass. He'd never met anyone like Allie, so totally without selfish agendas. He found himself longing to protect her from others who would trounce on her unrestrained joy. Yet wasn't he the very type he should shield her from?

"I know you've probably already picked out something, and he's got a thousand toys better than this. I just thought—"

"Allie." Jake pressed a finger to her lips, her mouth satiny to the touch. "He'll love it. Thanks for thinking of him."

Her smile spread beneath his finger. His body tightened, the reaction lingering long after her smile had faded.

She clutched the bag to her stomach. "I'll tuck it in your suitcase for you to give him."

"Why don't you bring it by when we get back?"

Allie's jaw slid open.

Jake's wasn't far behind.

Where had the invitation to see each other again come from? Didn't he plan to grin and bear it through their days at White Sands, then bid farewell to the tempting whirlwind beside him?

But to retract the offer would hurt her feelings. He couldn't withstand another wounded look from Allison St. James in a single day. "You could give it to Robbie yourself when you turn in your official report that his old man isn't up to any shady dealings."

She studied him through narrowed eyes. "Okay."

"I can arrange for Robbie to come by your office." He couldn't stop himself from continuing, "Or you could stop by the house."

Allie swayed closer to Jake even though there wasn't a pothole in sight. "That sounds nice."

Anticipation gripped him, stronger than he would have expected. Perhaps he should see her again, back in the real world. Maybe the whole attraction was simply a result of the uninhibited atmosphere of the Keys. If he saw her in their regular environment, he could reestablish objectivity.

The most logical corner of his brain joined forces with his libido to label him a liar.

Jake half stood in the cramped confines of the trolley, pulling the flyer from his pocket and passing it to Allie. "What's next on the agenda?"

"Hmmm." She scanned her finger along the first page. Allie flipped to the back, her eyes flickering along the agenda bullets, and frowned.

"What?"

"Uh." She nibbled her lip.

Jake slipped the pamphlet from her hands and read

through to the chilling last event of the day for White Sands couples.

*Marriage Vows Renewal: Oceanside Ceremony At Sundown.*

Allie trudged with the rest of her bridal party to the west side of the island for sunset gazing. Sailboats dotted the coast with swimsuit-clad crews lounging on deck. A crimson haze shimmered through billowing sails. Plump clouds hung from the sky like those in a child's picture book.

A lovely end to a special day, or it could have been if she weren't walking to her wedding.

Critically, she assessed her "bridal" wear, a bright red tank top covered by a loose jean shirt and shorts. The witnesses consisted of Tipsy Tonya and an entourage of sunburned tourists sipping everything from margaritas to Coronas. Just the fallout she would expect from one of her lame schemes.

At least she'd adhered to one wedding tradition. She'd worn something *old.* The *new* bagged shell animals hanging from her arm were *borrowed* until she could scrounge the five bucks she owed Jake. And heaven knew, she was feeling *blue.*

"Jake," she whispered. "We don't have to—"

"Allie, not now."

She should have left when she'd had the chance. Now the impulsive decision to stay with Jake for the afternoon would cost her, big time. They couldn't skip the ceremonial proceedings without causing a scene.

Perhaps a scene might be just the ticket out. She could start a shouting match before storming away in a theatrical huff. Given the pained, stoic expression on her handsome "husband's" face, no one would doubt the authenticity of their spat.

Allie turned to Jake, prepared to snap her wifely ire over not being allowed unreserved use of his gold card. "Jake, the twins are going to be so disappointed you wouldn't let me get them the—''

His clenched jaw preceded his arm locking around her waist and plastering her against his chest. He dipped to nuzzle her neck. ''Forget it. It's not worth creating a stir. Just play it through. The service isn't legal anyway.'' He pulled back. ''We'll buy the twins a swing set when we get home. Now, come on.''

''Okay, *dear.*'' She plodded beside him. He was right. What did it matter? It wasn't a binding service. Even if it were, didn't she know from her parents' experience that marriage only counted if feelings and commitment were involved? Blessings from a cast of Bishops didn't validate a marriage without love, and she could never love a distant man like Jake Larson.

Inhaling a bracing breath, Allie looked at the floral bower perched on a rocky overhang. Boats bobbed along the shore. A lone sailboarder skimmed by.

Her stomach knotted, and she knew it wasn't from fear of the ocean just beyond the arched latticework of hibiscus vines. Her palms grew slick with sweaty apprehension. She couldn't do this. She would almost rather swim to the mainland than go through the motions of pledging herself to this man.

Images of the tucked away bridal portraits from her mother's first marriage drifted through her mind. Heaven only knew why they hadn't landed in a trash can. Her mom insisted they would mean something to Allie.

They represented something all right, just not the happy mementoes her mom had intended.

Allie's feet refused to move. Jake ambled ahead a stride before their arms reached clothesline extension. ''Jake—''

He pivoted, his unguarded eyes flashing with anguish before he unhooked his sunglasses from the neck of his shirt and slid them onto his face. How could she have been so self-centered? This man had real wedding photos of his own, pictures of the mother of his child.

Allie closed the gap between them and let her hand flutter to his chest for comfort, not because she needed to touch him and ease the ache in her own heart. Her palm absorbed the increasingly familiar texture of him. She leaned her chest against his and angled her face until their mouths were a tiptoe lift away. "Jake, we don't have to do this. I can stage a diversionary fit without straining two brain cells. No one will be suspicious."

Jake shrugged. "Don't waste the effort. A few simple words and we're done. You won't want to miss their seafood reception. I told you. It means nothing."

His words slapped her. *It means nothing.* She meant nothing to him.

Once she'd caught her breath and could think more rationally, she remembered he didn't always say what he meant. Instinct told her she affected him. He'd always been so cool, she hadn't considered he might lash out because of the reminder of the woman he'd loved.

She wished she could see his eyes. At least they offered the rare glimpse into his thoughts. Why was he so unwilling to accept comfort, even to the point of gritting his teeth through the offer of a simple ice pack? To push the issue would probably only start an authentic argument.

Allie slid her hand free with a glide longer than needed. "Okay. You're right, of course. Like you said, it's just a few words. With everybody else in the group answering, no one will notice if we don't speak."

"Sure. Come on." He twitched his head toward the bower.

Neil Phillips loped up the four steps, wearing shorts and flip-flops while holding a service book. "Is everyone ready?'' he shouted into the portable microphone clipped to his Hawaiian shirt.

A drunken cheer swelled from the crowd.

Jake tugged her hand. ''Let's get this over with.''

Allie lagged behind as they joined the cluster of ten other couples. The melting crimson sunset cast a hazy glow over the casual congregation. Reeds bowed their blessing in the light breeze.

Tonya lifted her umbrella drink in toast. ''Tear him up, girlfriend.''

Allie winced.

''Friends...'' Neil Phillips's voice echoed from the sound system. ''Having been through a wedding or two myself—''

Onlookers rumbled with chuckles. Allie didn't find divorce at all amusing.

Phillips waved the group silent. ''I'm an expert on telling you what not to do. And I can follow the printed words in front of me. So let's begin.''

The speakers wafted undertones of violin music that Allie might have found soothing, had she not been fighting a bout of nerves that threatened to spill into nausea.

Jake followed the lead of the others and clasped Allie's hands in his, his touch warm and strong. She could do this. Just chant through a few words that meant nothing, then they would be feasting on the packed buffet waiting to the side. Except she wasn't hungry.

''We're gathered today to reaffirm the commitment already made by these couples....''

Allie and Jake mumbled answers to Phillips's call for responses. She told herself the promises meant nothing, words without feelings behind them. But she did have feelings for Jake, inexplicable, convoluted yearnings that left her more confused than ever.

Phillips gestured to the crowd. "Couples, will you share your worldly goods with each other?"

Big joke for Phillips of all people to tout that one. At least her father had been prompt with his child-support payments. Good old Al had been generous with his money if not his emotions.

"Will you give your bodies and your lives to each other?"

Jake's grip tightened around her. His rumbled "yes" mingled with hers. She wanted to give him her body, even trusted him to treat it with care, but not her heart.

"Will you be faithful to one another?"

Allie repressed the urge to snort with derision. She doubted Phillips had learned his lesson. How many times had he read the list of vows to honeymooners and not gotten the message for himself?

Watching Tonya's eyes wander over the other men present, Allie wondered if perhaps Phillips was about to receive his comeuppance. The thought didn't bring her joy, merely made her sad.

"Will you care for each other in good times and bad?"

Jake and his wife had repeated the same promises, yet she hadn't been able to care for him when he'd needed her most. How unfair that Phillips had thrown away what Jake couldn't have. Apparently what she couldn't have either.

She'd waited to meet "the one," so certain he and her houseful of children would materialize if she hung on long enough. What a joke. She was twenty-six years old, barely making her rent payment, and her only marital experience involved a seaside, drunken ceremony with a guy she could never spend her life with, but desperately wanted to share her bed with for at least a week.

"Will you love each other?"

What a typical Allie mess. The only thing that could

possibly make it worse would be if she actually fell in love with the guy.

Her mouth went drier than the rugged stretch of beach beneath her feet.

She couldn't be falling in love with Jake Larson, could she?

# Chapter 8

"Will you love each other?"

Jake absorbed the impact of the unshielded emotion glistening in Allie's eyes and thanked God for his sunglasses. She wouldn't find what she sought in *his* eyes.

Every spoken vow reminded him of the ways he'd failed Lydia. He'd been faithful, even happy. They'd had what most would call a good marriage. But he knew he'd taken far more than he'd given in return. He'd pacified himself with thoughts that Lydia didn't want demonstrative displays any more than he did.

But he should have told her he loved her. What the hell was the matter with him that he hadn't been able to give those simple words when he'd pledged to share his life with her?

He accepted that he didn't feel things like others did. The very element of his personality that had made him a top-notch agent, even now made him a driven, successful businessman, had made him a distant husband. He'd tried to compensate for the lack in himself with actions, but had failed Lydia when it counted most.

A woman like Allie would never passively accept half-measures of affection. She would expect, demand, more.

Phillips cleared his throat. "Now you can take a moment to offer your own vows to each other."

Great. Another landmine for him to step on.

"Jake, I promise to be honest with you." She paused, studying their hands, before sighing. "I'll give you my smiles, share my laughter, sing off-key to you when I think your frown has grown a bit too deep. And I will be your son's friend. I will be your friend."

She'd danced around her landmine quite neatly.

His turn.

He stared into Allie's near-purple eyes, her dark lashes sweeping over an expression so open he could dive straight into her soul. Her generous spirit went beyond conch shell gifts and ice packs. How easy it would be to take from her. But what did he have to give her?

Not what she needed.

He couldn't imagine how she'd convinced herself she might have feelings for him, but her eyes didn't lie. Maybe her generous ways led her to collect strays. At the moment, he certainly felt like a lame, lost cause. He needed to make her understand why that glimmer directed at him was totally misplaced.

Jake straightened, returning his attention to the debacle at hand. "I promise to keep you safe."

As expected, disappointment flickered through Allie's honest eyes. Unexpectedly, a similar stab of disappointment shot through Jake.

Neil Phillips closed the book and smiled out over his "congregation." "Gentlemen, you may kiss your brides."

*   *   *

Allie walked beside Jake, thinking they looked more like a couple on the verge of divorce than newlyweds. She had to leave. First thing in the morning, she would pack the pig into Jake's suitcase and hit the road for the airport.

She would simply soak up the extra fare since she feared sticking around would cost her far more than she could afford. Her heart. No doubt, Jake's was encased behind a wall of reserve she could never hope to erode.

Allie resolved to put as many miles as possible between herself and a certain golden-haired enticement. He could make his own ice packs, and she would buy her own pretzels.

Definitely, no more kisses from Jake.

When Phillips had called for the bridal kiss, Allie's intentions had been the best. She'd perched on her toes and brushed a quick one across Jake's mouth.

Except she hadn't been able to lower herself to the ground. Her lips had clung to his, their hands trapped between them, the back of his wrists branding a hot imprint against her tender breasts.

Stupid. She might as well have pasted a note on her head asking the guy to go to bed with her. Part of her wanted to do just that, go to bed with him, put an end to questions, and move on with her life. But what if afterward she wanted him again, perhaps even wanted him to stick around?

Not a chance. Their worlds simply didn't mesh.

Jake didn't look much happier with the situation. She should be glad, but she couldn't stop the flash of resentment. She might not be a glamour girl, but she wasn't exactly dog food.

"Hey, Jake," she snapped, turning to him. "Would you please take off the sunglasses. It's rude to wear them after dark."

Jake's brow raised slowly. "Rude?"

"Yeah." She knew her irritability had little to do with his glasses and everything to do with the sexual frustration tightening through her with every step closer to their hotel. The other couples were stumbling back to their rooms for mind-numbing sex, while she would watch another movie and eat her body weight in chocolate.

She tapped a fingernail against an opaque lens. "I can't see your eyes. You should look into someone's eyes when they're speaking to you. If Robbie stared over your head when you were talking to him, you would tell him that was rude, wouldn't you?"

"Fine." Jake swiped his glasses off and hooked them on the neck of his shirt, unveiling flat, emotionless eyes.

The dispenser of pretzels was long gone.

She was glad, since that made her decision easier. "I'm going home tomorrow."

That wasn't so tough. She'd be back in her office enjoying the work she loved without an uptight businessman in sight.

"No you're not."

"What?" Allie jerked to a stop. Damn him for being so appealing. What would a wedding night with Jake be like? How would it feel to have his strong hands explore every inch of her? Frustration fueled her anger. "Who do you think you are? I've finished my casework here. So I'm leaving. Tell everyone the twins have strep throat and I'm passing out Popsicles. You can have your bed back after tonight."

His arms crossed over an impossibly broad chest. "What about the threatening notes?"

"That's not your problem."

"Lady, you made it my problem." He stepped forward as if to intimidate her with his height.

Allie wasn't the type to back down, in fact, she found the challenge of his stance impossible to resist. "How did I do that?"

"By telling me. Until I know those letters have been taken care of, you're staying with me."

"You've got to be kidding. That's the most Cro-Magnon thing I've ever heard." But kind of romantic, not that she planned to tell him. "I'll stay with my folks for a while. Everything will be fine."

Allie plowed up the steps to their dime-sized patio, ready to pack and then hide in one of her jerseys. Jake rested a hand on her shoulder and gently moved her from in front of the door.

He slid his card into the lock and made a quick visual sweep of the room before waving her inside. Why hadn't she noticed that he always checked before letting her enter? Of course, any business traveler's guide indicated such as a proper safety measure. Jake had probably written the manual on safety and protocol.

Jake strolled to the bedside table and tossed his wallet and room card. His arm froze midtoss. Allie peeked around Jake, careful not to touch him.

A cellophaned gift basket waited for them beside the bed, complete with champagne, canned oysters, cheese, crackers—and a box of condoms. A dangling card broadcast hotel congratulations on the evening's ceremony.

Jake pivoted to face her. "Do you want to go for a walk?"

Allie only just heard his voice since she'd already hit the patio deck.

Jake considered staying in the room since temptation had jaunted out the door with a too damned enticing twitch. But he couldn't leave Allie alone after dark with any number of drunken beachcombers.

One more night. He could hold out for another few hours until he had a chance to check with Morgan about those notes. He'd promised to protect her, and that included from himself.

After he shrugged into a quick change of pants and shoes, Jake stepped onto the porch and scanned the dimly lit horizon. The moon's reflection splayed over the ocean with illuminating fingers of lights.

Where the hell had she gone? He wasn't sure he had enough reserve left in his ankle for a lengthy search. Pride had prompted him to suggest a walk rather than opting for an ice pack after the full day of sight-seeing. He'd needed to put as much space as possible between himself and the image of Allie's wild hair fanning over the pillow, pre-packaged safe sex waiting on the bedside table.

"Over here." Allie's husky whisper carried along the salt-scented air and the roaring tide.

Jake pivoted on the heel of his good foot to find her sitting on a lounger, her bent legs clasped to her chest, her chin resting on her knees. He sagged into the chair beside her and hooked his aching ankle over his knee. The mock wedding service had taken more out of him than he liked to admit. He rested his head against the back of the chair and stared into the night sky.

He would let her talk, since she seemed more adept at chitchat than he. Odd how he'd managed interrogations with ease during his years with the Air Force. He knew how to ask questions, just not how to converse.

More than once he'd wondered why. Was it a by-product of growing up an only child of subdued parents? Or simply a quirk of genetics he couldn't escape? He'd done his best to channel what some would consider a weakness into professions that suited his reserve.

A moot point anyway since Allie could easily carry the conversation for both of them.

"Did I ever tell you I'm afraid of the water?"

Jake tipped his head along the back of the chair to look at Allie, her face mellowed by the moonlight. He couldn't imagine her balking at anything. "You seemed fine in the pool."

"Not that kind of water. The kind without a bottom, or rather without one I can see or hope to touch." She furrowed her brow, staring out over the murky, white capped breakers. "I wasn't much younger than Robbie when we went on our first family picnic to the beach. I was so excited. You see, I knew how lucky I was to have landed in this big, noisy family."

She glanced at him, then away again. "Mom packed ham sandwiches, a bag of apples and a big cooler of lemonade. Nothing fancy." A sigh merged with her chuckle. "I couldn't remember ever feeling so happy."

"Sounds great." Jake couldn't help but think that after her lonely-little-girl need to belong, to blend into that new family, she deserved the security of those memories.

"It was. We built sand castles and tossed the football around. I was a part of the family. It was perfect, until I followed my brothers out too far, got swept up in a wave and couldn't tell which way was up. My stomach flipped. I couldn't find any air."

Her breaths took on a studied, even pattern Jake recognized too well. "You must have been scared."

Allie scratched her knee and kept her face averted. "Being around you feels like that."

Jake's gut lurched as if someone had knocked the ground

from beneath him. "I don't know what you expect me to say to that."

"Nothing. I don't expect anything from you. But I can't stop myself from caring about you."

Of course she couldn't. She was Allie, so willing to give of herself. "It's not me you want. It's just the whole romantic setting of the Keys and the hotel."

She smiled slowly, with a tender condescension. "Whatever you want to tell yourself."

He raked his fingers through his hair. God, she was stubborn.

"Jake, be careful around Neil Phillips."

His head snapped up. "What?"

She shrugged. "I told you. I care what happens to you. Watch your back around him."

Allie never ceased to surprise him, or frustrate him. He was supposed to be protecting her, not the other way around. "Why do you say that?"

"This is what I do. Remember? I just—well… I'm not much of a fan of what *you* do for a living, but I have got to believe you're honest."

"Good call, detective."

"So why are you doing business with someone like him?"

He could reassure her on the issue of Phillips, but it wouldn't change that fact that she wanted him to be some white knight. Eventually she would see him for what he was. He couldn't pacify her with vending-machine gifts forever.

What the hell was he thinking? He didn't want forever. But women like Allie did—a woman who made it her personal quest to avenge marital betrayals. "Is he who you're here to check out?"

"Answering a question with a question. Wow, careful or

I might mistake you for an old gumshoe like myself rather than a suit.''

"It wouldn't be a mistake."

Allie froze. "What?"

Jake couldn't recall the words, so he decided to make the best of his revelation since it had led her away from the subject of Phillips and protecting Jake's back. "I haven't always been a 'suit.' Apparently you didn't dig too far into my past or you'd know otherwise."

"What were you, Jake?" She leaned toward him. "Who are you?"

"An Air Force Officer, an OSI agent."

Surprise flickered across her widened eyes.

"The accident forced me to take a medical discharge." His hand instinctively massaged his ankle resting on his knee. "I'm from Florida, so I decided to settle in Fort Walton since it's close to my folks. That made it easier for them to help with Robbie. I went to the base to finish rehab."

"Did your wife die in the accident?"

Jake swallowed so he would have to breathe and nodded.

Allie swung her legs to the side, her hand fluttering to his knee. "You lost a lot all at once."

This time, Jake didn't bother to swallow or nod, just stared out over the ocean and let Allie's hand rest warm, vibrant, and innocent on him. "I have Robbie."

Her lengthy silence made him edgy. He turned his head to the side, the back of the chair rubbing along the base of his neck. The moonlight wasn't near dim enough in Jake's estimation. Tears hovered on Allie's eyelids, needing only one blink to set them free.

"Don't," he whispered. "I'm not worth it."

"I know." She blinked, releasing two tears with friends ready to take their place in her eyes.

"Damn it, Allie, stop."

"I can't." She sniffed, just the sort of inelegant, uninhibited type of reaction he would expect from her.

"Ah, damn." Jake pushed to his feet and crossed to the railing around their small patio. "I don't want pity."

"Tough! I feel sorry for you. There's no great sin in that. What kind of a heartless person would I be if I didn't ache for you and all you've lost?" Her voice cracked. "You break my heart with your great restraint and moments of understatement."

Jake pivoted to face her. He was a heartless bastard, and he knew it. Time for her to find out as well. He had to do something to wipe away the expectations in her eyes. Given the least encouragement or any more of his maudlin revelations and she would box him up to take home like a pathetic pound foundling.

The only person who needed saving was Allie before she made the mistake of confusing a romantic getaway for the real thing. Life wasn't about moonlight and margaritas.

Jake crouched in front of her. "What do you want from me? Because I can tell you restraint is the last thing on my mind when I'm around you."

Her tilted chin brought her lips a whisper away from his. "I want you to stop confusing me. Let me in or slam the door shut."

"Allie," he said, pinching the bridge of his nose, "I wish I could."

"Which one?"

He didn't have an answer for her or himself. He cupped the back of her neck and rested his forehead against hers. So much for his great resolve for distance.

"Jake," she whispered, her breath caressing his cheek, "if I'm the one we have to count on for self-control, we're in big trouble."

Wavering forward, she pressed her lips to his. A surge of desire flooded him, an impulsive rage against the thought of losing anything more. Everything he'd suppressed since meeting Allison St. James slammed through him with a body-tightening ache that no amount of breathing exercises could hope to overcome.

Jake gave up the fight. "Then we're in trouble."

He settled his mouth on hers and absorbed her shiver into his skin, even deeper. He slid his fingers into her hair and angled their lips for a fuller meeting, his tongue begging entry into the woman he'd waited what seemed like forever to taste to the fullest. It couldn't have only been two days ago when he'd sampled her in the lobby.

She whimpered and opened for him, her arms hanging at her sides as her body arched against his with warm, soft undulations. "Jake, more."

He slid to sit beside her on the lounger. Pulling her closer, he flattened her generous breasts against him until he could feel their beading response scorching through his shirt.

Suddenly, he knew exactly what Allie had meant about her near drowning. The sheer experience of her churned through his senses until he couldn't have found reason if he'd tried.

Jake lowered her, and when she didn't protest, he allowed his weight to anchor her with the most primal protection, his body covering hers. "You've had me on edge since the minute I saw you."

"Good. We're even."

He tunneled his hand beneath her tank top and cupped the roundness he'd ached to explore since he'd seen her by the pool. Jake shoved up her top with a hurried, impatient grasp. He paused above her, his hands lowering for reverent caresses. "Beautiful."

Greedily, he latched onto the peak that strained against her satin bra. Jake nipped and suckled and reveled in her writhing beneath him. Incredible, feeling the hard tip between his teeth, against his tongue, but he needed more. He moved to the creamy flesh swelling over, nuzzling, laving the undiluted taste of her. She grabbed fistfuls of his hair and yanked his head up, guiding his mouth to hers.

"Jake, I— I need— I can't—" She gasped disjointed phrases against his lips.

Urgency gripped him as tightly as her fingers clutching his hair. What had happened to his resolve for distance? Hell, maybe this would be the best way to work through the madness. He knew he was only telling himself what he wanted to hear, but he needed more than anything to lose himself in her smile, bury himself inside her.

Allie looked up with eyes so dark the purple turned near black, like the midnight ocean. And in a flash he thought of that little girl flipping underwater because she'd ventured too far from her safe boundaries.

"Jake? What's wrong?" Confusion flickered through her passion-fogged eyes.

There was so much he couldn't offer the incredible, infuriating woman beneath him. But he'd promised to protect her. That much, he could do.

He groaned, his forehead meeting hers. Jake struggled with each ragged breath.

Control returned, shaky, but present. "Do you want to go inside? We'll have sex, and it will be good—damned good. But that's all."

She'd been right earlier when she'd said he offered confusing signals. By giving her a choice rather than simply leaving, he'd kept his options open. He hadn't been able to close the door completely.

Jake chose his next words with care, knowing they would

send her running. "Is that what you want? A mock wedding night to go with the farce of a ceremony? Who knows, maybe they'll issue us a phony divorce decree on the way out."

Allie stiffened beneath him, and Jake enjoyed not even a glimmer of victory. She shoved at his shoulders until he hefted himself from her.

"You win, Jake. You've convinced me you can be a moody jerk." Allie leapt from the lounger. She combed trembling fingers through her snarled curls. "Too bad you can't convince yourself not to be scared of me."

She spun away, grappling with the handle on the sliding door until she stumbled inside their darkened room.

Jake flung himself onto his back, dragging in gasping breaths. Hell, yes, he was scared of her. It would take a long time before he could walk into that room alone with Allie and a basket full of condoms.

Why hadn't he kept his mouth shut? He stunk at conversation anyway. He should have let the tide take them both. They would have been in the middle of the best sex of a lifetime. Instead, he'd pushed her away as surely as if he'd tossed her into a pool.

Damn it, he'd done it to protect her, not for himself.

But he'd hurt her, as surely as if he'd taken her.

Their hotel-room light switched on, shining through the sliding door curtains. Jake tortured himself with images of Allie preparing for bed. Who would have thought he'd find overlong jerseys sexy? Her full breasts swaying gently beneath the fabric had sent him near insane the past two nights.

He would give her, and himself, at least a half hour before he showered and went to bed. A muffled thud sounded from the room, and it took every ounce of his restraint not to offer help.

A second thud sounded.

Followed by a muffled scream from Allie.

A scream. Not a yelp, or cry of pain. But a scream cut short.

Every muscle in Jake's body tensed. He shot to his feet, flinging aside the chair as he dashed toward the patio door and whoever had dared threaten Allie.

# Chapter 9

Allie clawed at the beefy arm restraining her. Terror clawed right back at her stomach. What the hell was going on?

She'd stepped into her room, dazed from the passion fog of Jake's kisses combined with the sting of his not-so-subtle rejection, only to be ambushed by some goon who looked like a college linebacker. Given the alcohol-tainted breath reeking over her shoulder, she feared a drunken mauling.

Allie gasped for air beneath the sweaty palm. How could she have gone from Jake's arms to this?

She wouldn't. Allie jammed her elbow in his stomach and stomped his instep. His yelp of pain rewarded her efforts.

A flash of movement snagged her attention, stirring a fresh bubble of panic. A second, stockier man wearing a battered ball cap pushed away from the wall. He whipped his cap free, swiping an arm over his oily, slicked back hair. "Geez, Bud, can't you take care of one little woman by yourself?"

Allie sagged against the restraining arm. One guy, she could have handled. Now, she would need Jake's help to handle Slick. Were there even more hidden or on their way?

Her teeth clamped down on the fleshy palm.

"Damn it!" Bud growled, shaking his injured hand. "She's tougher than she looks."

"Jake!" Allie shrieked with lung power that would have made her brothers proud. "There're two—"

Bud's arm undercut like a brace. Air whooshed from her lungs.

"Listen, lady, do that again and I won't be so gentle."

*Jake, where are you?* Had he gone for a walk after all? She had to buy time.

Slick grabbed her face in one paw, pinching until tears sparked unbidden in her eyes. "Doesn't look like your friend is coming."

Allie kicked out with both feet, catching Slick in the belly.

Damn. She'd been aiming for his crotch. And now her legs hurt. The man was a brick wall.

He gasped, straightened and stopped a rancid exhalation away from her face. His hand shot forward, and he squeezed a breast, hard. Allie couldn't hold back a yelp of pain.

The patio door smacked the wall. Jake charged into the room with a primal roar. He dipped his shoulder low, plowing into the men restraining Allie.

All the advantage Allie needed, even odds.

They crashed to the floor in a tangle. Jake ripped Slick off her. He jammed his knee in the man's gut before slamming his head to the floor in a lethal flash. Slick's ball cap tumbled away.

Allie fought to win, with nails and fists. She gouged at Bud's eyes, punched his Adam's apple. She wouldn't let Jake down.

Having the thug on the defensive, she kneed her assailant, with truer aim this time. Bud rolled to his side. He curled in a fetal ball and heaved. Gasping, Allie notched her knee in his back and yanked his arm around and up, not that he seemed able to protest.

Jake spared a glance for Allie, his jaw so tight the skin whitened beneath his beard stubbled face. "You okay?"

Allie nodded, unable to push words past the wheezing breaths shuddering through her.

With a brisk nod, he turned away. He braced his arm against Slick's chest and pinned him with a glare as forceful as his bulging arms. "Talk."

The man coughed a laugh and tried to buck himself free. Jake plowed a fist across his jaw. "Fine. I'll call the cops and let them deal with you."

A movement from the bathroom snagged Allie's attention. A third man stepped into the room, no drunken collegiate this time. A man with the feral eyes of one seasoned in threats leveled a gun at them.

With a chilling certainty, she realized this wasn't some haphazard rape attempt gone wrong. She'd known Phillips was a creep, but she hadn't imagined her digging would evoke such a violent backlash. She'd been so careful. How had he found out?

Allie's gaze skittered to Jake. His bunched muscles, delineated through the cotton shirt, pulled taut across his shoulders. Had it only been minutes before he'd covered her so gently with that same powerful body?

"Not so fast with that phone call." The lanky man strolled across the carpet with seeming lazy strides, one-hoop earring glinting in the dim light. "I have got to admit.

I'm pretty impressed. Maybe I should hire you two. But, I've already got these goons on the payroll, and they're nothing if not loyal.'' The roguish glimmer of his smile completed the pirate aura of his earring. ''Let them loose, please.''

Allie could see Jake mentally weighing the options. If one of them could tackle the third guy, could the other take care of the two wounded bouncers? Allie tensed, ready to act on Jake's cue.

Adjusting his revolver, the Pirate centered it on Allie's forehead. Jake's muscles twitched in small, convulsive jerks under his shirt.

The Pirate had chosen well.

She stared at Jake and shook her head. His cool eyes showed no sign he'd registered her message.

The Pirate sauntered closer to Allie, gun unwavering. ''No need to make it ugly. We're just here to give you a message about nosey private eyes. Boss's orders. No one has to die if you're willing to listen. You decide.'' He pressed the cool metal to Allie's forehead. ''Soon, please.''

Jake kicked free and pushed to his feet. The gun eased away an inch. Allie sagged, then straightened. She wouldn't turn into some wilting flower now. She'd gotten them into this mess, and she owed Jake her strength in return.

Slick scooped his ball cap from the floor, struggling to stand, until he swayed in front of Jake. Sneering, Slick swung an arm back and punched him in the gut. Jake huffed with the exhalation, but didn't wince.

Allie did.

She clutched Jake's arm and glared at the men. ''Okay. Give us your message.''

The Pirate gestured out the door. ''Not here.''

A hint of smile tugged at a corner of Jake's mouth. ''Of course.''

Jake extended a hand to Allie. Reluctantly, she let him pull her toward the patio door, stepping on Bud's hand on her way past.

"Ouch, damn it!"

"Sorry." She wanted to offer the same to Slick for hurting Jake. Rage and fear warred within her.

Jake squeezed her fingers. "Careful, Allie. Stay calm. Think."

The Pirate paused in the doorway. "Yeah, listen to your guy there." He gestured with a flick of the gun. "Outside."

Allie clung to Jake's hand, her only constant at the moment, and steadied her focus. She lagged, looking for something, anything to delay until they could attract attention. Surely her screams would have solicited some response. "Why can't we talk here?"

Looking into Jake's eyes, Allie saw in his darkening depths what she'd feared. These guys weren't interested in talking. They wanted to get them away from the hotel, which could only mean they planned to hurt them.

*Oh, God, please no.* Jake had been hurt enough.

The Pirate nudged the revolver in her side, shielding it with his body as they left the room through the patio door. She swallowed the acrid taste of fear. Her breast still burned from the thug's brutal grip. It didn't ache near as much as the thought of anyone harming Jake, and even worse, because of her. "Jake, I'm—"

"Not now."

A full moon cast crazy, merging shadows as they walked. Jake swayed into her, his ambling limp pressing heavier with every step. She hitched her arm around his waist and tried to support him.

His gaze flickered down to her. "I'm fine."

Allie stared at him, mesmerized. God, he looked magnificent, a wounded lion, but ferocious nonetheless, as if the pain only goaded him.

Why hadn't she stayed on the porch with him? Why had she ever kissed him and lost her ability to think? She'd allowed her emotions to blind her to business. No wonder she couldn't become a cop. She would probably get herself and everyone else killed.

She'd plunged into that room with no regard for safety, and now they both had to pay the price for her lack of control. *Jake, I'm so sorry.*

Thoughts of Robbie blindsided her, a sweet kid who worried about his dad. A sense of failure constricted her lungs. Even if Jake escaped with little more than a few bandaged injuries, would the child who had already lost one parent ever feel safe?

And it was her damned reckless fault.

Frantically, Allie searched for some way to send a message for help. The near-deserted beach offered few options. Too far in the distance to be of any use, a group of revelers surrounded a bonfire that licked toward the sky. An occasional strolling couple was either out of reach or too ensnared by romance to enlist.

She scoured the oceanfront rooms, wondering if any occupants might happen to gaze out and somehow realize—

Who was she kidding? There wasn't anyone but a lone man lounging on a patio, chair tipped back as he sipped a late-night drink.

Neil Phillips. She should have guessed.

Of course, if confronted, he would say he hadn't known anything was wrong. The gun was hidden from sight. But Phillips had broadcast his victorious message of power anyway. Lord have mercy, Neil didn't scrimp on getting his point across. The show of force seemed exorbitant, even considering what she'd uncovered.

Through the patio door, Tonya joined Neil. A flicker of hope seized Allie, until Tonya planted a kiss on Neil and enticed him inside before Allie could manage a diversion.

"This way." The man yanked her arm, pressing the gun deeper. Her gun-toting escort led them to a deserted niche in the coastline. "We're going for a ride."

Allie wove past palm trees to their destination, a dock, with a low slung cigarette boat tied and waiting. All bravado and resolve gushed from her like a receding wave. Her heels dug deeply in the sand.

Jake halted behind her, gripping her shoulders. "Come on, Allie. No scenes now."

His soothing caress barely made a dent in her immobilizing dread. Allie pressed her spine into Jake's solid chest as if she could somehow meld herself to him. He nudged her forward. She pushed back.

These goons weren't going to rough them up. They were going to toss them into the ocean.

The bottomless ocean.

She screeched like a banshee. Her clenched fists flailed wide. She kicked out at the thugs, Jake and the world.

Allie's screams echoed in Jake's head. He wrapped his arms around her waist to restrain her. If he'd assessed the situation correctly, their attackers wouldn't hesitate to put a bullet in her back if she ran.

He couldn't waste time wondering how Phillips had been tipped. Jake would have been prepared if he hadn't been panting over Allie like some teenager.

"Allie!" Jake lifted her off the ground, stumbling back a step. Pain clawed up his leg. "You have got to control yourself!"

He freed an arm to pin hers. Her bunched fists pummeled the air. He caught an elbow in the jaw. Damn, but she packed a surprising punch. Too bad she hadn't directed it at someone else.

"No!" She arched her back, legs kicking. "I'm not getting in."

The gunman looked too enamored with his weapon for Jake's peace of mind.

"Allie," Jake whispered, since shouting obviously wasn't working. "I won't let anything happen to you. Come on, Allie, play along. Pull out one of your acting jobs. You can do it."

His words weren't getting through. This woman wasn't afraid. She was terrified, her panic bordering on a phobia. A roaring sense of frustration echoed through him, stronger even than when he'd seen the man attack Allie.

Their only hope was in being dumped from the boat alive. He was bargaining on the gut instinct that these guys didn't want to shoot until they were out on the ocean, away from witnesses. Sometime after they left the shore, Jake could make his move. His Air Force survival training made a swim to shore the better option than a shoot out on the beach. He had an edge their captors didn't know about.

Or he would if he could get Allie to stop screaming long enough. Her head jarred under his chin. Grunting, Jake fielded the latest of her struggles.

The Pirate sauntered toward them. "Shut her up, or I'll do it for you."

"Allie! Allison!" Jake loosened his hold and turned her in his arms. He gripped her face. "He's going to shoot you if you don't stop."

She sagged, her eyes filling with tears. "Jake, don't you know they're going to kill us anyway? At least then I'll die touching ground."

"Shhh. Hush for just a minute." He cradled her head with his hand. She felt so right against him in the midst of situation gone so damned wrong. "You've got to trust me. Okay?"

Her chin dipped in what he hoped was consent, but he couldn't be certain. At least she wasn't screaming.

Jake turned to the Pirate and nodded. Could the guy actually think he was dumb enough to believe they were only going to talk? Jake hoped so. He couldn't fight three of them and a revolver on land, not with his leg pushed past its limits. They'd been lucky back at the room. A second brawl would be too risky.

He tucked Allie under his arm as they walked down the planked pier. Their footsteps echoed in the silence. The water lapped against the edge, splashing their feet as if already eager to receive them.

They settled into the sleek cigarette boat in silence, the engine roaring to life without a splutter. Bud took the controls. Jake chose a bench seat and kept his arm locked around Allie.

He'd somehow lost sight of how small she was. Her exuberant approach to each day gave her more presence than the shivering woman huddled against him. She had so much life stored inside one petite package—a fierce defender of children, connoisseur of the simple beauty of a conch shell, giving lady full of passion.

The weight of responsibility for what he'd allowed to happen threatened to steal his concentration.

With each chop of the boat against the waves, Jake steadied his breathing. He focused on staying alive, preparing for the ordeal he knew was ahead of them. He almost managed to ignore the flowery scent wafting from Allie's hair.

The shoreline lights grew fainter, but still offered a beacon for navigation. He estimated they'd covered three miles. The full moon provided more than enough illumination for him to keep track of Allie once they landed in the water.

What would Allie do when the time came to jump? He refused to worry about that now.

While he would prefer not to leap from a speeding boat, driving more than five miles out substantially decreased his chances of making it back with Allie in tow. Her swimming skills weren't stellar, and her fear of the ocean would further diminish them.

He'd exaggerated his limp on the way to the boat, hoping the trio would underestimate his ability. A slim hope, but the best bet he had going at the moment.

Four miles out. Not much longer. Jake ducked his head to warn Allie to prepare to jump, then reconsidered. Her pale face didn't inspire confidence that she could stay calm at his announcement. A gunshot wound in the water would attract sharks.

He allowed himself to skim a kiss across the top of her hair. Regret ripped through him at the possibility of never seeing her smile again. He hadn't been able to prevent Lydia's death, but he would get Allie to shore if he had to drag her the entire way.

Bud cut back the engine's power. The boat gurgled to a halt.

The Pirate frowned. "Why are you stopping? We're not out far enough."

Stepping away from the wheel, Bud braced his feet to absorb the swaying rolls. "I've got a debt to settle, and I don't feel like waiting another few miles." He jerked a thumb at Allie and Jake. "Get up."

Allie shuddered.

"I told you to stand."

Jake pulled Allie to her feet and assessed the deceptively calm waters. While he longed to slug the leer from Bud's face, he had to be thankful they'd stopped early. Jake savored breaths, readying for the impending moment of deprivation.

Bud nodded toward Jake. "Not you." He unsnapped his shorts. "Just her."

Jake's focus narrowed to a pinpoint of steely rage. He swiped the man's feet out from under him. Yanking Allie by the arm, Jake charged up a seat to the side of the boat. His ankle screamed in protest at the abuse.

He would rather dive. But he couldn't risk releasing Allie's hand and having her balk. He wasn't swimming to shore alone.

Jake wove his fingers with Allie's and hurtled them both overboard.

# Chapter 10

The ocean swallowed Allie like a murky vat of chilly retribution. Her nose stung. Briny wash clogged her mouth.

She lost all sense of surface and ground. Her world centered on Jake's hand gripping hers. She clutched him with a desperate strength born of panic.

A scream within her pleaded for release. Churning water and bubbles swirled against her skin, brushing her with terror. Her arms thrashed. She tried to will herself to stop struggling, but couldn't.

An insistent tug from Jake as he surged upward unfurled her body. The world righted itself. The fear didn't go away, only eased a bit, but at least she knew which way was up.

Another jerk from Jake stopped her from resisting. Her arm extended as she trailed him, gripping his hand. Allie's lungs burned. Her chest constricted. How much further to the surface? And what awaited them?

She just wanted out of the ocean.

Jake adjusted their underwater path. He steered them toward the boat's looming hull, a faintly distinguishable black shadow. Relief trickled through her. At least they would have a momentary respite to breathe beneath the protective overhang. She shook her sandals free and pumped her legs.

Nearing the surface, they slowed. Allie eased her head into the humid air, her shoulders bobbing. The speedboat's sleek nose shadowed them from sight. Waves slapped the drifting craft. She gulped in air, carefully quiet gasps laden with salty spray and fear.

She was alive. For how long? Her teeth chattered, but she wasn't cold.

Where was Jake? Her hand convulsed around his. She found him waiting beside her, steady, breathing.

"Jake?"

He pressed a finger to her lips.

"Hey, Bud." The Pirate's voice cut the air. Flashlight beams flickered over the water. "Where the hell are they? The boss is gonna be mad that your hormones screwed this up."

"Why would we tell, huh? Who cares as long as they're dead? They can't survive under water much longer. Even if they do, that guy isn't going to be able to make it to shore, especially with his little piece in tow."

The boat rocked above Allie and Jake as the men moved about. "You'd better be right. Maybe we'll luck out and the sharks will destroy the evidence."

Sharks. The single word plummeted her into the smothering terror she'd felt on the beach. Allie gulped down nausea. She even contemplated climbing back into the boat until Jake pulled her close. Reason returned, shaky, but present. The sharks in the boat posed a far more imminent threat.

The engine slid from idle to a deafening growl. Jake shoved Allie under water, deep and hard. The gushing wake from the passing engine pounded along her body with frightening intensity.

Jake held them both under until shards of light prickled behind her eyes. The sparks faded to a narrow pinpoint, and she feared losing consciousness.

With a tug and kick, once again Jake propelled them toward fresh air, exploding free this time. Allie inhaled greedy breaths as the cigarette boat roared toward the slim horizon of lights.

Jake turned to Allie, his face catching the rays of the full moon. "You all right?"

"I think so." She nodded, her legs working a jerky pace. Would she ever be able to stop, or would she have to swim until she died? Stories of shark attacks were oversensationalized, weren't they? She swallowed and coughed, choking on another rolling wave. "What do we—"

"No energy to waste arguing." His clipped words slid between even breaths. "Listen. Okay, Allie?"

"Okay."

"Two choices. Float until someone picks us up."

Which of course probably wouldn't happen until morning, at least eight hours away. "Or?"

"Or we can swim in. Regardless, the closer we are, the better our chances for rescue. No one's going to miss us anytime soon."

She steeled herself for a glance at the too distant shoreline. It was just the two of them with a few little stars and the huge yellow moon for company. Her lashes fluttered closed as if that might somehow erase reality. Already her arms ached. But what choice did she have? She gave him a small nod.

"May not have to swim long," he explained, his choppy phrases matching rhythm with the swipes of his free arm visible just below the surface. "Allie, I'm not winging it here. I've been through water survival tougher than this. Do what I say. You'll be fine. Are you listening?''

Of course she was listening. His ability to talk at all inspired confidence. His even tones rumbled over the ocean, warming her with hope.

''Jake,'' she gasped, ''sorry. My fault. I—''

''Allie. Not the time for this. Tell me on the shore.'' His voice held no hints of condemnation, only a calm as smooth as the gentle night waters, and just as complex with the frightening undertows beneath.

His hand slid free from hers. Panic shot through Allie stronger than the moment when they'd plunged into the water. Her hands thrashed at the surface, groping for Jake's solid body.

He slid his palms beneath her arms and steadied her. ''Allie, you can't afford to panic. Hang tough.''

She wanted to. Where had all her spunk gone? This wasn't like her, but she didn't know how to scrounge inside herself for her infamous grit. She sniffled, hating the pathetic, self-pitying tears. ''You go.''

''Damn it, Allison!'' His voice turned steely, offering the first hint of frustration. ''I'm not leaving you here. If you sink, I sink, too. Come on, I've got a kid at home. Don't do this.''

Tears stung and spurted free. ''Oh God, Robbie! Jake, sorry—''

He gave her a gentle shake. ''On the shore. Okay?''

Allie focused on his regular breaths, willing herself to relax. This was her fault. She owed it to him, and to Robbie, to make sure they came out alive. ''Okay.''

A sigh shuddered through him as if he'd expected less from her. Disappointment stabbed through her that he thought so little of her. She couldn't blame him. She hadn't performed up to standards, first at the beach with her tantrums and then with her lethargic acceptance. "I can do this."

"Of course you can. You're an athlete. That endurance will carry you through. There's no hurry. Easy and steady strokes. Ready?"

She nodded. His fingers tightened before sliding away, slowly, as if he didn't trust her not to panic again. She gritted her teeth and willed herself not to sink, grab for his hand, give up. The hardest thing she'd ever done.

Allie peeled off her sopping wet jean shirt, leaving only her tank top and shorts. She stared into Jake's eyes and gulped. "Okay."

"Good, girl. Pace yourself with me." Jake's body leveled with the surface, a long, powerful line of muscle and will. Allie slid beside him and dipped her hand into the water.

She swam, the slicing swoosh of Jake's strokes, the sting of water in her eyes, nose and mouth becoming the entirety of her world. If they made it to shore, would Phillips be waiting to toss their exhausted bodies back into the ocean? If they were picked up by a boat, would it merely be another of Phillips's henchmen?

Allie swam until even her skin burned. The drudgery of swimming gave her too much time for self-recriminations. Without her, Jake could double his pace. Without her, he wouldn't be stuck in the ocean at all.

She'd scoffed at Jake's reserve, yet wasn't that very cultivated self-control saving them? Her impulsiveness had almost gotten them killed. She had judged him as unworthy, deemed him not the right kind of man for her, yet never fully comprehending how totally wrong she might be for him.

Sure, she knew she wasn't the glamorous type suited for his lifestyle. But on a deeper level, she hadn't considered how her impetuous approach to life would eventually erode any tender feelings he might develop for her. She'd only thought of how little he could give her, never considering how lacking her offering might be in return.

Allie trudged ahead a stroke before she realized Jake had stopped. She was afraid to stop, fearing she'd never be able to start again.

Jake clutched her foot and halted her with a gentle tug. "Quit for a minute. You need a break."

"I'm fine," she insisted through huffing breaths. How long had they been swimming? Did she even want to know?

"You're doing great. But this isn't a sprint. It's a marathon."

"That sure sums up our differences, huh?"

Golden moonlight highlighted a smile kicking up one corner of his mouth. "We can reserve energy by resting with the occasional dead man's float."

Allie flinched.

"Relax. We're gonna make it. Changing strokes will help, front to back, dog paddle, floating. Okay?"

"Okay. I just want to be through."

"I know, Allie. Don't give up. You're a strong woman."

Empty praise? She hoped not.

After a short respite, they resumed their pace. Her arms ached. Even her toenails hurt. Their swim became a symbol for the ways she'd failed to channel her life. She'd always thrown all her efforts into one kind of stroke, not realizing she needed to adapt her techniques over the long haul.

Each weary slap of her arms against the water reverberated through her body. How often she'd bemoaned her brothers' overprotective ways. But had she ever made a genuine effort to stop them? She'd used their protection as a safety net to avoid the risk of relationships, just as she'd used Jake's dependability as a shield for her own impetuosity at White Sands. Just as she was using him now.

God, she was tired. Her arms thudded against the water like leaden logs. Her quivering legs begged to stop, to sink, weighting the rest of her with it, spiraling her to the bottom.

But Jake would follow her down. Strong, steadfast Jake would never give up. For him, she would keep swimming.

Allie's resolve strengthened.

Somehow, she arced her arm over again, forcing it through the water. Then the other arm and the other, following in an endless pattern. She found a sense of Jake's rhythm and adopted it as her own. Every turn of the head to gasp for air rewarded her with the whisper sounds of his strokes hitting the water, steady beside her.

"Allie."

Her arm smacked the water—for Jake.

"Stop!"

Her other hand cut a trembling wake. She turned for a breath. Jake, she would find Jake. Dependably, he waited beside her.

Not swimming, but treading upright.

How could that be? Had she started hallucinating? Her arm whacked the water. She swam. But Jake wasn't moving.

And neither was she.

Her body had betrayed her restored will and given up. She'd failed Jake. She'd failed Robbie.

She'd failed herself.

Jake knew Allie had exhausted her endurance. She'd lasted longer than he'd expected. He'd hoped they might just ride the tide in, or at least come across a boat. No such luck.

He didn't have energy to waste on regrets that threatened

to drown him more effectively than the cresting waves. "It's all right. Rest a minute."

Wrapping his arms around her waist, he pulled her toward him. She sagged into him, her arms limp around his neck, her breasts pillowed against his chest.

Damn, if he had to die, this wasn't a bad way to go.

He frowned. Where had the humor come from, the odd flashes of distracting emotion?

"Jake. Sorry. So sorry. Tried," Allie said through spluttering gasps. "Really tried."

"I know." His tread wasn't nearly as strong as he would have liked, nor his concentration, but he didn't have a choice. He had to support her. Her soft, wet body melded to him, her bare feet tangling with his. If he let go, she would sink. His mind raged against the possibility with a roar that defied the screaming pain in his weakened leg. More disrupting emotions. He had to get himself under control or he wouldn't be of any use to her. "I know you tried. It's okay."

"No! It isn't. Whole thing's my fault," she cried into his neck. "Jake, please go. For Robbie. Go."

Thoughts of his son knifed at him, the strongest distraction of all. He refused to consider the possibility that he and Allie wouldn't both make it. "Doesn't work that way. We stay together. Can you tread on your own for a minute?"

Her chest moved against his with heaving breaths before she eased away. Determination shone in her eyes, glinting in the moonlight. "Yeah. I'll be fine."

"I know you will." Jake reached below the water. He scooped his wallet, change and keys from his pockets until his fingers clutched his dog tags. How ridiculous to take reassurance from something so insignificant. He slipped them over his neck and tucked them inside his shirt, a reminder of the man that still lived within him. "Okay, lady. That's it for swimming. We're gonna make you a float."

"Huh?"

"I'm going under for a second." Jake unlooped his belt and slid it free. "Not gonna panic on me, are you?"

She bit her lip, shaking her head.

"Atta, girl." Jake inhaled, sealed his mouth and ducked below the waves. Mesmerized, he felt the swirl of water against him as Allie's legs churned a jerky rhythm. The hypnotic lure of the movements filled him with a lulling lethargy, urging him to surrender to the fatigue.

With a twitch, he startled from the near trance that could kill them both. Ignoring the exhaustion, he slipped his khakis free. Not exactly how he'd hoped to shuck his pants around Allie for the first time.

A grin tugged at his mouth in spite of his exhaustion.

Jake broke through the surface. Allie's sigh trembled. He hoped she wouldn't cry. He didn't think he could handle tears. His khakis floated in front of him.

"Jake?" Confusion tinged her voice. "Don't you think your timing's a little off?"

"I was starting to miss your mouth."

Her weak laugh was the most beautiful sound he'd heard in a long time.

Jake knotted the end of each pant leg. Holding the waistband, he draped the legs backward over his shoulders. He whipped the khakis forward, inflating them, then cinching the waist with his fists. The pants floated, bobbing along the surface.

"Works as advertised." Jake tightened his grip. "I know it looks crazy, but I read about a sailor who fell overboard and used this as a survival device. He reinflated the thing for three days."

"Three days?" Her voice wobbled.

"Not that I expect we'll be out here that long," he re-assured her. "Okay, Allie. Swim in. Tuck a leg under each arm. Grab the front. Seal the air."

Allie paddled forward with uneven, choppy grapples. She sprawled into the makeshift float, her fingers folding over his. Her hands trembled. "Thanks. This'll do it. I'll be fine in a minute. Just need—to catch—my breath. You next. Okay?"

"Sure." Not a chance. Jake allowed himself to keep his hold on the waistband, as close as he would come to accepting the buoyancy, as close as he would come to accepting the comfort of her touch. "The inflation is good for about fifteen minutes. We'll keep repeating it. Our effort wasn't wasted. We made progress with the swim. Being nearer to shore increases our chances for pickup."

"Good." Allie propped her forehead on her extended arms, her eyes sliding closed.

He was beyond tired, but his grip on the makeshift raft gave him the edge he needed. Minutes passed, and the pants deflated. Allie swam free, her strokes surer, but not strong enough while Jake reinflated the pants.

"Your turn," she huffed, pumping her arms. "Jake!"

"Come on." He nudged the raft toward her.

"Not any good to fight you, huh?"

"Nope. Don't worry. I'm getting as much as I need holding on."

Sighing, Allie settled back into the float's embrace and rested her cheek on her arm.

Jake repeated the process countless times. Although dawn seemed imminent with a hazy glow edging just on the horizon, he worried about Allie's endurance. The ocean rolled, calm and gentle now. But gale force storms could blow in with little warning.

Her slow blinking gaze grew glassy. What would he do

if she fell asleep and slipped from him? He could remain afloat until help stumbled on them, but he couldn't institute an underwater rescue. He had to keep her talking.

"Allie." Was that the best he could do? If they had to depend on his conversational skills to stay alive, they were in bigger trouble than he'd originally thought. "What are you thinking?"

There, that was better.

"About stuff." Her voice eased along the waves, husky and scratchy.

"Like?"

"Regrets." Her eyes fluttered closed, but her fingers held tight over his. "The whole life review thing if this is going to be it for me."

His hands twitched under hers. "It's not."

"Could be."

"You could climb out of this and die in a fluke accident." Hadn't that happened to Lydia? He'd faced life-threatening situations for a living and survived unscathed, but she'd been taken out by a careless driver.

"Yeah, I could. But the present seems a little more dangerous."

"You've got a point." Jake chuckled, then realized where the erratic breaks in concentration had come from—more of Allie's influence.

"Do you have regrets, Jake?"

"Sure." Big ones. Not that he planned to discuss them. He settled for sharing the obvious. "I want to see my son grow up, go to his college graduation. What about you?"

"Lots of the regular ones. I never nibbled croissants for breakfast in Paris. I never devoured a whole box of Godivas, since I could only afford one at a time."

How like Allie to have dreams centered on junk food.

"I'll treat you to a box when we get out of here. What else?"

"I wanted to be a cop."

She never stopped surprising him.

"A cop?"

"Yeah. I actually applied to the police academy before I chickened out. Oh, I convinced myself it was all because I didn't like the confining rules and structure. Being a P.I. would better suit my personality." She wrinkled her nose with an inelegant snort. "Bull. I was afraid. Afraid I wouldn't measure up. My dad and brothers would know what a fraud I am. Then I would never belong."

Her eyes were fluttering again. He had to keep her talking. Jake scrambled for something else to ask her, anything to keep her alert. "What do your dad and brother have to do with it?"

Her eyes opened, and she seemed to rouse. "They're all police officers. Like I should be."

"Allie we're going to make it. You'll get that chance if you really want it," he vowed. He absolutely would not let her die. Jake blinked hard against the sting of salt water. Damn, it was tough to swallow. "Okay, chocolates and a new job. Any other regrets?"

"I've never made love."

His hands twitched around the float, almost releasing the air. Allie a virgin? More unwanted mishmashes of sentiments chugged through him—relief that he hadn't given in to her allure after all so he wouldn't have further regrets to add to a list already too damned long.

And a primal urge to be the first—hell, the only—man to hear her sigh with satisfied completion.

She extended a trembling hand and brushed a lock of damp hair from his forehead. "I don't regret that so much as the fact that I didn't make love with you, Jake."

If he hadn't felt the salty air weighting a path into his lungs, he would have sworn a rogue wave had washed over him. More than the words, he heard the emotion in her tone, just as he had during the vows renewal, and he panicked. "Allie, we're going to get out of this alive. We made it through the night. Someone will pick us up soon, and you're going to be sorry you said all of this."

"No, I won't, because it's the truth."

"What do you expect me to say?"

Bittersweet acceptance traveled through her touch into him with an odd connection that would have scared the pants off him, if he'd been wearing any.

"Not a thing, Jake. I just didn't want to regret never telling you."

A roaring sounded in Jake's brain. He couldn't answer her. They could very well die. Why the hell couldn't he make himself utter some romantic words she obviously wanted, even if they were a lie?

For the same reason he hadn't told Lydia how much she'd meant to him, a woman he'd cared about more than anyone. Even as her torn body had lay dying beside him in the wreckage of their car, Robbie's hysterical screams pulsing through the silence, Jake hadn't thought to say he loved her.

He thrived on success, had for as long as he could remember. Innate intelligence and control had helped him achieve every goal, except when it mattered most. He'd failed Lydia, himself, probably even Robbie.

And now he would fail Allie as well.

The roaring inside his brain increased. Rather than ignoring it, he accepted it, concentrating on the predictability of its drone. He compartmentalized his past away from the present, fixating on the need to survive. Jake resurrected his walls of reserve until he eased past the pain, beyond the disappointment, into a single point of focus.

The sun had risen, but Jake knew it was already too late for him to harbor hopes of salvation.

# Chapter 11

The roaring increased in Allie's ears. The rumbling transmitted into a pulsation battering through the water, along her skin. She wondered if perhaps she'd lost control of her senses. Had her body finally given up?

A thrumming drone mingled with music.

Music?

A raspy rock ballad wailed softly on the breeze. Realization energized Allie.

"A boat. Jake! A boat!" She scrambled to turn, loosening her hold on the float. A twenty-four-foot sloop chopped lightly across the water, puttering out to sea with minimal motor power. Neon orange and yellow sails flapped uselessly in the early morning calm. "Tell me I'm not hallucinating!"

"You're not. It's a boat. About damned time." Jake slung his deflated pants around his neck and waved an arm. "Hey! Hey, over here."

"Help!" Allie hollered, her hoarse tones a weak version

of what she normally would have blasted free. "Please! Help!"

"Over here!"

The nose of the hull seemed to shift. Allie redoubled her screams. "Hurry! We're here!"

Two of the boat's crew, a college-aged, bathing suit clad couple holding hands, loped to the bow. Lean and tan, they stood like mastheads surveying the horizon. The gangly man nudged the woman and pointed.

Hope surged through Allie. "Yes! Help us!"

The woman cupped her hands to her mouth, her ankle bracelet glinting in the morning sun. "We see you! Hold on! We're coming over."

Allie turned to Jake to hug him, squeal, perhaps celebrate with an impromptu water dance. "Jake, can you believe it?" She spluttered sea spray, no longer caring about the taste now that she knew it wouldn't be her last. "I'm going to take a hot shower and then order— Jake?"

He stared at her with one of those condescending looks that made her want to splash him in the face, which would only further prove his point.

Silently, she waited beside him. Why was he so hesitant to talk now when help had arrived and endurance was no longer an issue? They'd wasted precious energy on sense-less conversation over the past hours.

She acknowledged the obvious. He'd been trying to keep her awake and alive. He'd promised to protect her, and he'd accomplished his goal. But he'd never promised anything more. Not even to be her friend.

Allie shook off the depressing thoughts. He'd saved her life. She should be grateful. How ridiculous to expect that simply because they'd been rescued he would throw his arms around her and spit out some flowery declaration of his undying devotion.

The white hull eased closer. A second, bronzed man with sunglasses dangling from a cord around his neck pitched the roped lifesaver. It whizzed through the air before plopping a few feet out of reach. "Can you get it? Do you need me to come in?"

Jake shook his head. "We're fine."

Allie and Jake swam in synchronized strokes, a habit impossible to break after the past hours. Both grabbed for the ring and looped an arm through, their elbows touching.

A yank from the two men on board jerked the rope taut until Jake and Allie skimmed along the water. Her head fell to rest on her elbow, and she allowed her feet to stop moving. A sigh trembled through her. She yielded to the pull, her weightless limbs dragging behind her as if the water wanted to keep a part of her.

Slowing, they reached the back of the boat. Allie raised her head, a task almost more difficult than the swim itself. She looked up into the unfamiliar faces, grateful their thug pals hadn't returned. Two sets of hands reached overboard and grasped under her arms, hauling her inside.

"We've got you," one of the men said, his sunglasses swaying from the string in front of Allie's blurry eyes.

She collapsed onto the floor, her body shaking uncontrollably. Every muscle burned, hummed, then began cramping. She curled into a ball and simply breathed.

The woman knelt beside her, an anklet chiming as she draped a blanket over Allie. She lightly dabbed dry Allie's waterlogged body. "Hi there, I'm Marie. You're going to be fine."

While the water hadn't been cold, Allie knew that wasn't a safeguard against hypothermia. Shivering, she glanced up with a weak smile. "I'm..." Her voice rasped, a hoarse croak. She cleared her throat and tried again. "I'm Allie."

"Hello, Allie."

Marie couldn't have been more than twenty, with shoulder-length blond hair clipped back from her face. Allie felt unaccountably old. "Thank you, Marie, so much."

"Glad we were here for you two."

The boat shifted in a rolling undulation. Allie swept her fuzzy glance to the men as they pulled Jake from the water. Strained grunts resounded as they hauled his bulk inside, then sunk to the deck with the force of his weight.

His khakis slapped the damp floor.

Everyone stared. Allie watched the woman and two men try to contain their curiosity. Certainly questions could wait. More than anything, Allie wanted to crawl to Jake for one of his broad chested, all encompassing hugs, a comfort she knew wasn't her right to claim. She hurt so much she wanted to cry.

So she laughed.

Marie knelt beside her, patting her back. "Are you okay?"

"Perfectly awful." Allie laughed, at her own stupid behavior, her screwed up life and at Jake's pants draped sopping wet on the deck while he sprawled on his back in a polo shirt and navy blue boxer shorts. His beautiful sleek body stretched muscular and glinting before her, not too different from the first time she'd seen him.

And she wanted him, not the body, but the man inside who gave her pretzels, worried about his son and still winced at the mention of his wife after five years.

Tears stung, and she laughed harder, uncaring of the creeping edge of hysteria stealing over her. She held her sore sides and watched Jake struggle to recapture his regulated breathing pattern. His chest heaved with gulping breaths until he flung his arm over his face, chuckles rumbling free.

The trio exchanged hesitant looks. The lanky man slung

an arm around the woman's shoulder and smiled at Jake. "Hey, dude. What a time to be caught with your pants down, huh?"

Jake's hoarse laughter tripped over a snort of amusement. "That's an understatement."

Marie thunked her companion's hairless chest. "Warren, why don't you do something useful and call ahead for help?"

Jake's arm slid from his face, thudding to the deck, the controlled man returning. "Police. Call the cops to meet us, but not here. It's not safe. Go up to Key Largo."

Warren stared, then shrugged. "Whatever you say, dude."

Allie clutched the blanket. They would soon have the protection of the police, complete with an investigation and retribution. Phillips would pay. They'd cheated the consequences. She would have the chance to make it right. A chance to go to Paris, eat Godivas…make love to Jake?

Desperate to touch him, reassure herself of his warm vitality, she inched along the deck, a strenuous trek of probably not more than eight inches. She rested her hand on his chest, his heart echoing beneath the rigid wall of muscle. "Jake, thank you."

He winced, jaw tight. He turned his head to look at her, traces of laughter long gone, his eyes as opaque as the night ocean. A foreboding whisper of wind chilled her.

Marie returned with a drink and extra blankets. "Warren's calling while my brother hunts for extra clothes." She knelt beside Allie, offering a cup of juice. "This should perk you up."

"Thanks." Allie struggled to sit with Marie's hand pressed between her shoulder blades for support. She tried to hold the glass, but her hands trembled and she had no choice but to let Marie tip the drink for her. A single taste sent nausea roiling through her. "That's plenty. Thank you. I feel better."

Marie's brother tossed Jake a pair of running shorts and stopped midstride. "What happened to your leg?" He dropped the blanket beside Jake and moved a step closer. "Your ankle's really wrecked."

The chill turned to a cold core. Jake's foot. Why hadn't she thought of what the long swim would cost him? Knowing what she would find, Allie let her gaze travel down Jake's powerful thigh to his ankle. Already it had swollen until normal shape and definition were lost. No wonder he hadn't felt like talking.

Exhaustion shoved aside, she ripped her blanket from her shoulders and rolled it around her arms into a pillow. "Oh, Jake, why didn't you tell me?"

"Wouldn't have made any difference."

Leave it to Jake to be pragmatic.

"Stupid male ego. You could have taken your turn with the float," Allie grumbled, sliding her hand behind his knee. She looked into his eyes for signs of pain, but found nothing except his emotionless mask. What more would she expect from Jake?

So she cried for him.

Big, silent tears leaked from her eyes as she gently lifted his leg and slipped the blanket under his foot. Her hand hovered over his battered ankle. She could feel every excruciating stab he must have endured during their hours in the water, her conscience aching in response. Not once had she helped Jake. She'd let him save her, just as she'd allowed her brothers to persist with their overprotective ways.

In the water, she'd acknowledged her responsibility for the whole White Sands debacle, and then had made the same mistake. She'd had a chance to redeem herself, emerge a better woman. Again, she'd failed and still had no idea how to make restitution.

No, she wasn't at all the right woman for Jake.

Allie clutched her knees to her chest, her eyes sliding closed, kicking more tears free. The image of Jake's stoic face haunted her from behind her lids.

With Warren half carrying her, Allie followed Marie down the hatch for dry clothes, leaving Jake above deck talking with Marie's brother. What would it be like to go the rest of her life without hearing Jake's voice again? How odd to treasure the time they'd talked, floating in the middle of the ocean on a pair of inflated pants.

Warren left the two women, and Marie offered her arm for support as Allie sunk to the cushioned bench. She looked around the cabin, small, musty and wonderfully water free.

Marie offered her a dry sundress. "Sorry I don't have anything warmer. Do you need help?"

"No, thanks. I think I can manage."

Marie turned her back to give Allie privacy. "What happened to you two out there?"

"I can't believe you waited this long to ask." Allie knew she would have already exploded with curiosity. Of course, her impetuousness had put Jake's life at risk. "Long story. Basically, I'm a private investigator. I came a little too close to solving a case, and it got us dumped in the ocean."

"Wow. That sucks."

"Sure does." Allie finished struggling out of her wet clothes and into the dress, the simple task exhausting her. "All set."

Marie pivoted, sinking to sit cross-legged beside her. "How does your guy feel about your job?"

"Jake? Oh, he's not mine."

"Hmmm." Marie passed Allie a towel for her hair.

"He's not," she mumbled from beneath the towel, scrubbing her tangled curls dry.

"I believe you." Marie's eyes twinkled.

"We're not, but—"

Marie leaned back against the side of the boat. "But you want to be."

"Maybe." Allie let the towel fall to her lap, wanting a nap more than anything, except perhaps Jake's forgiveness.

The sails billowed, taut with propelling gusts. Each bump of the boat along the waves jarred through Jake. His body throbbed with a pain no amount of regulated breathing could control. But he'd survived. More important, he'd kept Allie alive.

Who had sold them out? He'd been too focused on survival to consider where the threat might lie, but now, he couldn't risk leading Allie into a trap. He couldn't relax until he had a wall of police protection around her.

Warren supported Allie as she climbed through the hatch and slumped on the cushioned seat across from Jake. She clutched her knees to her chest and sipped a drink, but refused food.

That worried him.

It shouldn't have. Allison St. James wasn't his responsibility. She would find some other man to take her to Paris, buy her Godivas…and introduce her to sex.

Jake let his head thump against the cabin. The sting of regret threatened to overpower the ache of his leg.

Wind whipped along his skin, a welcome distraction after hours spent in the water. He counted each sloshing dip of the hull that brought them closer to shore.

Apparently Warren's call for help had netted results. The beach drew nearer with each chop along the water, police cars already parked and waiting. Uniformed officers stood along the pier. Sirens blaring, an ambulance pulled into sight while Marie steered the sloop smoothly to the dock.

The jostling transfer from the boat was agonizing, but bearable. Allie's sympathetic whimpers weren't. He'd endured countless surgeries. He could withstand whatever came from this. Pity, he could not take. Prideful perhaps, but he didn't particularly care at the moment.

Hazy from pain, Jake provided terse answers to police questions while an EMS technician stabbed him with an IV needle, excavating for a vein. Jake barely felt the stick, having been a human pincushion for months following the accident. The technician issued an order to delay further interrogation until they reached the hospital.

As they wheeled Jake away, Allie struggled against the EMS worker tending her. "No! I'm riding with him."

"Listen, ma'am—"

"No, you listen!" She swayed in front of the technician, jabbing a finger at his chest. "After the night I've had, you don't want to mess with me. I'm going with Jake."

"O-kay." In the face of her heated determination, the technician gave up and allowed them to ride together.

Jake pulled a tired smile. His spunky Allie had returned. He sagged on the stretcher, finally giving into the exhaustion.

He battled the urge to sleep as they settled in the back of the ambulance. Jake lay on the stretcher like a damned invalid. Yet, he couldn't stop the wash of relief that they hadn't been separated. Allie perched across from him, pale, ragged, and beautiful. An IV line of glucose dangled from her arm.

"Allie? Are you okay?" The ambulance rocked along the rutted paved road. Jake gritted his teeth against the shards of white heat stabbing up his leg.

"Yeah, I'm fine." She glanced at the technician who was busy checking Jake's vitals. "Why wouldn't I be?"

"I'm sorry for landing you in this. I shouldn't have let myself get distracted by—" He mentally cursed their lack of privacy. "I let you down. I'm sorry."

"Jake! Would you quit with the martyr act?" Allie straightened, her old spark shimmering in her violet eyes. "You're not responsible for carrying the world on your impossibly broad shoulders! It's my fault. I was investigating Phillips. I got a little too close, and he found out. I didn't think he was dangerous. My mistake and you paid."

It had never occurred to him that she might blame herself for their midnight boat ride. How much could he tell her, and in front of some unknown EMS tech? A few minutes more and the police would be questioning them both, then she would understand. Fighting sleep became an increasingly difficult task. "There's undoubtedly more to this than that. Who could have known?"

Allie brushed her hair from her forehead, her untamed curls a tangled snarl around her face. "I should have seen it coming. I can't believe I ever thought I could actually cut it as a cop."

That snapped him from his drowsy fog. He wished his head was clear, his body rested and his instincts not dulled by exhaustion and pain. A deep pothole jolted pain though him. He swallowed a well of nausea. "A cop?"

"Remember? Like my stepdad and stepbrothers. I tried to tell Sam about Phillips and my suspicions regarding his drug connections, but my rock-headed brother wouldn't listen. He said there wasn't anything there and for me to pack it in." She shrugged. "So, I set out on my own."

"Police officers. All of them? In the Fort Walton Beach area?"

"Danny's over in Tallahassee. Trent and Matt work out of Atlanta. But yeah, Dad and Sam live in Fort Walton."

Jake's muddled brain shuffled information, and the emerging picture made him distinctly uncomfortable. Before he could finish adjusting the pieces into a clean fit, the ambulance jerked to a halt. Jake bit back a groan.

The ambulance doors flung wide, revealing the Emergency Room entrance and a cluster of police officers. A man in a coat and tie broke away from the crowd. The badge clipped to his waist broadcast his status as a detective. Apparently Jake's call to the state police the day before had garnered personal attention.

Robbie's creepy Officer Samuel Morgan lumbered toward the ambulance, his craggy features set in an ominous scowl. He braced an arm against the frame, blocking most of the outside light.

But Officer Morgan didn't seem to be looking for Jake. The detective's gaze zeroed in on Allie. "Well, hello, Allie Cat. I should have known I'd find you in the middle of this."

Allie's face creased into a wry smile. "Hi, Sam."

Jake looked from Allie to her stepbrother, and thought yet again how Allison St. James attracted more than her fair share of hits from Murphy's Law.

# Chapter 12

Allie slouched in the wheelchair as the nurse rolled her down the hall toward a cubicle where she would wait until her room was ready. She was glad to be finished with the Emergency Room poking and prodding so she could finally find out how Jake and her brother knew each other.

She'd submitted to the E.R. doctor's once-over. He'd diagnosed a mild case of hypothermia, ordering an overnight for observation with the fluid-replenishing IV. She'd landed on her feet, typical Allie Cat style as Sam would say. Someone else would pay for her impulsiveness—Jake.

She'd finessed information from a nurse that Jake's tentative diagnosis had been a severe sprain. He would be transferred home so the Eglin Air Force Base Hospital could determine if he needed surgery.

The grandmotherly nurse wheeled her into another cubicle. "The E.R.'s really swamped today," she said, rolling Allie past the glass supply cabinet and the closed privacy curtain to a gurney. "Sorry we have to keep you and your friend in here until your rooms open up. It shouldn't be long."

"Thanks." Allie smiled over her shoulder while climbing onto the gurney. The paper covering crackled as she settled on the edge.

"Buzz if you need anything." The nurse skirted out of sight around the curtain. "How are you doing, Mr. Larson? The doctor ordered some pain medication."

Jake's grumbling response as he rejected the shot brought Allie a needed touch of whimsy. Typical stoic Jake.

Only a drape of fabric separated them. Allie stared at the blue-and-green striped pattern. It might as well have been a resurrected Berlin Wall since Jake was an expert at building barriers.

Immediately after arriving at the hospital, she and Jake had been separated for individual statements. Sam had stood to the side, listening without commenting as she'd relayed the circumstances leading her to White Sands. The only time he'd shown emotion was at the mention of her sharing a room with Jake. The tic in the corner of Sam's eye had been disgustingly predictable.

What had Jake told them during his statement? And what was Sam doing in the Keys?

She heard the nurse's shoes squeak as she left. The door swooshed, only to hiss open again midswing. Allie looked up just as her eldest stepbrother lumbered toward her. He filled the room with his brooding bulk, dark hair spiking as if he'd worried his fingers through it a hundred times.

Allie slid off the edge of the table and into his bear hug. "I'm not sure how you knew to come, but I'm so glad you're here."

Sam gripped her with an almost painful strength. "Lord have mercy, Allie Cat, you've gotten into your fair share of scrapes, but you scared me big this time."

Allie sunk into the familiar comfort of his embrace and all the associated memories of home. She would give just about anything for the escape of a disorganized picnic. What would Jake think of her crazy, loud family where gourmet food and reserve were unheard of, but potato salad, grilled burgers and love flowed in abundance?

What was he thinking now, laying one insubstantial curtain away?

Pulling back, she tapped a finger on the bridge of Sam's slightly crooked nose. "Yeah, well, I told you Neil Phillips was up to something. Maybe you'll listen next time I give you a tip."

Sam yanked one of Allie's curls before stepping away. "I heard you the first time. You told me to take care of Phillips and I did."

"You did?"

"Of course, I did. Larson and I have spent the past month trying to nail the guy, and you blew it all in a couple of days!" He leaned until his bumpy nose stopped a mere inch from hers. "Allie Cat, what were you thinking coming down here?"

"Hold on just a minute," she snapped, rising on her toes with an ease born of numerous sibling battles. "Don't lecture me, you big lug. I was thinking about earning a living!" While not totally true, she managed to keep her gaze locked with his. Then his words filtered past her instinctive defensiveness. She thumped her brother on the chest before jerking her thumb toward the curtain. "You and Jake?"

"Jake? *Jake?*" Sam grabbed the edge of the curtain and flicked it open to reveal Jake. "Time to talk. Larson, are you up to it?"

Jake stared at Allie as she stood rigid and defensive, shadowed by hulking Detective Sam Morgan. Jake knew he should have sent her packing that first day at White

Sands, and now the reckoning had arrived in the form of a suspicious brother, who just happened to carry a revolver, if not a shotgun.

"I'm fine. We need to clear up a few things." Jake raised the bed so he wouldn't be caught downed and vulnerable. He stuffed an extra pillow behind his back, his ankle wrapped and immobilized in a sling.

His teeth ground with each excruciating movement. Pain pills could wait. The medicated stupor would come soon enough. He didn't need his senses muddled until he'd ensured Allie was protected from Phillips and whoever had been sending her threatening letters. "Allie, what about you? You okay?"

"The doctor ordered an overnight in the hospital with this stuff." She jiggled the IV line. "And you? The truth this time."

Jake ignored her question, refusing to risk something as weakening as sympathy, and looked past Allie to Morgan. "So you're Allie's stepbrother."

"When she'll claim me." Morgan glanced between the two with ill-disguised interest—and censure. "Thanks, Larson. I owe you for taking care of her out there."

"You don't owe me a thing. I never should have let it get this far. I intended to fly her home before you moved in on Phillips. If it hadn't been for those damned threatening letters, I would have sent her packing the first day."

"Sent me packing?" Allie perched her hands on her hips, her hair batting the air as she looked from Jake to her brother. "No one 'sends' me anywhere!"

Morgan glowered at Allie. "Threatening letters?"

"It's nothing." Allie tossed a quick scowl at Jake before transferring the force of her glare to her brother. "What's this with you and Jake and the whole Phillips deal?"

Damn, but she was sexy when fired up. His foot hurt like

hell. He had never felt so exhausted. But he wanted her and no busted foot full of pain could douse the heat.

Allie quirked a brow. "Well? Pony up some facts, boys."

Morgan hooked his hands on his hips, his thumb tapping his badge absently. "Phillips had business dealings in the area, was even an old neighbor of Larson's. He'd approached Larson's parents with some questionable condo investments, swampland in disguise sort of thing. Larson reported Phillips to the cops. The case was referred over to my desk since you'd already given me the tip on Phillips anyway. This offered us the perfect opening. With his investigative background and established connection with Phillips, our man here was the practical choice to assist us. Satisfied, Allie Cat?"

"You could have told me something instead of patting me on the head like a kid and 'sending' me on my way."

"And if you had used some common sense instead of plowing—"

"Common sense! When did you ever—"

"You're not on the force, so I'm not under any obligation to tell you—"

"Listen, Sam-the-Mule-Head, it's about time you quit treating me like—"

Jake sliced the air with his hand. "Stop! Both of you. Quit throwing blame around so we can figure out who's leaking information. Morgan, what's the word from your end?"

"We've already got someone searching for your thug pals. With your information, we should have enough to pick up Phillips for questioning so he can't skip the country while we nail down the rest."

Jake relaxed into his pillows. Morgan tugged at his tie. The guy had the neck of a pro athlete, and a scowl that would send a Doberman running. Except when he looked at Allie. His face creased into an affectionate smile. If the other three brothers looked anything like this one, Allie had a considerable blue wall of protection until he recovered.

But didn't he plan to walk away?

Of course not.

There wasn't a chance he could stop himself from checking on her, not that she wasn't able to take care of herself. During their ordeal in the ocean, she'd certainly held her own for far longer than most would. He'd known she had spunk. But a newfound respect built within him for her tenacious strength of will. "Good. With the leads I found on some account numbers, we're almost there. All we need is the name of one of his banks to tighten the noose."

Allie cleared her throat. "I've got a copy of an electronic transfer to his girlfriend's account."

Both men turned toward her.

"Phillips's bank transfer. A big one." She grinned. "I found a copy."

"And where is this bank?" Morgan's words slid through tightly clenched teeth.

"The Cayman Islands."

Didn't Morgan realize what a stupid risk Allie had taken? Jake cursed the restraining sling that kept him from shaking some sense into both of them. "And what were you doing snooping around Phillips's office? He wouldn't have been near as accommodating as I was when I found you in mine."

"I wasn't in his office. I, uh, found it in Tonya's pool bag while she was in the bathroom."

Only mildly placated, Jake asked, "And where did you stash it?"

"I hid it in our room."

Morgan's chin thrust forward. "*Our* room."

Allie sighed. "Back off, Sam."

Jake noted the looming detective's jutting jaw. Morgan didn't seem to care that Jake had placed Allie at risk, or even that she'd been rifling through other people's bank statements. Yet, he was ready to burst a vein over the thought of his twenty-six-year-old sister sharing a room with a man.

Jake's admiration for Allie's independence increased tenfold. She'd obviously battled long and hard for every inch of it. "Phillips has probably torn apart our—the—room by now. So it doesn't matter anyway."

"I doubt he found it." Allie swiped a lock off her brow. "Sam, when you get the search warrant, look inside the conch shell decorated like a pig. But be careful and don't break it, okay? It's kind of special to me."

An image of Allie with her bag of souvenirs and carefree air battered Jake's already weary body. Once again, the need to protect her gripped him, then gave him pause. Allie had plenty of protectors. She wouldn't want another, and didn't seem to need the efforts of the ones already in place.

But he had nothing else to offer her.

"Bye, Allie Cat." Sam shuffled his feet as if hesitant to leave her, even overnight in her own hospital room with a guard posted outside the door. "I'll be back in the morning to take you home. By then, we should have some word about your..." he paused, barely stifling a chuckle "...pig."

"Thanks." Allie tucked into his hug, then patted his cheek. "Try not to worry the family when you call home. I'm fine."

"Are you, really? You being here with Larson, well, I'm not comfortable with that. I don't know what's going on with you two—" He held up an open palm to silence her protest ready to spring free. "And I really don't think I could handle any gory details without further injuring an already incapacitated man. Be careful, okay?"

"Why the warning?" She twined the sash of her hospital robe around her fingers. "You trusted Jake enough to bring him into your investigation."

"That's a case. You're my sister."

"Ah, come on. I've only just met the guy. It's not as if I'm going to do something impulsive—"

Sam quirked a brow.

"Okay, so I've been known to be, uh—"

"Impetuous?"

"Spontaneous."

He stayed diplomatically silent.

"Not with relationships, Sam. Never that." When she committed, it would be forever. She would never settle for less than a hundred percent from any man. For too many years she'd settled for whatever leftover attention her father could spare for her. "Yeah, Jake's a good-looking guy, smart, funny—"

"Larson?"

Allie quelled him with a look. "Yeah, Jake can be funny sometimes. But it's not enough to make me jump into bed with the guy."

Sam winced as if he'd taken a bullet. "Okay! I get your point. No need to be graphic."

How could he be so infuriating and sweet at the same time? Allie grabbed his necktie and wrenched it up into a light chokehold. "Just worry about getting my pig back in one piece, all right? I can take care of the rest."

"Yes, ma'am." He carefully extracted his tie from her fist. "See you in the morning." Shooting a wave over his shoulder, he eased out the door.

Allie sunk to the edge of the hospital bed and stared at her ugly, green hospital slippers.

Jake was working with Sam.

Her brother didn't trust her enough to bring her in on the case, just Jake. For that matter, Jake hadn't trusted her enough to tell her about the investigation either. Of course they hadn't had reason to. It wasn't like she was a real cop or some hotshot OSI dude.

It all made perfect sense, all logical, neat and totally heartbreaking. Fort Walton was a small community. She and Jake would have crossed paths during the investigation anyway. Their meeting had nothing to do with fate.

Jake had told her of his history as an agent, and she'd been too caught up in the appeal of his broad shoulders to register the significance of his revelation. Of course he wasn't a money-grubbing suit like her father, having only turned to his current profession when life had limited his options.

Her momentary relief faded as she remembered his reserve had little to do with his job. His inescapable habit of slicing away emotion without notice was a hurdle far larger than his substantial bank account. He wasn't the type of guy she could be interested in long-term. And what of his feelings for his dead wife?

Allie sniffed and scrubbed her wrist under her nose. Geez, she hated turning into some weepy sap just because it was time for her and Jake to check out of their honeymoon suite.

Because they would never enjoy a wedding night together.

Regardless of how much Jake's touch made her burn, she couldn't go for a one-night stand. Not that he'd offered.

Heat stung her face as she remembered all she'd said out on the ocean while floating on his pants. Had she actually told the guy she wanted him to be her first? Mortifying embarrassment urged her to duck into a supply closet.

Her greater sense of honor told her she owed Jake her thanks. The guy had saved her life, after all. She needed to thank him, genuinely, not in some throwaway line as they left the hospital.

And she needed the chance to tell her temporary "husband" goodbye in private before they returned to the real world and their real lives.

Allie pushed to her feet, her legs still wobbly. She held the IV stand for support and rolled it out the door. The uniformed guard, a husky man with steely gray hair, sat between her room and Jake's. He glanced up from his magazine and waved her through.

She slipped into Jake's room. A privacy curtain had been pulled even though he didn't have a roommate. She hobbled across the floor, each step a monumental task. The sensation of being in the water hadn't diminished. When would she ever feel steady again?

*No regrets,* she reminded herself. Jake's sacrifice deserved to have recognition, meaning. She had to believe she'd learned something out there in the ocean.

Allie gripped the edge of the curtain.

"Jake," she whispered. "Are you awake?"

"Yeah." His voice came low and fuzzy.

"Is it okay if I come in?"

"Sure."

She rounded the curtain. Flat on his back, he rested his head on his crooked arm, his eyes heavy-lidded. She glanced at his IV. "Did you finally give up being so stubborn and agree to the pain meds?"

He nodded, his long, powerful body outlined by the sheet. His bare leg was suspended with his battered foot bandaged and cradled in a sling. "Didn't want to, though."

"You'll rest better."

"Whatever."

The room echoed with a cave-like silence. Only periodic, muffled noises from the hall filtered through, a cart rattling past, a television from another patient's room. The sounds so far removed merely served to accentuate their solitude.

While hours had passed since their rescue, they hadn't been alone. She needed to touch him, reassure herself he was alive, and then sleep for at least a day or two. "I'm sorry about your foot."

"It'll heal."

"That doesn't make me any less sorry. I guess I'll have to add it to my list of regrets." Inhaling a bracing breath, she crinkled her nose with a smile and met his gaze dead-on. "Should I lock the door so we can do away with my virginity and get rid of one of those regrets?"

Jake's brows raised, before a lazy smile notched his face. "Your timing stinks, but if you promise to be gentle with me, who knows?"

She nearly lurched back a step, then noticed his slow breaths, cloudy eyes, all signs of the lulling haze of pain killers. He didn't know what he was saying. "Jake, there you go again, opening and closing that emotional door."

"You're a tough one to resist."

"Thanks, I think." She liked Jake all warm and fuzzy, even if it was the by-product of Demerol. But the medicine would wear off. The world would intrude, and he would pull away as he'd done before. Already the sting of the inevitable rejection made her throat close, her eyes burn.

He lifted his hand, the IV line trailing from his wrist as he brushed her hair from her face. His stroke was gentle, but lethargic. "Allie, just so you know. I regret it, too, not having been with you."

"Oh, Jake." She couldn't hold onto her smile or her feelings. Tears chased each other down her cheeks.

*No more regrets.* She swiped them and her tears aside.

Jake stared back at her, his eyes filled with pain for the first time since she'd walked into the room. Callused knuckles skimmed her cheek, his caress making her long to climb into the bed with him. With or without sex, she needed to be closer to him than his injury or her wary heart would allow. "Thank you for what you did for me out there."

"You held your own."

She wasn't sure about that at the moment, but she planned to fix it in the near future. "Think what you want, but I know I couldn't have made it without you. Thank you." She studied his face, the strong planes of cheekbones, beard-stubbled jaw, honey rich eyes, locking away the memory. "Bye, Jake."

Allie spun away before she did something stupid, like cry all over his hospital gown. Why was this so darned difficult? She'd only known the guy for a few days.

A few days, a fake marriage and an intense wedding night that had stretched into a life-or-death struggle.

Stumbling, she clutched the IV pole for balance.

Jake caught her hand. "Be careful. Stick close to your brother until Phillips is in custody and those notes are cleared up. Promise me you won't do anything impetuous, just this once."

His voice warmed her, but his words so similar to Sam's chilled her. She'd had protectors. What did she want from Jake?

Her head lolled forward. She would hold strong and just say her goodbyes. She wouldn't cave to temptation....

His thumb rubbed the vulnerable inside of her wrist, a simple touch that stirred much.

She was going to weaken. Already she could feel the heat of his skin steal up her arm, pooling into a low swirl of longing. "I'm not your concern anymore."

"My gut tells me otherwise."

"Just focus on yourself and recovering. I can take care of a disgruntled note-writing client with sloppy penmanship." Her fingers fluttered to rest over his lips before he could protest. "But thanks for worrying."

"How do I stop?"

His lips moved under the sensitive pads of her fingers. Breathing became a monumental task. "What?"

"When you leave, how do I keep from wondering what happens to you?"

Allie wanted to close off that blasted IV drip and stop it from relaxing Jake into a man too enticing by half. "I don't have an answer for that one myself."

Her fingers feathered a path over his full bottom lip. He lifted a swaying curl and tucked it behind her ear, detouring his knuckle into her gaping hospital gown, trailing along her collarbone. His hand slid to cup the back of her neck.

She told herself she wouldn't lean in. She'd already tossed her pride aside so many times for this man and been rejected. No more.

But if he pulled her forward…

Allie sunk to the edge of the bed, draping her torso along him to bring their faces a whisper apart. "You're opening that door again, and I know you're going to slam it shut tomorrow."

He didn't answer, only stared. His lashes swiped lazy sweeps over his amber rich eyes. Like warm honey, his gaze melted over her.

"What do you want from me, Jake? And why can't I walk away from you? Or just give in—"

"Allie."

"Huh?"

"You talk too much." He nipped the end of her finger.

"No great news flash there." She combed aside a lock of hair from his brow. The white blond strands glistened in the showering of bedside light. She traced his lips one final time. "Goodbye, Jake."

She replaced her fingers with her mouth, a gentle brush that gave birth to a moan. His answering groan, not one of pain at all, provided the encouragement she needed. She nibbled his bottom lip. No hurrying, she intended to make this moment last.

Her hair fanned around them in a curtain, enclosing them in their own world of sensation. Slowly, he slid a heavy arm along her waist. His mouth parted beneath hers, and she tangled her tongue with his in languid, sensual strokes.

He was a man of such unrestrained passions. Why couldn't some of that intensity overflow into other aspects of his personality and sweep away her reservations? How could he be such a contradiction of what she needed and couldn't accept?

She felt not too different from the alley cat she'd been labeled, a bit battered and hungry for affection.

Her reserve of energy faded as quickly as it had bloomed. Her exhausted body wilted, settling on Jake just as his deflated khakis had melded to the boat deck.

His hand soothed a steady pace over her hair, contrasting with the erratic breaths raising and lowering his chest beneath her ear. "Allie."

"What?" she whispered without moving.

"Have I ever told you how good you smell?"

Not much of a romantic declaration, but it touched her all the same.

"No, Jake, you haven't." A flutter of panic tickled her insides. Such a small compliment shouldn't bring this rush of pleasure. She was losing control, fast. Her throat closed, tightened by the lost feeling she'd had all those years ago when her father had walked out the door for good.

"Well, you do." Jake's voice flowed over her, words slurring, slowing. "Like flowers—lots of flowers."

A smart woman would leave.

Reluctantly, Allie started to push to her feet. Jake palmed her back, holding her in place. She turned questioning eyes toward him.

His wide-awake stare greeted her as he increased his pressure on her back, urging her down beside him. "Stay."

"Why? There's a guard posted outside for the night. I'll be fine."

"Stay."

For a moment, she resisted, gripped by an irrational fear. Her stomach sunk with that lurching sensation of plunging into waters far too deep.

She swallowed back reservations, needing to tuck this one memory away for herself before she left. With a sigh, Allie fit her body to Jake's. Serenaded by the steady beat of his dependable heart, she slept.

# *Chapter 13*

Jake grappled through layers of drug-induced fog. He had to wake up, but he wasn't sure why. God, he hated taking medications and being subjected to the out-of-kilter feeling they brought. He preferred gritting through the pain if at all possible.

Sleep lured him, and he turned to bury his face in his pillow. Instead, he nuzzled sweet-scented hair. Allie's scent. Grogginess fell away in a heartbeat.

Jake opened his eyes and found Allie's sleeping face mere inches from him. She lay on her side, each curve tucked to him, her arm draped across his stomach. Her IV trailed back to the near-empty bag of glucose.

Blaming any impulsiveness on the aftereffects of the drugs, Jake gathered a hand full of Allie's hair and brought it to his face. The floral scent swirled through his senses with its now familiar power.

What would it be like to wake with her beside him, naked and warm? He'd always enjoyed morning sex, those slow, lazy couplings that launched a day—

Guilt slammed into him with a ten-ton impact.

He hadn't had morning sex since Lydia, because he hadn't slept with a woman since Lydia had died. He'd had sex, infrequent encounters, but he hadn't indulged in something as intimate as sleeping with a woman.

Until now. Until Allie.

He wanted to blame the whole incident on the pain meds, but he remembered well-enough when she'd walked into his room, his relief at seeing her. He also remembered the allure of her kiss, his need to make her stay.

So he'd pulled her down beside him and slept with her. And wanted to again.

Guilt slugged him a second time with double force. He'd given Allie something that had belonged exclusively to Lydia. It was almost like losing a part of his wife all over again.

He may not have been the best of husbands, but he wasn't the kind of man who committed his life to someone else impetuously. Shaking free that feeling of being married didn't come easily to him.

Of course Allie hadn't slept through the night with anyone either. She'd made that quite clear in her confession out in the ocean. A woman waiting for a romantic white knight and wedding night romance didn't need to tangle her life with his. The thought of hurting Allie lashed at Jake with a ferocity that rivaled his aching foot in the sling.

The thought of never holding her again didn't feel too great either.

A tap sounded on the door. Jake sat up and jostled Allie gently. "Hey, wake up. The nurse is going to be here in a minute."

Allie grumbled unintelligible words, then sighed, settling

back against him. He'd forgotten how deeply she slept. She snuggled closer. Her arm landed across his lap.

Jake scooted as far away from her as he could without falling off the bed. "Allie—"

The knock sounded again and Jake called, "Hold on a—"

His words came a second too late as the door opened and Allie's brother lumbered through.

Jake winced and sat up straighter. Allie's running average with Murphy's Law had struck again.

Morgan's eyebrows shot into his forehead just before his face turned to stone. He cricked his neck left, then right as he tugged at his tie. "Damn, but there are some things a brother just shouldn't have to see."

Jake didn't bother to explain that nothing had happened. Morgan wasn't a moron. Jake wasn't in any condition to take advantage of Allie—not sexually anyway.

But Morgan would understand as well as Jake did the vulnerability Allie had displayed by sleeping with him, and Jake didn't know how to offer an overprotective brother the reassurance he sought.

Jake reached for Allie's shoulder to wake her.

Morgan held up a hand. "No need to embarrass her. Let her sleep," he said softly. "She's all but hibernating. She'll never hear us talking."

Jake had to agree, but wisely refrained from telling Allie's brother he knew her sleeping habits well after their nights at White Sands.

Morgan stuffed his hands in his pockets. "I just wanted to let you know I've brought the Fort Walton Department up to speed. The powers-that-be have scheduled a meeting first thing tomorrow to take statements from you and Allie. I convinced them to cut you some slack so you don't have to head straight from the airport to the police station. The flight back will likely wear out you and Allie anyway.''

''I chartered a plane for us last night—''

''No need. I'll take care of Allie.''

Jake tossed out the ultimate argument. After all, he understood well the urge to protect Allie wasn't easily suppressed. ''The quiet and extra space of a Chartered flight will be easier on her.''

Morgan's jaw flexed twice before he nodded. ''Makes sense. Thank you.'' He scratched behind his ear, looking anywhere but at the bed. ''I'm going to run downstairs and grab a cup of java before I come back up to check out Allie.''

Giving Jake enough time to wake her and send her to her room. ''All right.''

Morgan pivoted away, grabbed the door handle, then paused. ''Hurt my sister and you'll need a sling for the other foot.'' He yanked the door open and disappeared into the hall.

Jake glanced down at Allie curled so trustingly against him and knew the last thing he wanted to do was hurt her. Too bad the only thing he could do to protect her was walk away.


As the plane taxied along the runway in Fort Walton Beach, Allie unsnapped her lap belt and grabbed her backpack from beneath her seat. Too bad she didn't have on her good running shoes, because she couldn't get home fast enough.

The plane ride back had been miserable with its stilted silence, although it had started out well enough. She, Jake and Sam had used the time to review their case against Phillips so the charges would stick—hard. Otherwise that scum could be out on bail and out of the country before the courts could say "off-shore accounts."

Talking about the case had been great. She loved that stuff, and couldn't help but yearn to be a cop for real.

With a butterfly sensation of realization, Allie remembered her discussion with Jake in the ocean about going to the police academy. She'd been hiding in her private eye office, afraid she couldn't measure up to her brothers. She may have made mistakes in her life, but she would have never considered herself a coward.

She hated cowards.

Maybe the time had come to give the academy another try. The thought shuffled around inside her mind until it settled into a clean fit. She pressed her hand to her stomach, nerves tap dancing double time.

But like she'd told Jake, no regrets.

*Jake.* She still felt weak-kneed with relief to have found out he wasn't mixed up with Phillips and his money-laundering legions. Jake truly was as gorgeous on the inside as out.

Which made him all the more tempting, damn his great pecs and honorable mind waiting across an aisle that might as well be a mile wide.

How would she get through the rest of the investigation and all the times she would meet with Jake, work with Jake, want to jump right back into Jake's bed? Waking up in his arms had been beautiful for thirty wonderful seconds before awkward self-consciousness had kicked in and she'd rushed back to her room.

The plane slid to a stop, and the captain pulled back the curtain to announce temperature updates and good-day wishes.

Jake stood, bearing his weight on one foot while grabbing for the crutches. Allie winced with guilt. She'd done that to him, robbed him of his already treasured store of mobility with her carelessness. She couldn't bear to watch him struggle, instead walking across the plush carpet toward Sam. Her brother had snoozed off midway through the flight and hadn't stirred during the whisper smooth landing.

She nudged Sam's shoulder none too gently. "Get up, Mule Head."

His snore tripped on a snort before resuming its rhythm.

"Hey, Sam." Allie opted for a stronger wake-up call. "Danny's hitting on your girl again."

Sam bolted upright, blinked twice and rubbed a hand over his scowling face. "What time is it?"

"Three in the afternoon. I'll meet you outside, okay?"

"Sure. Go ahead. I'll be there in a minute."

Turning, Allie sighed at the sight of Jake's broad shoulders filling the open doorway. His thick, perfectly combed hair begged her fingers for mussing. She would keep her hands to herself from now on. "Would you like me to carry those?"

Jake glanced over his shoulder, pride stamped across every strong feature. He paused, then acquiesced with a curt nod. He passed her the crutches and grasped the handrails, hefting himself down the steps. His muscles rippled beneath his jacket with each lifting grip of the rail. His arms bulged, strong arms that had held her through the night. What would it be like to have those arms hold her again?

Her stomach fell to her toes as if she'd plunged right back into the ocean again.

After tackling the last step, Jake pivoted to face her. Allie stopped so close she could have leaned into his chest as she'd done in the water, absorbing the warmth and scent of him.

She held the crutches, a fence between them. "Here."

''Thanks.'' He placed his hands on top of hers.

Her arms refused to move away. She flipped her palms to clutch him, holding firm.

For a moment, Jake opened the door to his feelings, and she saw the hint of regret in his eyes, a need that seemed perhaps even stronger than hers. Steam radiated from the asphalt, burning upward, a physical manifestation of the scorching link between them.

Confused by the intensity of his stare, she studied their twined fingers. Her rings glinted, now upon their correct fingers. She thought of Jake's wedding ring, a band that would never again be in its rightful place.

Her emotions were so jumbled she wasn't sure what to think. Surely it must be an adrenaline let down from all they'd been through. She would be fine after a long nap and plateful of her mother's brownies.

*Yeah, right.*

Allie eased her hands away. ''I guess this is it. Tell Robbie 'hi' for me.''

''Hold on. Morgan's not out yet.'' Jake cleared his throat and looked around the tarmac, still blocking her exit.

''He will be any second.'' She should simply circle past. And she would, as soon as she could will her feet to move. What was she procrastinating for? She would see him again in the morning.

But that special connection they'd felt at White Sands would be gone. ''Thanks for the ride. I'm not sure I would have had the energy to battle airline hassles and gate changes today.''

His amber brown gaze snapped back to her. ''Are you okay?''

''Fine. Just a little tired. Nothing a hot soak and some pampering from Mom won't fix.'' She pulled a half smile. ''Guess I'll see you later.''

Allie sidestepped him, ready to run before she embarrassed herself with more tears.

"Wait!"

She spun back, unable to staunch the futile flow of hope. For what? "Huh?"

He frowned, as if stringing words together were some monumental task. "Nothing… See you at the station tomorrow."

"Goodbye, Jake." Holding strong, she shrugged her backpack into place and walked away, each step more difficult than an hour of strokes in the water.

"Allie!" Robbie's squeal broke through her haze of self-pity.

An irrepressible smile crept over her face as Robbie hurtled through the airport doors. "Hey there, cowboy!"

Jamming his hands in his pockets, Robbie screeched to a halt. His face widened with a gap-toothed grin. "What are you doin' here?"

Allie ruffled his corn-silk hair, before jerking a thumb over her shoulder. "I was checking up on your dad like you paid me to."

Robbie deserved a refund. But what could she do, refill her trash cans?

Jake powered past her toward Robbie, injured foot swinging with each thump of the crutches. He juggled his crutches to the side so he could kneel and hug his son.

"Hi, kiddo." Jake's forehead settled on top of Robbie's tousled hair. "I missed you."

The towheaded youngster wrapped his arms around his father's waist and squeezed hard, his face buried in his father's chest. "Me, too."

Jake's arms trembled, as if restraining the need to hold tighter. Clearing his throat, he pulled away. "What did you do while I was gone?"

"Weeded Gramma's flower garden," he said, grinning. His smile faded as he touched his father's crutches. "Gramma told me you hurt your foot again. Are you gonna be okay?"

"Just a sprain. No big deal. We'll have to put our camping trip on hold for a few weeks, but then I'll be fine."

Robbie's gamin grin returned. Jake's ease with Robbie was obvious. Jake was a good father. His reserve didn't spill over into his parenting.

Of course Robbie only added another reason for Allie to steer clear of Jake. Even if she tossed caution out the window and chased Jake around the block, she had to think of Robbie. Odd weren't good from the get-go that she and Jake could have much of a lasting relationship. Once a kid bonded with someone, it hurt when that person left if things didn't work out.

Allie shuffled backward, memorizing the image of those two blond heads huddled together discussing their camping plans. She twisted away from the too-enticing sight.

Turning, she plowed into an elderly couple. There could be no mistaking Jake's parents. "Excuse me."

"No harm done," said a broad-shouldered older man with gray-blond hair.

*Wow!* If this guy was any indication, Jake would be one hot sixty-year-old. Life just wasn't playing fair today.

From the lined face of a soft-figured woman, Jake's honey-brown eyes stared back at Allie. "Are you all right, dear?"

"Just fine, thanks," she mumbled before bypassing the couple. "Have a nice day."

Allie hefted her backpack over her shoulder, her collection of slogan pins chiming a discordant tune. So focused on finding the shortest path out of the airport, she barely registered the approaching footsteps until a heavy arm slung around her shoulder. She glanced up into Sam's craggy face as he gave her a comforting squeeze, for once keeping his brotherly advice to himself.

"Hi, Mule."

"Hi, Allie Cat. Are you okay?"

She glanced up into his concerned eyes. "Of course," she lied. "Why wouldn't I be?"

His brow furrowed as he glanced at Jake, then he shook his head. "No reason. Want to stop for a pizza on the way home?"

Somehow she knew pizza and a plate of brownies wasn't going to make her feel better anytime soon. "Thanks, Sam. But I'm not very hungry."


Limping down the hall, Jake listened to the even thud of his rubber-tipped crutches interspersed with the balancing thump of his good foot along the hall floor.

*Thud—thunk. Thud—thunk. Thud—thunk.*

The familiar rhythmic serenade from his year of recovery after the accident didn't offer the reliable forgetfulness he'd found after Lydia had died.

Where was the thrill he'd expected to find in bringing down Phillips? Phillips and his goons were in custody. Already, Jake had received a call from the U.S. Attorney's office in Miami, requesting his help in assembling the case against Phillips.

So what the hell was wrong?

He missed Allie. They'd only been apart for a few hours, and the quiet threatened to smother him. She definitely had a way of filling any silence, and his bed and his every thought.

She'd also left him feeling as off-kilter as when he'd been hooked up to the IV.

Jake shrugged through kinks in shoulders and focused on

his son. Robbie had watched over him with wide, worried little eyes all day, bringing pillows, drinks and an endless supply of magazines. Robbie needed reassurance. Having lost one parent, it was only normal he feared accidents more than most kids.

Jake planned to make damned sure his son's world stayed stable.

Balancing the crutches under his armpits, he nudged the door to Robbie's room with an elbow.

Sheets rustled as Robbie flipped onto his back, eyes wide. "Hey there, Dad."

"Hi, kiddo." Jake stared into the blue eyes so like Lydia's. He hadn't given himself time to think of her over the years, always too busy caring for Robbie, building a new career. Or had those been excuses? "Shouldn't you be asleep?"

"Just waiting for you to tuck me in."

"Wouldn't miss it." Jake thumped across the room, using a crutch to swipe aside Matchbox cars littering the floor. He stacked his crutches against the computer desk and hopped to rest on the edge of Robbie's bed. "Sorry about the camping trip. Tomorrow night we can rent some videos—"

"And eat junk food?"

An image of Allie plunked on the sofa with them, munching a bag of chocolate-covered pretzels blindsided him. "We can grab some burgers and shakes."

"And chips."

"And chips."

"Cool!"

"It's a plan then." Adjusting the covers over his son's foot protruding from the blanket, Jake didn't take for granted the simple act of saying good-night to his kid. Jake's jaw clenched as he thought of how close he'd come to never seeing Robbie again, worse yet, how close his son had come to losing both parents. He held out his arms, and Robbie launched forward without hesitation.

He hugged Robbie, trying not to frighten him with a hold too tight to be explained away by a short business trip. Robbie didn't know about Jake and Allie's night spent in the ocean, and Jake didn't intend to tell him, at least not until they were both a hell of a lot older.

Robbie wriggled free and Jake let him go, swallowing the suffocating lump in his throat, a sensation not unlike the oxygen deprived time spent under water. "'Night, son."

"Don't forget the prayers!"

"Oh, uh, yeah right." Jake clasped his hands between his knees and bowed his head. *Thank God Allie's alive to enjoy more pretzels and family picnics.*

Robbie sat, shuffling a nest into his racetrack patterned covers before he folded his hands. "Thanks, God, for bringing my dad home and help his foot get better fast so we can go camping. And please hold off on the rain for a while, 'cause it makes Gramma's weeds grow faster. Bless Dad, Gramma and Gramps. And say 'hi' to my mom. Amen."

"Amen," Jake echoed, before he retrieved his crutches and padded across carpeted floor. "'Night, kiddo."

"'Night, Dad." Robbie whispered one last request, "Oh, yeah, and bless Allie 'cause she looked awful sad today. Amen again." He flopped on his stomach and burrowed under the light summer blanket.

Jake accepted the well-deserved mental sucker punch as he stepped into the hall. Slumping against the door, he pressed two fingers hard against his closed eyes. Not twenty-four hours ago, he'd been in a bed with Allie, could have been in bed with her again if he hadn't been so torn apart by those vulnerable violet eyes.

His head thunked back against the wood as he exhaled.

Why couldn't he make a clean break? He'd been alone most of his life. Sure, he had parents and a child, but unlike Allie's overpopulated childhood, he'd spent little time on relationships with people his own age. He and Lydia had only been married four years, and he hadn't excelled as a husband, a failure that rankled still.

He stared down the hallway at his bedroom door. He'd slept alone for five years without questioning his choice. Why should now be any different?

How senseless to get sappy over a woman he'd known less than a week. He would see Allie in a few hours at the police station anyway. They would meet countless times in Fort Walton and Miami putting together the case against Phillips. Bland, impersonal fact-finding meetings instead of moonlit walks along the beach.

Jake shrugged aside distracting emotions, tucked his crutches under his arms and limped to his bed. Alone.

# Chapter 14

Two weeks later, Jake waited in the police department corridor. Allie should be finished any second. He wanted a minute to talk with her alone, make sure she was all right, an impossible task to accomplish during their other meetings at the department with Watchdog Morgan hovering just behind her.

Morgan had Thursdays off.

The case against Phillips was mounting with reassuring ease. Allie had been more help than even Jake had expected. She packed a sharp brain under all that hair.

He was in constant contact with the U.S. Attorney's office down in Miami, phone calls that would be followed up with a meeting in a couple of weeks. He'd spent hours scouring bank statements and wire transfer documents, helping assemble the money-laundering case in a way a jury of lay people could understand.

His trip to Miami would cinch the noose around Phillips's operation and sever his last tie to Allie.

Jake flexed his ankle, healing without surgery, but still stiff. The doorknob turned, and he stood straighter. The force of his need to talk to her, just talk, left him shaken.

Allie stepped into the hall. Jake took in her bare arms, the curves beneath her sleeveless jean vest and scrunched fabric long skirt.

"Hello, Allie. Got a minute?"

She glanced down the hall at the Exit sign as if it were a portal to paradise.

*There's a real kick in the ego, pal.*

"Sure, but I'm meeting my mom for lunch soon."

Now that he had her alone, he wasn't sure what he wanted to say. He only knew he'd missed her, missed their late night conversations and her quirky wit.

Her high cheekbones seemed more pronounced with her curls swept away from her face. No haphazard topknot, her hair was restrained in a tight braid secured at the base of her neck. Only one small spiral had escaped to brush her forehead hinting of the impetuous woman who'd knocked him flat. Damn but he wanted to press his mouth to the vulnerable curve of her neck and breathe, reacquaint himself with her flowery scent. Not that he'd forgotten.

Curiosity bit him, hard. What had prompted these subtle changes in her, such as a more reserved dress? She'd even ditched the slogan pins on her backpack. Had she dressed up for some other guy, some burly cop type at the station like her brothers? Jealousy bit him a hell of a lot harder than curiosity.

Allie fidgeted with her backpack strap. "How's your foot?"

"Fine. I won't need the crutches in a couple of weeks." Allie glanced down the hall toward the exit again, and Jake found himself saying, "Actually, it hurts like hell, but the doctor says that will pass in another month or so."

Her eyes flickered with surprise, but at least she was looking at him. "Will you be able to take Robbie camping soon?"

"After I get back from meeting with the U.S. Attorney's office down in Miami in a couple of weeks. Robbie's due a little R and R. The kid's had too much to worry about."

She pleated the skirt between her fingers, a nervous motion at odds with her bright smile. "I bet he'll have a blast."

"We both will."

Uniformed officers brushed past, some waving or tossing greetings to Allie. Jake flexed his foot and stepped back. What kind of reassurance was he looking for? She was obviously all right. He should just go. But he couldn't seem to force himself to walk away.

"Oh, here, I almost forgot." Allie shrugged her backpack from her shoulder, unzipped it and withdrew a wrapped package the size of a shoebox. "It's Robbie's pig."

"Thanks." He stared at the package and couldn't suppress the irrational stab of disappointment that she wouldn't be delivering the gift herself. Back at White Sands they'd made plans for her to bring it to his house, but things had changed since then.

Jake inched closer to Allie. "How have you been? Any more threatening letters?"

"They stopped when I closed up the office. I guess we'll never know who sent them."

"You closed the office?" He straightened. She still managed to surprise him.

"I'm reapplying to the police academy." Her shoulders braced back, her chin tipping up. "I decided to give it a try, and you know, I really think I'm going to make it this time. All the things that women usually wash out for, the

PT course, the firing range, well, I've basically had on-the-job training for years, thanks to my brothers and my dad.''

Jake tried to imagine Allie in a uniform, a police uniform. Officer St. James. She would make one tenacious cop. He couldn't stifle thoughts of his own service dress uniform in a musty hang-up bag, the shoulder boards that would never carry a rank higher than captain.

Allie had wiped away another of her regrets. He was happy for her, even though he couldn't ignore the sudden realization that he hadn't come to terms with what he'd given up professionally. ''Congratulations.''

''It was time.'' She continued to fidget with the folds of her skirt and eyed the exit again.

Jake blurted, ''Why don't you give Robbie the gift yourself?''

Where the hell had that come from? Like the odd flashes of Allie-induced humor he'd experienced during their time in the water, he now wondered if some of her impulsiveness may have rubbed off as well.

While the request left him questioning his own sanity, he couldn't help wanting her to agree. The police station hall chat hadn't satisfied the need to talk to her. He wasn't sure what would. He only knew the past two weeks had been the loneliest ones he'd lived since just after Lydia had died.

''Jake—''

''I can't manage the package with these crutches.'' He charged right over the denial he could see forming in the furrows along her brow. ''I know Robbie would like to see you. Maybe you could bring it over to the house. We picked up a stack of videos yesterday. We could order some burgers.'' He shamelessly tossed in the enticement of junk food.

''Jake. Stop.'' She held up a hand. ''Thanks, really. I

appreciate the invitation, but I don't think it's such a smart idea.''

''Why?'' And why was convincing her so important?

''Because we're not in the Keys anymore. Things are more—complicated—now.''

''But they don't have to be. The whole thing seemed so convoluted down at White Sands. We were both riding an adrenaline wave. It didn't help that we were sharing a room.'' And a bed.

He grasped her hand, the softness of her flooding up his arm, his senses absorbing the feel of her like a cracked beach soaking rain. The more he thought about keeping things simple, the more he warmed to the idea. He was an expert in control after all. ''But now, we're in the real world. We can back things up. It doesn't have to be so convoluted.''

Her chin jutted with that familiar Allie spunk. ''So you want a quick hop in the sack, and then we move on?''

Leave it to Allie to lay it on the line.

Was she right? *Hell, no!* His mind raged at the thought of anyone, even himself, treating Allie callously.

''I want you to come over and hang out with Robbie and me for an evening.'' He held her hand tighter to keep her from bolting down the hall. He also ignored the niggling, guilty voice that told him he'd promised himself he wouldn't do this. ''That's all I'm asking.''

''For now.''

''Your call. Your pace.''

Uncomplicated sounded better and better by the minute. He wouldn't be lonely. Robbie already thought Allie was the greatest. And if he kept it simple and let Allie take the lead, she wouldn't get hurt. Perfect. Right?

Her eyes flickered with uncertainty before she tossed her shoulders back. ''We can't back it up, Jake. You're right that the time in the Keys was intense. We packed years worth of living into less than a week. You saved my life, and I'll never forget that. Thank you.''

Slumping against the wall, Jake studied her set features. ''I guess if you're willing to turn down junk food, you must be serious.''

Allie stared at him so long Jake wondered if she might change her answer. His fists tightened as he realized how very much he wanted that. It was just a video and take-out burgers for crying out loud, not a marriage proposal. Even thinking of walking down the aisle brought a tic to the corner of his eye.

A grin crinkled her freckled nose and lightened his mood.

''Well, Jake, I have to admit to being tempted by your...junk food.''

God, he'd missed her smart mouth. ''But?''

''But I think I'd better hold strong against temptation. Thanks for the offer though.'' Allie backed away. ''I'll just leave this box at the front desk. You can pick it up any time.'' She backed another three steps, then spun away.

Jake watched her leave and told himself it didn't matter. That didn't stop the ache in his foot, throb in his pants, or odd awakening sensation tightening his chest.

The Miami hotel lobby sprawled before Allie, blessedly different from White Sands. Rather than chrome and opulence, this hotel sported an island theme of wickers and rattans, browns and muted creams. Towering palms added warm shadows. The effect should have been relaxing, certainly was intended to be so.

But she was strung tight as a fishing line fighting a trophy-sized marlin. Jake hadn't let up since their conversation at the police station two weeks ago.

Of course he wasn't annoying or blatant. He didn't touch her or even so much as brush against her in passing. He simply slid a candy bar her way in the middle of a meeting, placed a soft drink beside her when he walked into a room, or casually mentioned having an extra ticket to a ball game that just happened to serve kick-butt hot dogs.

Much more and she would club the man over the head with a two-liter soda bottle.

Or take him up on his offer for a no-strings relationship and run the risk of ending up with her heart trounced.

Allie picked at her sundress, then fanned her face. Wasn't the air conditioner working in this place?

Having rushed straight from the Miami airport to the hotel, Allie longed for a shower and a change of clothes. It was just the heat, right? Not sticky-palmed apprehension about being alone in South Florida with Jake again. She scrambled through her backpack for ID to check in.

Memories had plagued her all day, Jake's stunned expression when she'd waylaid him at the Miami airport over a month ago, their drive to the Keys. As she approached the counter, she remembered with a touch of whimsy the frantic look on his face when she'd finagled her way into his suite.

The government was picking up the tab for this one since she'd come to assist with the case. She and Jake would spend hours together with local attorneys pouring over their statements to ensure nothing had been missed.

She would get through the next two days and go home. She would love her new job, wasn't even overly apprehensive about starting training.

All well and good except lately life held a flat quality, soda without the fizz. Maybe once she finished with Phillips's case that would offer her the closure to move forward with her life.

Allie signed in and gathered her room card, hitching her hang-up bag more securely. She walked backward, listening while the hotel clerk gave her directions to her room.

"Thanks." Turning just before she reached the elevator, Allie slammed into a rock-solid chest. Palms pressed flat against the man, she recognized the owner of those fabulous pecs without even looking up. "Hi, Jake."

"Hello, Allie." His breath ruffled her hair.

She'd known she would see him soon, but thought they would have the distance of meeting at the federal courthouse. No such luck.

She shivered and pulled away, plastering a fake grimace of a grin in place. "A bit different than last time, huh? No Honeymoon Cove." She forced a little dance step. "No calypso beat."

His face creased slowly into one of those perfect toothed smiles that melted her knees. "Certainly not with my parents and Robbie in tow."

"Your parents?"

"Some wise lady suggested I should bring Robbie along on business trips."

He'd remembered. He'd listened to her during their oceanside walks and had remembered. God, the man was good. How did she stand a chance?

"I'm sure he'll have a great time at the beach. Tell him I said 'hi.'" She tucked her head to plow forward.

"Hold on a minute and you can tell him yourself." Jake stepped aside, calling into the crowd still unpacking from the elevator. "Robbie, look who's here. Mother, Dad, this is Allie St. James."

Just behind Robbie, Allie saw the elderly couple from the airport. She circled around Jake toward Robbie.

"Hello, cowboy." She nodded to Jake's parents, aware

of their son looming just behind her. "Mr. and Mrs. Larson."

The other Mrs. Larson. A burning sensation heated over Allie as she remembered her short tenure owning that name.

The woman with Jake's amber warm eyes clasped Allie's hand and shot a curious look from Jake to Allie. "We've heard so much about you from Robbie."

But not from Jake. Not surprising, yet annoyingly hurtful. "How great you could come along to help."

Robbie nudged his ball cap back and smiled, the gap closing with permanent teeth. "Hiya, Allie."

"Wow! It looks like you're giving the tooth fairy a chance to recoup some losses."

His puckish smile widened. "Thanks for the cool pig."

Seeing all those shiny new teeth glinting in the overhead light, Allie couldn't stifle a sense of loss that she hadn't witnessed the change, silly when he wasn't even her kid. "Glad you like it."

"Whatcha doin' here?"

"Same thing as your dad. Putting away bad guys." In spite of the awkwardly curious stare of Jake's parents, Allie couldn't fight the infectious quality of Robbie's grin. "Well, I really need to get going."

Jake's hands fell to rest on her shoulders, his touch warm, heavy and exciting after a month without it. He squeezed gently. "I'll see you later."

Allie knew it wasn't a question, or even a threat. Just a statement of fact. She tilted her head to look into his eyes and discovered the determined businessman, the corporate shark she'd glimpsed cutting deals with Phillips, or rather leading Phillips into incriminating grounds. Suddenly, with heart stopping clarity, Allie realized she was Jake's next target and her resolve was in short supply around him.

No doubt, she would be buried in candy bars by sundown.

Allie took a shower and changed into shorts and a loose purple T-shirt, hoping the restless tension would ease.

Her hotel room seemed too empty without Jake. The oceanfront room window lured her with picturesque views of the late night tide. The two double beds with tan, striped spreads bore no resemblance to the Honeymoon Cove back at the Keys, not that it helped her forget anything.

She clicked on her television, only to find Bergman and Bogey speaking their tearful farewells at the airport.

"Ugh! Like I need this torture!" Allie mashed the remote's off button with undue force.

She didn't bother with her shoes, merely tucked her room card in her pocket and headed for the beach.

Allie strolled barefoot, the rolling tide lapping her feet. Thunder rumbled in the background, and she knew she should go back to her room, but she wasn't ready to let sleep silence her memories. Kicking through the breakers, she passed a bonfire party, an empty lifeguard tower, a thatched roof cabana. Had any of the couples walking arm in arm ducked inside for a moment of privacy?

Lights from the hotel shimmered along the tumultuous, crashing waves. How odd that she'd lived her whole life near the water, yet had spent so many years avoiding the ocean. Oh, she'd toyed with it, lounged on the beach, dipped her toes into the tide, but never plunged in to meet the challenge.

Rather like living in the same town with Jake for the past month and refusing to see him.

Was she protecting herself from drowning or merely hiding? Was Jake right when he suggested they keep things simple? But her feelings for him weren't simple or uncomplicated.

She thought she'd come so far since they'd climbed from the ocean. She'd enrolled in the police academy, closed her office, liquidated and consolidated her limited finances.

Yet, she'd still ended up right back where she'd started, on the shore of a Florida beach aching for Jake Larson.

Uneven footsteps sounded behind her and Allie stiffened, momentarily questioning her easy dismissal of the threat of men like Neil Phillips. She jerked to look back, then relaxed.

Jake loped past the cabana toward her. Even though he no longer needed the crutches, his stride canted more to the right since his latest injury. He eased to a stop beside her, his arm naturally falling to rest along her shoulders. She didn't even bother ducking.

Her body knew his touch, the cup of his broad hand, the tangy scent of his soap mingling with the ocean air. Although certain she should shrug free with some lighthearted quip, Allie settled against his side, her head lolling to rest against his chest. "Hi, I was just, uh, thinking about, well…"

"Remembering?"

"Yeah."

He stayed silent for the expanse of three crashing waves. "You're good at that, taking the most from the moment, learning from mistakes and moving forward with your life. I'm better at cutting my losses when I move on. I've always found it's easier if I try to keep things simple. Focused. Memories can be one hell of a distraction."

Allie chuckled. "Make that much of an impression, do I?"

"Yes, Allie, you do."

The deeper tone in his voice made her look up at him. "Jake?"

His eyes darkened to near black, and she suspected he was about to offer her something far more important than candy bars.

"I've missed you."

That beat chocolate, hands down. "Really?"

Jake scratched his head. "Not much of a persuasive argument to get you to share a pizza with me, huh?"

"It's not bad."

He stared out over the ocean again. "I've never been good with the emotional stuff."

Jake dug into his pocket and the extended his hand. The chain dangled from his finger, dog tags and two rings swaying with the ocean breeze.

Allie gasped in a breath of salt laden air. Any man who carried around his wedding rings for five years must be packing some heavy emotional baggage. Her throat closed at the poignant beauty of the gesture.

"Her name was Lydia. It's easier not to think about her, but then sometimes Robbie has questions and he deserves to know about his mother." Jake exhaled slowly.

Allie held her breath and waited. Finally, he was opening up to her with something real, substantial. And suddenly she was shaking, her mouth as dry as sand.

"We'd been married for four years. Robbie had just turned two. I needed to use up some time off before I lost vacation days, so we decided to see my folks, kind of a belated birthday celebration for Robbie. I didn't take leave often, and we wanted to make the most of it. We left right after I got off work and planned to drive through the night while Robbie slept."

He twirled the chain around his finger bringing the rings

closer and closer until he clutched them in a white-knuckled fist.

"You don't have to—"

He stared straight ahead and continued as if she hadn't spoken, his arm a heavy, delicious weight along her shoulders. "Robbie was getting fussy. Lydia unbuckled to get his pacifier. A drunk driver crossed into our lane."

Jake cleared his throat. "Those first weeks after Lydia died, I rescripted the night a thousand times. Why didn't I just pull over? Or stop for the night? React faster." He let the chain trail from his finger again. "Yeah, I understand all about regrets."

Suddenly she wasn't sure she wanted to hear more about the woman who held Jake's heart, the reason he held himself away from committing to anyone except his son. Jealousy was a really ugly emotion, especially when directed at a dead woman.

Allie twisted her hands together until her knuckles numbed. "No wonder you're not over her yet. To lose someone you love like that—"

Jake's gaze snapped to hers. "Hold on a second. You're missing my point altogether. Don't read more into this than I'm trying to say. It was five years ago. Yeah, it was tough. But you can do away with the romantic notions, Allie. Didn't you hear me say I had too much leave time accumulated? I never took off work. I was one of those married-to-the-job types. We didn't fight, never would have gotten divorced, but your idea of love and fairy-tale marriages…" He shook his head wearily. "I failed her. She didn't expect much from me, and that's all I could give her."

"What are you trying to tell me?"

Jake stuffed the chain back in his pocket. "That I want you, and I've missed you, but I'm not ever going to be the kind of guy you're looking for. All I can offer is something simple, uncomplicated. You should probably keep flinging those candy bars right back into my face. Do you understand?''

She understood far more than he'd meant to say. How many times had she watched Jake shut down rather than acknowledge pain? When his foot hurt, he clenched his jaw and steadied his breathing. At the moment, his jaw was set so tightly he could have flattened nails with his teeth. Each breath pumped out in that too-steady pattern she'd come to recognize.

How could she have missed the intense emotions churning beneath his cool exterior? He was just as torn up by this crazy attraction as she was.

Glancing down and away, Allie slid her focus back to the ocean. Fighting her longing for Jake had left her so frustrated, she sometimes lost sight of why she needed to resist him.

He rested his chin lightly against her hair as they stood together, taking in the play of the moon against the endless stretch of darkening ocean. Another shoreline scenario unfolded in her mind, an exchange of vows. *Jake, I promise to be honest with you. I'll give you my smiles, share my laughter, sing off-key to you when I think your frown has grown a bit too deep. And I will be your son's friend. I will be your friend.*

She told herself the ceremony hadn't been legal. There wasn't any real commitment between them. Yet, standing on the beach, she felt linked to him by promises and the water, by their words and their struggle to live.

Either she needed to get over Jake or accept his offer of an uncomplicated relationship. She couldn't live the rest of her life floating as she'd done the past month, bobbing while waiting for some miraculous rescue. Allie knew she may not have always made the right choices, but being still had never been an option.

Even if her answer was to walk away for good, she needed closure to their time together to be certain. And that meant finishing what they'd started.

Allie tipped her head until she could see Jake's eyes. Wind ripped at her hair, twining it around them both. "Jake, I promise to be honest with you."

His gaze delved into hers as he waited. When she didn't finish her earlier vows, he tucked a curl behind her ear. "I'll try to make you smile," he continued with his own adaptation, "share my laughter, not frown when you sing off-key. And I will be your friend."

He'd come a long way from his stark vow of protection. Allie smoothed her fingers along the roughened skin of his near too-perfect face and told herself not to think about how much more she might have hoped for.

She slid her hand around to the back of Jake's neck, urging him toward her as she eased up on her toes to meet him. The heat, a need to meld her body with his, flamed within her. Desire denied now tingled along every nerve, requiring only the simple brush of her chest against his to reignite.

If she walked away tomorrow, or even if she had more tomorrows with him and ended up with her heart trampled, Allie would have her wedding night with Jake.

## Chapter 15

Jake's control snapped at the mere touch of Allie's lips against his. If she wanted to call a halt, he would stop, somehow, but he couldn't imagine anything more agonizing at the moment.

He wouldn't waste thoughts on why she'd suddenly changed her mind. He swiped his tongue through her mouth with bold, greedy possession. No objection came from Allie, merely a moan of impatience. An arch of her back brought her closer, her hands grappling at his shoulders, his arms, his face.

Waves crashed and swirled around their ankles as if luring them back to a place without equilibrium. Sand slipped from beneath his feet, stealing reason with it. Jake didn't care. He only knew it would be now. No more waiting, he wouldn't let another chance pass.

Thunder carried along the ocean, echoing the deafening drum of his heart. Allie's hand tunneled under his shirt, her fingers digging into his back as she drew him closer, their damp clothes clinging. Blood pulsed in his ears. Jake pulled his mouth from hers, traveling kisses across her cheek, to her ear and down her neck. He drank her sweet taste flavoring the drops of water on her skin.

Slowly, he realized, the waves weren't responsible for all the moisture, but rather rain sprinkling over them. A quick glance at the ocean confirmed the storm blowing in with its inevitable tropical speed. "Allie, honey, it's raining."

Her chest heaved against his. "Inside. Let's go. My room."

"Are you sure?" It hurt even to ask.

"Absolutely," she gasped as another couple sprinted past them toward the hotel. Others ran with hands overhead to protect themselves from the increasing shower.

A fresh frustration throbbed through Jake. His wait for Allie would be that much longer. He couldn't run, sweep her into his arms and carry her across the beach as he once could have done. Of course, only since knowing Allie would he have even thought to behave spontaneously.

Allie had never seemed to care that he would slow her. She'd simply dispensed her ice packs and healing touch. This time, she offered her smile and her hand. The soft giving of her touch seared along his senses, burning away regrets. They walked, kissed and stumbled through the rain, accepting the drenching.

Unwilling to wait the fifty yards to her hotel room, Jake paused at the lifeguard tower, molding Allie against the frame, anchoring her body with his. He filled his hand with the supple roundness of her breast, his thumb circling the peak straining against her damp shirt. "Allie, you're so beautiful."

"Jake, you don't need to—"

He stared into her star-speckled eyes. "I may have left out things, but have I ever lied to you?"

"Never." Her rain-spiked lashes fluttered closed, her sigh whispering over his mouth.

"I wanted you the first time I saw you."

"Me, too." Her hands skimmed along the T-shirt molded to his chest by the downpour, then down to his belt, tentatively moving lower until she cupped him in her palm.

A groan slid past his clenched teeth. He was tempted to take her then, unsnap his pants and hers and steal the moment cloaked in darkness. But she deserved better. "Allie, not here. Need to get inside."

"Yes, here. I don't care." She nipped his lip.

His forehead thudded to rest against the wooden beam. He hated being practical and reasonable, for once longing to dive into Allie's world of mayhem. "Lightning. It's not safe here."

Did lightning strike twice? Because he sure as hell felt like Allie had jolted clear through him the first moment he'd seen her.

She lolled into his chest, shivering. He gulped in breaths of rain-tinged air and found no steadying comfort. The hotel looked too far away looming past the cabana.

The cabana.

A thatched hut full of privacy waiting only a few steps away.

He grabbed her hand, barely registering her complaint as sheeting rain battered them. "Come on."

"Jake!" She tugged back, her body limp against the wooden frame.

He cupped her face and kissed her hard and fast, impatient to get her somewhere, anywhere, safe and private. Jake nodded toward the hut. "Come on!"

She glanced over her shoulder at the cabana. Suddenly, he wondered if he'd expected too much from Allie. It was her first time. Should he rein himself in, take her back to the hotel for a slower, tamer initiation? She'd finally stopped turning him away, and he didn't want to lose the chance with her. His body rebelled against his mind at the thought of delay and restraint.

Her face lit into a powerful siren smile. "Perfect!"

"Yes, you are."

"I thought you never lied!"

"I don't."

Like children, they scrambled toward the rustic changing room. Jake flung the latch back, winging a desperate prayer that it would open. He didn't want to add a breaking and entering charge to their evening, because that door was going to give way, regardless.

It swung wide. The cubicle, large enough for a small family, waited empty except for an inviting bench and dangling beach towels.

She lured him inside, walking backward as she kissed him. Needing no further encouragement, Jake followed her, slamming the door behind them. He locked her against him with one hand and locked the door with the other.

Allie heard the click of the latch sliding into place and knew she'd committed herself. She didn't regret her decision in the least. She would have something of Jake, if only a memory.

The primitive hut held an elemental air. Sultry humidity blended with the woodsy scent of damp thatching. The muffled patter of rain on the roof obliterated sounds from outside. She heard only Jake breathing and her heart thrumming.

Dim light filtered through the vents circling the top of the paneled walls. Her eyes adjusted until Jake took shape before her, the strong beauty of his features coming into focus.

"This is perfect." On tiptoe, she sprinkled kisses along his unshaven jaw. "So much better than some cliché old hotel room."

"You're certainly easy to please."

"Let's find out."

Growling low, Jake boldly reclaimed her mouth. She loved this new hint of wild abandon in him, loved that she could unleash the man she knew hovered beneath his cool exterior.

Allie tore at his clothes, scrunching his wet shirt up and free to expose the body she'd drooled over since their first meeting over a set of barbells. Droplets of water clung to the hair sprinkling his chest. She licked tastes from him, flicking her tongue over his hard, flat nipple. As she nipped along the cut of his muscles, tendons jerked in reaction. She'd seen many men's bodies but had never known one, and she gloried in the discovery.

With impatient hands, Jake peeled away her T-shirt, her bra falling to rest beside it on the sandy ground. His mouth closed over her breast in a hungry swoop that pulled the thread of desire taut within her. He cupped each swell, lifting her to him as he feasted, suckling, tugging the hardened peak, rolling it gently between his teeth as he flicked it with his tongue.

Allie thought she would die. At the very least, she would pass out. Her gasping pants left her light-headed. Her knees weakened, turning weightless as if she were once again in the water with Jake and he was the only force keeping her from drowning in a whirlpool of sheer pleasure.

Over her head again with Jake, she could only surrender and let herself be swept away by his introduction to a new world of sensations. He transferred his mouth to her other breast, laving equal attention upon it as he tended the abandoned one with the circling strokes of his callused thumb.

She hooked her leg around his and flung her head back. Her damp hair tickled along her bare back, adding another scintillating shiver to her already overloaded senses.

"Don't stop," she gasped. "Please don't become the honorable Jake who tries to tell me what I should have rather than what I want—"

"Allie."

"What?"

"It's time to quit talking." He nipped her earlobe.

"Okay." She had never so willingly given in on anything.

Unable to fight nature, she rocked against him, the hardened steel of his thigh between her legs sending tingles rippling through her. Jake leaned against the wall, bearing their weighted balance with his good foot. He cupped her buttocks and nestled her closer. Their legs entwined as he nudged his other thigh more firmly against the core of her, his mouth still bathing delicious moist fire over her breasts.

Pressure built within her, an escalating need riding the scream welling within her throat. Like lightning snapping through her, desire exploded in an expanding umbrella of sparks.

Allie wilted against him. He cradled her as each wave of completion shook her until she simply shivered with aftershocks.

"I'm so glad," she gasped. "So glad you didn't stop."

A chuckle rumbled in time with the thunder. "Me, too."

Allie buried her face in his neck, a little embarrassed by how quickly she'd peaked, but she'd never felt anything remotely like Jake's touch.

He dispelled any uneasiness without pause. He didn't offer tender words. That wouldn't have been Jake's style.

Instead he stroked her hair with a gentle hand, kissed her forehead, rested his beard-roughened cheek against hers until her breathing steadied into a normal rhythm. Only then did she realize his chest rose and fell at a pace double hers.

Allie threaded her fingers through his tousled, damp hair, writhing a languid wriggle against him. "Your turn, now."

Jake bracketed her face with his hands, his lowering head blocking the meager light. "No. It's our turn."

His words weakened her already shaky knees. She lifted herself from him, perspiration and water linking them, then giving way. Air caressed over her moist skin, making her impatient for Jake's more insistent touch.

Reaching beside them, he grabbed towels dangling from the hooks and flung them to the sandy floor, creating a cottony bed better than any mattress. "Are you sure you wouldn't rather go to the room?"

He stared at her, his tenuous restraint apparent through the dim light, even if she hadn't been able to feel the evidence of his arousal straining against her.

"I would really regret it if we didn't finish this, right here, right now." She couldn't wait any longer to grab her bit of happiness. She didn't ponder overlong why she trusted him with her body, but not her heart.

Lowering her to the floor, he gifted her with one of his rare, full smiles that made her want to cry. The sandy ground, padded with toweling, didn't make too shabby a bed, not that Allie particularly cared at the moment. Her back bowed upward so he could wrest her shorts from her. He kicked his own free, before fitting his body over her again.

She savored the solid weight of Jake against her, a pleasure she would have regretted never having. She refused to let even a hint of embarrassment steal a second from her.

Honed, muscled man contrasted with her curves. She

could feel her own softness giving way to accept the bulk of him. The roughness of his skin scratched an exciting abrasion. His broad hands explored her with tantalizing thoroughness. Just as she'd expected, Jake's methodical attention to detail had definite advantages.

No inch of her went untouched or untasted until he settled over her once again. The hottest part of him pressed against her leg insistently. Curiosity compelled her to reach for him. Wrapping her fingers around him, she couldn't staunch the well of surprise, and perhaps the first twinges of nerves. If only he would sweep away her worries of inexperience. "Uh, Jake. Here's where my knowledge gets a little shaky. Rather, uh, nonexistent."

"Allie—"

"I know. Hush. But will you stop being so patient, please?"

"Soon, honey, soon."

His hand slid between them, his finger dipping into her, rekindling her need until she forgot how to think, worry, doubt. He shifted more fully over her, the thick, blunt prodding of him foreign, wonderful and almost no longer a mystery.

She dug her heels into the sandy ground, tipping her hips toward him. Slowly, he eased inside, nudging and stopping, stretching before edging further. Impatient, she writhed against him with greedy whimpers.

Jake nuzzled aside her hair and whispered against her ear. "Hold on, I want this to be good for you."

"It is, Jake. Hurry." Her need for completion, for utter possession by Jake, of Jake in return, shook her almost as much as the desire that swept through her.

"Shhh. Not going," he said through gritted teeth, "to hurt you."

How she wished he meant that the way she wanted him to.

Jake gently pushed the rest of the way inside her with only a slight sting, Allie's life of athleticism perhaps paying off. She looked straight into his eyes and watched the shutters fall away, awed by the glimpse of the stormy man. "No more holding back, please, Jake."

He pulled almost completely free and returned. Her body gripped him, tight and unyielding. For once, she would have all of him, even if only in the most basic of ways.

Then she lost the ability to think or reason, each thrust urging her closer to another completion, except this one would be better, because she wouldn't go alone. She locked her legs around his, clasping his hips in her hands as their sweat slicked bodies danced against each other.

"Allie. Allison. I need you." The words seemed ripped from him with begrudging intensity.

She couldn't unscramble her mind to answer or fully comprehend what he might be trying to tell her. The tide swelled within her, filling her as his pace increased, his breathing growing heavier as it blasted over her. His muscles bunched beneath her hands in time with an answering clench within herself. A hoarse growl building to a shout tore through him, filling the hut, merging with the pounding rain and crashing thunder.

That sound alone would have sent her over the edge, knowing she'd given Jake a measure of the pleasure he'd given her. The echoes of his shout brought an answering cry from her. Her orgasm flowered free as Jake continued to pulse within her.

Shuddering, Jake's arms buckled until he blanketed her. His bristly face scratched against her neck as he kissed her, then her tender breasts, before returning to her swollen lips.

Allie had always known Jake hid his emotions behind a

mask of control. While her body had reaped the benefits of his unrestrained passion, experiencing Jake's unleashed power only made her realize how much she was missing by not having that same intensity poured into love.

Jake relaxed into the stack of pillows piled against the headboard of Allie's hotel bed. Contentment was rare for him, but he'd somehow snagged the elusive commodity, thanks to Allie.

Everything would be fine. He would buy her boxes of Godivas and make love to her until they both couldn't breathe, much less think.

He needed to follow his own advice and not complicate things. Focus on the moment.

The rest would only be a distraction.

Jake turned his head on the pillow to stare at the exciting woman beside him. Allie provided more than enough distraction for any man. Sitting cross-legged and wearing an overlong jersey, she feasted on a bag of cheese puffs, licking the orange stain from her fingers with decidedly wicked meticulousness.

She trailed her other hand over his propped ankle with soothing strokes. "I'm about ready for another snack run. Do you want something?"

"No thanks." He lifted a curl from her bare shoulder. The lock, still damp from their shared shower, twined around his finger, not unlike the way Allie swirled through his concentration—soft, sultry, smoky. "Do you want me to go for you?"

"No need, I'll get it." She tipped forward to press a quick kiss, followed by a lingering one before pulling back. "You should head back so you're there when Robbie wakes up."

''Kicking me out of your bed already?'' he asked, in no hurry to move.

''Of course not.''

''Good. My parents are watching him from the connecting suite.''

''But you should be there.''

He knew she was right, and while he was well past explaining his behavior to his parents, he didn't want Allie embarrassed. Still, he couldn't will himself to roll out of her bed and put on his clammy pants. ''In a minute. I'm not done touching you yet, and I won't be able to indulge myself with a wide-eyed audience tomorrow.''

A tiny, whimsical smile lit Allie's face. ''It's amazing my mom and dad ever managed to find a minute alone with my brothers and me tagging along on all their dates.''

''How long were you and your mother on your own?'' He wanted to know more about her and she liked to talk, not a bad combination. Perhaps if he could unravel the convoluted paths of Allie's mind, he could keep the contentment that much longer.

''Mom met my dad, my stepdad, a couple of years after she and my father divorced.''

''Divorced? I assumed—''

''That my father died? No. Al's a bank president. He lives in Mississippi with his new family.''

''So you have other brothers and sisters?''

Her brow furrowed. ''Yeah, I guess so. We're not really that close. The older I got, the busier I became with extracurricular stuff, like soccer camps or track meets. Anyway, it all interfered with visits.''

What kind of man wasn't willing to adjust his schedule to see his child? Suddenly, Allie's persistence tracking men like Phillips made sense. ''His loss.''

''No big deal. We managed fine without him.'' Allie

popped another cheese puff in her mouth. She stared down into the bag. "He left my mom and me for another woman."

"He left your mother, not you."

"Yeah, right. I have to give old Al credit for sending his checks on time. And he even tried with the visits for a while, but he just didn't know how, well, to be my dad. I don't think either of us realized it until Mom wasn't around to act as a buffer anymore."

The guy sounded like a cold fish. "God, Allie, I'm sorry."

"It's not some great tragedy. We went through the motions for a few years. I spent weekends, alternating holidays, and time in the summer there, sleeping in the trundle in my stepsister's room. He did try, but he just couldn't mask the ease he felt with his full-time family."

"I'm glad you found the Morgans."

"Me, too. I was lucky Mom got it right the second time around. The Morgans are always there for me. I can trust they always will be." She dangled a cheese puff in front of his mouth. "I don't want to talk about it anymore, okay?"

"Okay." Crunching the snack straight from her hand, he nibbled the end of her finger. So she needed reassurance. He could manage that. "What do you want to do this weekend to celebrate starting the police academy?"

She stared down into her bag and poked a finger around until coming up with an unbroken puff, which she ate while digging for another. "I'll probably spend some time with my family."

Jake waited, but no invitation followed. "I'd like to meet the rest of them. Are they, uh, all like your brother?"

She didn't answer, only studied her bag. What was wrong with her? Uneasiness edged into the corners of his brain. He should have offered her words, or some reassurance after they'd made love. Hadn't he learned anything?

He hooked a knuckle under her chin, lifting her face to his. "Allie? Are you all right?"

Her head tipped the side as she looked at him, her brow too furrowed. "What's going to happen when we get back home? Will it be like the past month?"

"No!" He had to be honest. "I hope not."

"Forget I said anything." She crinkled her nose with a grin that didn't reach her eyes. "I'm just a little tired."

There she went again with the hints to leave. He'd actually planned to indulge in something that a woman might call cuddling, and Allie wanted to boot him out of her bed. Damn, but women were confusing, changing the rules just when a man started to break the code.

"Okay. Fine." He swung his feet to the floor. "I'll call you in the morning, and we can ride over to the courthouse together—if you want."

"Jake." Her hand fluttered to rest on his bare back. "I'm sorry. I'm being moody." The bed dipped as she knelt behind him. Sitting on her knees, she wrapped her arms around his chest, her cheek falling to rest on his shoulder.

Her soft, but surprisingly strong arms, held him and the last thing he wanted was to talk or leave. Those curls of hers danced along his back, some falling forward to caress his chest.

With a twist at the waist, Jake turned and lowered Allie onto her back. He had to make her understand. He could never be the kind of man who would give her whispered romantic promises.

But he had something to offer her, damn it.

Why couldn't it be good enough for her? "Allie, I know you wanted some big-mouthed cop type like your brother, but here we are. And we're damned good together."

Her eyes glinted, but she didn't cry. "You're flipping my world again, Jake, and I need a second to find my footing."

He was afraid if she found her footing she would run again. "If it makes you feel any better, you churn mine all the time."

"Really?"

Jake almost laughed aloud at the obvious hope in her voice. "How can you not know?"

He yielded to the temptation to drop a kiss on her mouth, then the tip of her nose. "Let's go slow, okay? We've got something good started. Something really good. Let's not ruin it by moving too fast or looking for trouble. You have enough on your plate with the new job."

"You're probably right." The confusion in her eyes didn't ease.

"Yes, I am. You have another shot at your dream. Second chances are rare."

"I know." She stroked the side of his face, her eyes too tender for his comfort level.

"Don't go feeling sorry for me." His ankle ached. Funny how it hurt more when the subject had changed. "Yeah, I miss the Air Force, the job, but I've—adapted."

"I wasn't thinking about your profession."

Jake's skin chilled beneath her warm touch. He didn't want thoughts of Lydia intruding, not now, when he was ready to move on. He rolled onto his back. "Okay, I admit it. I still miss those Air Force days. I was damned good at my job. From the time I was a kid, I knew what I wanted to do with my life."

Would she push the issue and ask more questions about Lydia? Allie stared into his eyes, hers turning that near-purple shade a man could lose himself inside. "Tell me about one of your cases."

Relief eased over him as they settled on a common ground, their interest in law enforcement being something reliable between them. "Do you really want to hear?"

"Are you kidding?" She sat yoga style, burrowing into the covers as she leaned forward. "I live for stories like this."

He relaxed into his pillow, grateful for the reprieve. "The Air Force was running a MOOTW—military operation other than war—in South America. Troops and engineers were stationed down there on a humanitarian mission building hospitals and runways. The problem was, we suspected some of them were using their jobs and taxpayer dollars to smuggle drugs over the border." He could feel the heat of the sun, the thrill of nailing the bastards. "It took OSI a year undercover, but we busted them. They'd been filling their truck tires with cocaine."

"What a rush!" Allie's eyes gleamed with all the anticipation of a kid in front of a candy store display case. "I can't wait to get back to work."

The edge of excitement dulled. "Kind of ironic that I had to hang up my uniform and you're putting one on."

She stroked a finger over his brows. "Don't OSI agents wear suits most of the time?"

He'd never thought of it that way, and the new insight unsettled him. "Yeah. So?"

"I can't help but wonder why you didn't chose a profession like your first one after the accident."

"Allie!" He jerked a frustrated wave toward his leg. "Are you being deliberately dense?"

"No, really. You didn't use your foot for solving cases. Yeah, the PT part was important to being in the Air Force, but when you talk, all I hear you mention is the brainteaser untwisting of a crime or navigating the law. Think about the excitement of all those exotic, overseas settings. Why cut yourself off from a job you obviously loved? Why not open a security business? Or doesn't a securities investigator do basically all the same things you enjoyed about your other job?''

Jake frowned, looking for the flaw in her logic. But he couldn't find it. ''It's not that simple.''

''But what if it is? You have a partner. Shuffle things around in the office. You could be the one to check out foreign bonds for overseas investors, make sure the companies aren't bogus. Aren't you already paying someone else to do that for you now? Just think of what you might stumble across.''

Why hadn't he made the more obvious choice? He didn't know, and he'd had about enough soul picking for the night.

''Hmmm. Interesting thought.'' He gave her lock of hair a gentle tug and rolled from the bed to his feet. ''You're right about one thing, though. I need to get moving.''

Lumbering into the bathroom, he tried to ignore the sensation of her gaze burning into his back. Jake snatched his damp clothes from the shower rod and began dressing.

Her scent carried on the residual steam left from the shower they'd shared. He'd begun making love to her again against the shower wall, then finishing slowly in the bed. Already, he wanted to bury himself inside her again, couldn't imagine a time when he wouldn't want her, the silken softness surrounding him—

Jake straightened, his brows pulling together as he looked for the source of the niggling sense that he'd missed something. Something like—

Birth control.

Jake slumped back against the sink. How could he have been so careless? Even when he'd been married, he'd been careful. He combed a restless hand through his hair. Allie deserved better from him. He'd failed to protect her in the most basic of ways.

Yet, the thought of her pregnant didn't disturb him, in fact made him hungry with the primal need to fill her with his child. For the first time, he contemplated gritting through the panic brought on by thoughts of commitment. How far was he willing to go to ensure he didn't spend another lonely month without Allie?

Having the choice taken from them would certainly be the easiest way. He wouldn't have to worry about Allie bolting. He could simply have her forever.

Forever?

The word didn't stick in his throat anymore, not after the past month with only glimpses and brief encounters with Allie. Whether she realized it or not, she needed him.

Jake tugged his shirt over his head, unable to lie to himself. He needed her.

He stepped from the bathroom, buckling his belt. Seeing Allie, he paused. She sat, knees clasped to her chest, the sheet draped over her as she crumpled the empty cheese-puff bag. He was right. They would be good together.

She'd brought him light and laughter. He could offer her a constancy she'd seemed to yearn for growing up. They would be fine.

Cupping her neck, Jake dropped a quick kiss on her mouth. "I'll stop by in the morning. We can have breakfast together before we go to the courthouse." He stepped back before temptation led him into bed again. "See you in a few."

His hand gripped the doorknob when her voice stopped him.

"Jake?"

He pivoted to face her. That she sat utterly still clued him in she meant business. "What?"

"It isn't about jobs or uniforms. It's about the fact that you haven't said goodbye to Lydia."

Damned if Allie didn't go straight for the jugular. "You don't know what you're talking about."

"I know you can't just shut off the past, tuck it in your pocket like your dog tags and rings." The snack bag crackled in her clenching hand. "I don't expect you to care for me more than her. I just can't be second."

The bedside lamp, on its lowest setting, cast hazy shadows around room, not unlike those still smudging below Allie's eyes. Contentment fell away. Already he wasn't able to give her what she needed from him. He should have followed his gut instinct and stayed the hell away from her.

## Chapter 16

She couldn't let him open that door and walk away. Allie crumpled the cheese-puff bag and winced. She'd had the warm, fuzzy Jake back without the aid of pain medication, and now she'd ruined it with her big mouth.

Worse yet, she'd hurt him.

She should have been content. They'd had incredible sex. In spite of his talk of simple relationships, he wasn't a one-night stand kind of man. She had time to develop a relationship with him.

Why couldn't she stop herself from saying the very things that would send him running?

He turned, gripping the doorknob, but not moving. What would he do? Would he pull her close and reassure her?

Fat chance.

Most likely, he would walk out the door, and by breakfast he would pretend she hadn't spoken. All the while, her words would hover between them like a flashing neon sign.

She couldn't let him leave, not yet. Allie leapt to her

feet, launching herself against Jake's back, holding him until he turned, his arms looping around her.

His cheek fell to rest on her head. "Like you said, I can't just erase her from my past so you can be first."

"I know that."

His breath ruffled warmly through her hair. "Your mom found happiness the second time around."

"But she didn't love my real dad, not with a forever kind of commitment, and he sure didn't love her, not the way you loved Lydia—" Jake tensed in her arms. "I'm sorry, Jake. That wasn't fair to throw her in your face like that."

"Maybe. But it was honest. And that's okay. You don't have to apologize for saying what you're thinking."

A sigh shuddered through her. She should have known Jake would be fair. While she didn't think a relationship between them could ever be uncomplicated, she could bring him joy to smooth the furrows in his brow. It would have to be enough, for now, because she wasn't ready to let go just yet.

She offered him her best crinkled-nose grin. "I don't? Well, then, have I told you what a great butt you have?"

Jake pressed his forehead to hers. "Oh, honey, I've missed your smile."

For once, she welcomed thoughts of an uncomplicated approach. She was simply too emotionally raw for more soul searching. "Wanna make me smile some more?"

She circled her hips against his, her body still tender from their earlier lovemaking, but thirsty for another memory to store away. They seemed to have a problem returning to the real world, and she wanted to capture every moment left.

He quirked a brow. "So you want to, uh, smile again?"

She felt the tension ease from his hunk body, replaced

by a different, welcome tautness. Thank goodness he seemed as willing as she to put questions behind them for the moment. "Uh-huh. If you want."

"I always want to make you smile." Jake slid his hands beneath her jersey, palming both breasts simultaneously.

Their earlier encounters having eased the frenzied edge, Allie moaned as a more languid heat melted within her, like thick, rich chocolate sauce pouring through her veins.

Somewhere between the door and the bed, Jake swiped away her clothes before lowering her to the mattress. Her legs dangled off the edge as he braced over her, his head diving to graze his mouth along hers. She hooked her arms around his neck, her fingers twining lazy patterns in his close cropped hair.

Making love with Jake was incredible, bone melting. Kissing him was fun, unhurried, deep reveling in moist sips of his heady flavor. And Allie loved to have fun, needing lightheartedness now more than ever.

She slid her arms free, propping on her elbows to meet him more fully. She began creeping up the bed so he could stretch on top of her. Or maybe she could roll him to his back and—

Jake gripped her shoulders to stop her progress. Her eyes flickered open, but he had already transferred his attention to tracing a damp tingling trail down her neck. Gently, he tugged her nipples before resuming his tasting trek over her stomach, nibbling a detour along a hipbone.

"Jake?"

Without answering, he dropped to his knees between her legs. She had little doubt of his intent. He draped her feet over his shoulders, and she didn't resist or comment. In fact, she wanted the experience, but how embarrassing it was, this new first time, feeling more vulnerable and open to him than she had when they'd made love in the hut.

This seemed more intimate somehow. It involved an almost greater sense of trust to bare herself to him so completely. How like Jake to keep himself from her while she left nothing hidden.

She wished he would hurry up and start so she could stop thinking and—

He dipped his head and flicked his tongue over her once, twice, then more firmly circling the tender bud.

Thinking wasn't an option, or even a remote possibility.

Allie flung her arm over her eyes and surrendered. She forgot about embarrassment or restraint and granted her pleasure full expression with her moans.

Jake's persistence wasn't put to the test. All too soon she felt the tension in her womb foreshadow the building explosion. Already exhausted, her body didn't bother to resist or attempt to delay, but merely yielded to the rippling swells of release.

Weightless, her legs fell away. Jake pressed a final, nuzzling kiss against her, inciting an aftershock before he rested his cheek on her stomach. She wondered if she should be self-conscious, but decided it would be a waste of energy, and energy was in short supply at the moment.

Jake eased onto the bed, kneeling beside her and lifting her until she rested against the pillows. Her eyes fluttering closed, Allie burrowed into her pillow, but there wasn't anywhere to hide this time. She loved Jake Larson.

Allie stretched beneath the sheet, her muscles aching like after the first day of gym class. Memories of making love with Jake came flooding back. She blinked, trying to adjust her eyes in the still dark room.

Jake sat beside her, his back propped against the headboard as he stared at her. "Hi."

"Hi."

He dropped a kiss on her forehead. ''I really do need to leave now, but I didn't want to go without saying good-bye.''

Not ready for the world to intrude on her new feelings for Jake, she reached for him. ''Can't you stay for another few minutes? It's still dark out.''

He inched away with a groan. ''Tempting offer, honey, too tempting, but not a wise idea. I was going to wait to mention it, but we forgot about birth control and there aren't any White Sands complimentary baskets around here.''

Allie blinked fast while she processed the obvious. Why hadn't she considered condoms? What kind of modern woman was she to risk her health and body that way? ''I guess it's no secret I don't have any communicable diseases.''

''Me, either.'' His eyes darkened with a stormy, guilty cast. ''I should have protected you, though.''

She gritted her teeth against the temptation to argue with him. Had she ever met a man who wasn't obsessed with protecting her in one way or the other? She wanted something different from Jake. It took all her restraint not to club him with a pillow.

And pregnancy? There was nothing she could do about it. She would think about it if and when she had to. Meanwhile, she settled for a simple, hopefully non-combative, answer. ''It's a moot point now.''

Maybe she could divert him with an offer of reciprocal pleasure? Allie began her own tasting trek along his neck, the sheet falling away from her as she reached for the snap of his shorts.

He twirled a lock of her hair around his finger. ''Just so you don't worry, if you're pregnant, you know I would marry you.''

Passion effectively doused, Allie rocked back on her heels and clutched a pillow. She was willing to make allowances for Jake's reserved personality, but did he have to steal every one of her romantic notions? "Don't do me any favors."

"Huh? What did I say wrong now?"

He looked so totally clueless she couldn't stop the pang of annoyance, even anger. "If I'm pregnant, which I'm probably not given the timing, I'll take care of myself. I wouldn't hide it from you. But there's not a chance I would enter some loveless marriage like my mother did. Watching their marriage break up hurt a lot more than if I hadn't known what I was missing."

"Calm down." His hands fell to rest on her shoulders, massaging gentle comfort. "I was only trying to reassure you."

"Well, stop," Allie said, her chest heaving with frustration. His gaze drifted lower, settling on her breasts. His pupils dilated, and his breathing picked up speed.

Allie suddenly realized she was stark naked arguing with Jake. Once again, he sat with full shield protection while she waited, emotionally bare.

She snatched the sheet to cover herself. "This is a stupid conversation anyway. What happened to your 'keep it simple' attitude?"

"The consequences of this are a little more far reaching. I don't want there to be any misunderstanding." He cupped her bare shoulders. "Allie, I know you probably would have liked some prettier phrasing from me, but you've got to know, baby or not, we're probably heading toward forever. I doubt whatever's holding us is going to let go."

"Probably?" Why couldn't she have a genuine, all out expression from him, just once? Allie shrugged aside his touch and gave in to the urge to thump him with her pillow. A side swing caught him in the arm.

His shocked expression was worth it. "What was that for?"

"It's called 'love,' Jake! This thing that won't let us go is love. Why can't you say it? Why can't you admit it? Is it so hard to say the words to me?" As she raged at him, she saw him shutting down. But she couldn't stop the flow of resentment. She flung her pillow aside. "Am I a stupid virgin who misunderstood raging hormones for something more?"

"Allie, I just said otherwise. You're making this complicated again."

"Complicated? How complicated is it to tell me you love me like I love you?" Tears pricked at her eyes at the thought of losing him. But, he'd asked the one thing of her she couldn't give. She couldn't be the peaceful partner he'd found in Lydia. "Three little words. Either you do or don't. You're the one who's been in love before, so you can recognize the feeling. This is a first for me. Come on, Jake. Help me out here. Am I wrong?"

"Just because I don't put some label on it doesn't mean I don't have feelings for you. So why are we arguing about this? It makes me wonder if you're trying to shove me away." He stared back, brown eyes stilling her with their intensity. "Did you only say you loved me because I'm safe? You could tell yourself I'm just a cold jerk like your father, rather than admitting you're scared to take a risk on a real relationship."

Her spine stiffened. "That's not true."

"If you can't be honest with me, at least be honest with yourself."

When she didn't answer, he pushed away from her and crossed to the door, pausing as he had before, hand on the knob, broad shoulders raising and falling on a long exhale. "Allie, maybe you're the one who can't let go of the past."

The door eased closed behind him.

She started to fling his pillow after him, then clutched it to her stomach. He was wrong. Dead wrong.

But if he wasn't, what kind of person did that make her? A first-class coward.


Allie pushed awake through the gritty fog, a symptom of too little sleep and buckets of tears. Sun glinted through the slit in the hotel curtains, and she reminded herself it was a fresh day. Jake had said he would come to get her for breakfast. She would plaster on her best happy face and get through the day.

And if she was pregnant?

An image of Robbie and a new baby together was so bittersweet she bit her lip until she drew blood.

Jake would pursue her relentlessly. If she caved, she would have to live the rest of her life wondering if the ever-honorable Jake truly loved her or had simply done his duty. The thought only made her love him more. After years of tracking men who shed burdensome children as if they were no more than frayed clothing, she couldn't help but respect the innate goodness in a man who lived up to his responsibilities.

He would never abandon her, not physically. But were his vague offerings of unlabeled feelings enough to keep her love alive while she waited for him to catch up?

Her stomach grumbled, refusing to power her brain for further decisions until she downed some bacon and a stack of pancakes. She would show up at Jake's room and meet him for breakfast before he could come to her, giving her the edge of surprise.

Allie rushed her shower, combing through her hair and

leaving it free to air dry while she put on her typical lip gloss and swipe of blush. She took gulping breaths to steady her nerves.

She didn't waste a thought on glamour. Jake had left her with no doubts about one thing. He found her attractive, wanted her body, T-shirt wardrobe and all.

After a quick wriggle into her favorite purple dress, long, loose, flowing and suitable for her appearance at the court-house, Allie slid on one sandal, hopping as she put on the other. She snatched her purse and dashed out the door. She didn't want to give herself too much time to think. The chewing sensation in her stomach had nothing to do with hunger.

Inside the elevator, she stared at the flashing numbers increasing until she settled to a stop on Jake's floor. The doors swished open, and Allie charged forward, smacking into a brick wall chest. She braced a hand to keep from stumbling into the child the man held sleeping against his shoulder.

"Sorry about that." Allie glanced up, straight into the eyes of a face she'd hoped never to see again anywhere except in a courtroom.

The Pirate grinned back at her, Robbie nestled unconscious in his arms. "Hey, pretty lady."

Allie opened her mouth to scream and the goon, Bud, thrust her back inside the empty elevator. The force of his shove knocked the air from her lungs. Her shout muffled to a squeak.

Bud scowled as the doors slid closed. "I wonder what the boss is going to think of our two-for-one special?"

Jake stared in the bathroom mirror, splashing water on his freshly shaven face. He wasn't sure what his reception would be when he stopped by Allie's room, but he wouldn't give up. It wasn't in his nature.

Once Robbie woke, Jake planned to convince Allie to meet his parents in the dining room. Would she understand the significance of the gesture, or once again would she be disappointed by his lack of overt emotionalism? Why couldn't he simply make himself say the words she wanted since they meant so much to her and so little to him? The thought of losing her closed his throat.

Jake raked his change from the bathroom vanity to dump in his pocket. His dog tags and wedding rings glinted in the pile.

*You can't just shut off the past, Jake, tuck it in your pocket like your dog tags and rings.*

He hadn't shut off the past, merely moved on. Hadn't he? Allie's questions about his job choice rocked through him. She was right. He would be happier doing something along the line of investigating fraudulent investors. So why didn't he? Because it was easier to cut himself off from the past than think about it—or actually resolve it.

The job issue was easy enough to fix with an addition to his company. But what of the mess he'd made of his relationship with Allie? How did he start to fix that?

*I don't expect you to care for me more than her. I just can't be second.*

His feelings for Allie were just as strong as those he'd had for Lydia, different, definitely more tumultuous, but equally as constant. He should have told her that.

Damn it, he should have told her he loved her.

Jake stared at the rings in his hand and the truth whispered through his mind in a stilling realization. He hadn't feared loving Lydia more than Allie. Just the opposite. If he said the words to Allie that he hadn't been able to share with Lydia, he'd feared somehow betraying his wife again.

The chain dangled from his finger, the dog tags and rings swaying gently.

*It isn't about jobs or uniforms. It's about the fact that you haven't said goodbye to Lydia.*

How like Allie to make him blast it all out there in the open, unlike how he and Lydia would have quietly sifted through the issue, or have ignored it. He looked at both rings and realized Lydia had never said she loved him either, but he'd never doubted her for a minute.

His eyes slid closed, the guilt slipping away with it. Lydia had known, just as he'd known, because they'd thought alike.

But Allie was different. She had different needs, and he was failing her by not finding it within himself to offer her the reassurances the abandoned little girl inside her still required.

Jake set his course with a focus he knew would never waver. He would spend the rest of his life working to make Allie happy and secure.

He eased the chain into his shaving kit. Robbie might want the rings some day. The dog tags would make for good storytelling. But he didn't need the tangible reminders any longer. His past had reconciled itself with the man he'd become.

If only Allie could manage the same for herself.

The phone rang in the bedroom, pulling him from the past back to the present. Jake snagged his tie from the hanger as he ambled by the bed to answer before it woke Robbie. He watched the small form, curled and still beneath the covers in the other bed.

Tucking the receiver under his chin, Jake began knotting his tie. "Hello, Larson here."

"If you want to see your kid alive, you'll pay attention." His hands stilled on the tie. Panic twisted his stomach tighter than any knot. He launched the few feet to Robbie's bed and ripped aside the blankets to uncover two strategically placed pillows. The bed was still warm from Robbie's body. Jake swallowed down a mix of bile and rage. He'd been so close, only in the shower, yet he hadn't heard.

He clutched the phone, his only lifeline to his child. An inadequate calming breath later, he found the concentration to string words together. "Just tell me what you need. I'm sure we can work something out."

"No stupid stunts like calling the cops or your kid's gonna be in a world of pain."

Fury exploded within him until he wanted to claw through the phone line and pummel the man on the other side. "Listen you son of a bitch, if you hurt him there won't be a rock big enough for you to crawl under. Put my son on the phone, now."

"Calm down, pops. He can't chat right this minute. But there's someone here who can."

Crackling sounded as the phone shuffled hands.

"Jake."

Allie's voice punched clean through him. "Allie?"

"Jake, they've got both of us. Robbie's all right. They gave him something to make him sleep when they took him, but his breathing's good. I think he'll be fine. But Jake…"

His ears roared until he almost couldn't hear her speak. "Allie, keep talking."

Maybe she could slip him a hint, just some piece of information. And as long as she was talking, she was still alive.

"If it were just me, Jake, I'd tell you to nail these sons of a bitch. But there's Robbie…" Her voice grew distant as the phone was snatched away.

Jake willed his breathing to steady, his thoughts to stay clear.

"Listen up," the kidnapper said. "I'd be nice if I were you. We've got your kid, after all. But don't worry, he has your big-mouthed lady detective friend to keep him company. So if you want to see either of them again, you'll do what I say when you go to that courthouse today. And no funny business. We've got our man in the U.S. Attorney's office who'll be watching you every step of the way. The boss isn't at all happy with you and your snooping pal."

Jake's tie seemed to cinch around his neck. Lightning did strike twice. Once again, he could lose his family.

# Chapter 17

Sea spray stung her blindfolded face. Allie curled and unfurled her fists to restore circulation. She needed to be prepared for any chance of escape. With passing time, the possibility dimmed.

The gun in her side had kept her silent as the men escorted her and the still sleeping Robbie to a van. Bud had promptly bound, gagged and blindfolded her. An hour's ride later, they'd unloaded her into a speedboat. She'd almost panicked at the thought of drowning without the ability to fight.

She had to protect Jake's son, a child who'd already lodged himself in her heart. Given her feelings for Robbie, she'd had her first taste of maternal love, and it was a mighty motivator for survival. No way would she fall victim to the panic she'd experienced when the Pirate had stolen her and Jake the first time.

How far out to sea had they driven? With stalwart focus, she held on to her control for Robbie, for Jake.

The engine spluttered to a stop. Allie's stomach lurched. "Come on," Bud ordered, yanking her by the arm. "Quit dragging your feet and get moving."

She burned to ask him about Robbie, but the gag kept her from talking. Her idea of hell.

Bud's grip tightened as he propelled her forward. She listened for any reassuring sounds from Robbie as she struggled to board a ship or some large sailboat. Or at least it seemed such, given how far she walked to the stuffy cabin.

Allie sat huddled on the sofa for so long she lost all sense of time. Her grumbling stomach informed her she'd missed at least two meals.

The steady rolls of the couch beneath her felt all too familiar. Where was Robbie? What had they given him to make him sleep so soundly? Part of her was grateful they had thus far spared him the fear.

Could it have only been a few hours ago that she'd been in Jake's arms? Why had she wasted such precious time on stupid arguments?

Did it matter if she still harbored some resentment toward her dad for walking out on them? That had nothing to do with how she felt about Jake.

*If you can't be honest with me, at least be honest with yourself.*

She looked back over her childhood, trying to see it from Jake's perspective. As a child, she'd done her best to blend in with her new family so they wouldn't abandon her. As an adult, she'd opted for a no strings existence, a limbo state. Had she been any better than her father, dodging commitment?

The truth slid over her like a silky dress. She'd run the minute Jake had shown signs of genuine interest in a relationship.

She'd condemned her father for so long. How would she expect Jake to forgive her? And would they even have the chance to try?

Footsteps in the corridor grew louder until the door creaked open. Hope and fear duked it out inside her. At least she was through waiting.

"Time to talk," the Pirate's voice filled the cabin. Brusque hands untied her gag.

Once free, she coughed, swallowed and moistened her dry, cracked lips. "Where's Robbie?"

"All in good time. The boss wants to chat with you first."

The boss? Wasn't Phillips in jail, bond denied even though his goons had been released? "I'm not saying anything until you let me see Robbie."

Roughly, the Pirate yanked her to her to her feet. "You're not exactly in a position to bargain here, lady. But it's no skin off my nose if you see the brat."

Another set of footsteps clicked down the hall, stopping somewhere in the vicinity of the doorway.

"Allie?" The groggy voice wobbled.

"Robbie?" She stumbled toward the sound. A steely arm locked around her waist, and she nearly cried with frustration.

"It's okay," a woman said. "Let her see the kid. It doesn't matter anyway."

The familiarity of the voice niggled at Allie as the Pirate whipped off her blindfold. She blinked until her eyes adjusted to the light. They'd stowed her in small, but luxurious accommodations, even if she hadn't been able to appreciate them. Her gaze swept to Robbie, barefoot, pajama-clad, and wide-eyed with fear.

Holding Robbie's hand, tipsy, tacky Tonya stood silhouetted in the doorway. She sauntered into the room, wearing a bikini top and sarong, her sapphire belly-button ring matching the one dangling from the Pirate's ear.

With no time to waste on shock, Allie struggled to hasten the release of her hands. Once unbound, she held her arms out to Robbie. "I'm here, cowboy. It's going to be all right."

Robbie staggered across the cabin to Allie, apparently still muzzy from whatever they'd given him. "Where's my dad? I want my dad."

"So do I, cowboy. You'll see him soon, though." She hoped she hadn't lied. Gathering his wiry body close, she shuddered with relief. "Just be brave. Do what they tell you and be brave."

"How touching." Tonya sunk onto the opposing sofa, crossing her legs to reveal a perfectly tanned calf. "Sit. Let's indulge in some girl talk."

Silently, Allie perched on the edge of couch, tucking Robbie securely to her side, and waited for Tonya to set the tone.

"Well, Allie, it looks like I win the award for the most convincing bimbo act." Tonya smoothed back her sleek, gelled hair. "Although yours wasn't too bad. Getting that bank statement out of the planner in my bag was pretty slick. A shame Neil was the true moron for leaving a trail, and with something so insignificant, too."

Frustration threatened to overtake Allie as she struggled to unravel Tonya's motivations. The cop within her understood the need to discern the criminal mind in order to have any chance of getting out alive. "How could you have found out about that?"

"I have my people everywhere. Most everyone has a price, hon."

"Why? How much is enough?"

"It takes a lot of money to look this cheap."

Hysterical laughter bubbled inside Allie. A barrage of smart-mouthed quips zinged through her head, but for Robbie's sake, she had to stay in control. She doubted ''the boss'' would have revealed herself if she planned to let them walk out alive. The best Allie could hope for was to keep her talking until Jake found them. ''So you helped Phillips out with his operation?''

Tonya let loose an inelegant snort. ''How un-PC of you, Allie.'' She leaned forward. ''Neil works for me. He brings in the money from his little land scams, and I turn it into tax-free, clean cash in the Caymans.''

''Why are we here then? Why haven't you just left the country?''

Anger sparked in Tonya's eyes, just beneath her seeming calm. ''I don't like losing. You and your pal cost me a hell of a lot of lost revenues by shutting down my business.'' She glanced at her watch. ''Of course, he should have cleared all that up at the courthouse now. They'll be busy chasing their tails on the new lead he plugged in. Meanwhile, the half million ransom money for his kid will go a long way in soothing my anger.''

Which meant she planned to kill Jake once he arrived. Allie swallowed down a wad of panic. ''Just don't hurt Robbie, all right? He's too young to tell the police anything reliable.''

''Oh, my, all this maternal concern is really moving. Quite frankly, I never wanted things to get so ugly.'' Tonya smiled, the Pirate and Bud flanking her with protection. ''Those little notes we sent when you started digging around Neil's business had you on the run, even if you ran the wrong way right into our laps. I really felt bad about your little midnight swim, but you didn't leave me any choice, just like now. You should have listened to the messages, girlfriend.''

There had to be some way out. Jake must be working to find them. If only she could keep Robbie alive long enough. His warm body curled against her was such a sweet burden. "Maybe we can cut a deal. My private eye business sure didn't net me much of a profit."

"Tempting offer, but no thanks. What a shame we couldn't have been on the same side. You'd have made a much better ally than all these men. Never could trust any of them to multitask. As soon as Bud brings this little guy's dad— Well, I wouldn't want to upset the kid with the messy details."

Allie's mouth watered with fear for Robbie. Then the rest of Tonya's words penetrated. Jake knew where they were. Would he get to them before it was too late?

Her head pounded with a throbbing ache at the thought of never seeing him again. It was one thing to push Jake away when she could possibly have him back. But what if she died—or worse yet, he died?

Heaven help them all, she hoped he could disprove Tonya's theory on men being unable to multitask, because it would take more than a few miracles to save them this time.

Jake watched from the cigarette boat as they closed the miles between them and the looming luxury sailboat. Anger and rage waited, ready to surge free. He suppressed the impulse to wrestle the controls from Bud.

Were Allie and Robbie hurt? He refused to consider that they might be dead. He'd crawled out of the hellhole of grief after Lydia had died. He knew without question he wouldn't find his way free if he lost Allie and Robbie.

Jake gripped the suitcase with half a million dollars inside. He'd met the caller, Bud, at the designated pier with the ransom money. The fact that he hadn't been blindfolded only confirmed what he suspected. He didn't doubt he'd been lured into a snuff scenario by irresistible bait, Allie and his son.

He would either end the day with Allie and Robbie, or he wouldn't see the sun set.

The gap between Jake and the boat narrowed. A silent grouping of four on the bow's lounge deck eased into focus.

Like a beacon, Allie stood with her arms encircling Robbie in front of her. Her wild curls whipped around her head, lifted and tangled by the ocean breeze. A gun pointed at her side glinted like the cresting waves.

Jake swallowed back the metallic taste of nausea. He'd faced death more than once. This was worse.

How could he have ever doubted he loved her? Love for Allie and Robbie lashed through him with a painful, relentless momentum. He couldn't lose another woman he loved, he wouldn't. Again, he'd let time slip until he might not have the chance to go back and right the wrongs.

Yet, Allie looked so calm. How odd to take reassurance from her when he'd planned to supply it. Even from a distance, he couldn't miss her resolve, so very different from the way she'd reacted during their last experience at gunpoint.

Jake gripped the briefcase with the embedded tracking device. Now if only he could shield Allie and Robbie when the police and Coast Guard made their move. God, he hoped his parents were holding up as they waited with the authorities on shore.

Why had the caller thought he would actually adhere to the demands not to call the cops? Large withdrawals like he'd made would instantly flag the Feds' attention. With the Feds' help, he'd pretended to follow through on Tonya's request to plant information at the courthouse before withdrawing the cash. Coming alone wasn't an option.

To do so would have signed Allie and Robbie's death certificates. If he hadn't already.

Bud cut back the engine, gliding to rest against the side of the sailboat. Jake hauled himself up the ladder, the waves slapping his shoes. Bud trailed behind and secured the buoy rope.

On the lounge deck, Jake came face-to-face with his greeting committee gathered by the boat railing and nearly stumbled back a step.

What was Phillips's girlfriend doing here?

"Well, hello, big guy." Tonya slanted her painted mouth into a smile. She stood beside one of the goons, separating Jake from Allie and Robbie. "Glad you could join us."

Seeing the calculated gleam in Tonya's eyes, Jake felt the pieces slide into place. Too late, the hours of paperwork at the federal courthouse coalesced into the logical conclusion. He should have realized Phillips didn't have the brainpower to oversee such a large operation.

Jake risked a look at Allie, before shifting his attention to Robbie. "Hey there, kiddo."

"Hi, Dad." Robbie's voice trembled, his eyes filling as he moved to catapult forward.

Tonya stopped him with an extended arm. "Not yet, sugar. Your daddy and I have some business first. I need traveling cash for my trip out of the country."

At least Tonya had pretended she intended to let them live, saving Robbie from any more trauma while Jake planned his next move. One small thing to be grateful for.

There were too many guns around for his peace of mind. Their earringed pal looked trigger happy, gripping his weapon of choice, a Beretta. Bud's Glock waited, nestled in his waistband while he tied off the boat.

Robbie pressed his back against Allie as if he wanted to somehow climb inside her. Allie stood with one arm locked around Robbie, her other hand clutching the rail. Although Jake hated like hell that Allie was there, he couldn't regret the reassurance she'd brought his son.

The fierce light in her eyes awed him. God, they deserved a chance to be a family.

Jake's fist clutched around the leather handle. "I love you, kiddo. You just hang in there, okay?"

"Love you, too, Dad."

It was so simple to say, and he'd nearly blown the chance. Jake's gaze met Allie's and held. He didn't want to give these men more leverage by letting them know how much she meant to him. Would Allie see the love in his eyes? He certainly could see hers, and its strength humbled him. "Are you okay?"

Her smile was serene, belied by the rapid rise and fall of her chest. "We're fine. They haven't hurt us."

*Yet.* The word hung unspoken, but palpably real, between them. He hadn't found her only to lose her now.

He gathered his shredded concentration.

His best bet was in acting as if he believed they would let them live, delay the confrontation as long as possible. "Why don't we go below deck?"

A muggy ocean breeze coiled around them. Absently, Tonya flicked her belly-button ring with her thumb, then shook her head. "Right here's good. Open the case, handsome."

Jake swung the briefcase to a cushioned bench beneath the rail and popped the latch. Stacks of hundreds packed the case. Allie's gasp threatened his control. He couldn't afford another distracting glance at her.

He pinned Tonya with his best boardroom stare. "The full half million is there. I took care of your errand at the courthouse, so Phillips should be walking soon. Pick an island to drop us off while Phillips clears the system and you make your getaway. I'm not choosy.''

''Well, I haven't really decided yet. You know, the woman's prerogative to change her mind.'' Light splashes of fish in the background fused with the sound of Tonya clicking her nail against the sapphire-studded ring. The taps slowed as her eyes turned sultry. ''You wouldn't want to sway the odds in your favor, would you?''

A faint chop in the distance predicted the appearance of a helicopter. His time was running out. He needed Allie and Robbie out of the line of fire.

''As, uh, tempting as your offer is, I think I'll have to pass.'' Jake dangled the briefcase over the railing. He knew full well he would toss it overboard if it would buy him one minute to tell Allie he loved her. ''Let them go. Now, please.''

''Sorry, big guy, no can do.'' Tonya gave her belly-button ring a final click. ''As much as it pains me, I'm going to have to deny the world glimpses of your fine body.''

Tonya turned to the Pirate. ''Shoot them and unload their bodies where they won't wash ashore.''

Panic slashed through Allie. How could she ache this much, ripped in half by her fear for Jake and Robbie? She scanned the deck for options and found them to be next to nil. Her only choice would be to throw herself on top of Robbie and pray for Jake.

''The briefcase is wired for sound.''

Jake's declaration offered Allie a glimmer of hope. Of course Jake would have called the cops. Yet, even knowing the cops to be on their way didn't stop her respect for the lethal power of a bullet. Jake's broad chest made too perfect a target.

The briefcase swayed from Jake's hand out over the rail.

"The Feds have every word on tape. They're only waiting for my signal to take you. A signal you gave by threatening to kill us."

"Cops?" Just beyond Jake, Bud held the buoy rope in his hands, scanning the horizon with panicked eyes. A cutter loomed just in sight. Helicopter blades slapped a choppy rhythm in the distance. "Damn."

Bud tossed the line overboard and leapt into the boat.

The Pirate's gun wavered.

Allie saw her chance. The gun wasn't pointed at Jake after all, only her.

She shoved Robbie out of the way and kicked the nine-millimeter from the Pirate's grasp.

Jake sprung forward, the briefcase still clutched in his hand, and scooped the gun from the deck. "Let them go."

Her sense of victory lasted all of two seconds.

Tonya had Robbie. She held him securely in front of her and backed toward the railing, her Pirate pal cursing beside her. "I don't think that's a shot you're going to risk."

"Jake?" Allie looked into his eyes across the deck and in a flash, she knew her role. She didn't need him to say a word. Their combined strengths would get them through. Jake would keep Tonya distracted, while Allie closed in from behind. They could do this, together.

They had to.

His hand steady, Jake alternated his gun from the Pirate to Tonya, keeping both in place while Bud roared off out to sea. "You can't expect to stand there holding my son forever. We'll wait you out. Just give up before anyone gets hurt."

"Good advice. Not that I intend to take it." Tonya forced Robbie perilously close to the rail. She hefted him up and sat him on the brass bar. "Give my friend the gun and the money or your kid goes overboard."

Terror iced Allie. She stood on one side of Tonya, Jake on the other. Surely one them could get to Robbie.

She steadied her focus and inched closer. Not much further.

Slowly, Jake walked beside the boat's edge toward Tonya, gun in hand. Two fast blinks of Jake's eyes told her he wasn't as calm as he pretended to be.

She shook off the distraction.

Something in the Pirate's eyes bothered her. What was he planning? She scooted closer to Robbie.

While Jake had his gun trained on Tonya, the Pirate lunged for the briefcase. He sailed through the air clutching the briefcase as he jumped overboard. The dip and bob of the boat as the man went over the side jarred Tonya—and Robbie.

"Robbie!" Allie screamed. "Don't move!"

She launched forward, grabbing for Robbie's pinwheeling arms as he flailed backward. Her feet slid along the wet siding as she struggled to reach him.

She grabbed his wrist as he toppled over the side. Her grip slipped. She caught his fingers.

One tiny hand clutched hers as he dangled from her grip. His feet pumped at air.

Robbie. Jake's child. A child who'd smiled his way into her heart.

Help was so close, the helicopter whipping through the air. A police bullhorn sounded a call for surrender.

"Easy, son," Jake whispered, his voice deep and rich. He moved carefully, as if the least roll of the boat might dislodge Robbie.

Allie squeezed Robbie's hand. "Don't let go, cowboy! Whatever you do, don't let go!"

The roll of a deceptively small wave rocked the boat.

Allie spread her legs for balance. Jake grabbed Allie's waist to steady her. She tightened her grip.

Robbie's small, sweaty hand slid free.

"No!" Allie's shriek mingled with Jake's hoarse shout.

She grabbed for Robbie, but slipped sideways on the ocean-slick planking. Her head cracked against the deck. Dizzy with nausea, she could only listen in horror for his splash so minute, almost unheard.

Jake dove overboard only seconds behind his son. Allie cleared her foggy senses.

Leaving Tonya to the approaching Feds, Allie clambered onto the railing. She inhaled a breath, more for confidence than air, and jumped. For Jake, for Robbie, for the love she held for them both, Allie plunged into the briny ocean without fear.

*Well,* she conceded as water surged up her nose, *maybe a little fear, but without reservation.*

She propelled herself toward the surface, refusing to allow herself the luxury of closing her eyes against the salty sting. She searched, desperate for any sign of Jake and Robbie.

Allie scanned the rippling waves. She tread frantic, choppy kicks, until she spotted a splash.

Jake or Robbie?

Her arms sliced through the water as she kicked toward the movement. Her soggy dress tangled around her legs, slowing her. Jake resurfaced just ahead, seemingly unharmed. Beyond him, a small figure bobbed. A flash of blond hair kindled hope.

"Jake! Behind you!"

He jerked around, plunging toward what she prayed was Robbie. She swam toward them just as Jake emerged, clutching a spluttering Robbie to his chest.

"I've got you." Arm extended, Jake gathered Allie into

the circle. "I've got you both. Won't let you go. I love you. Do you hear me? I love you."

Allie heard and allowed herself to hope the words were for her, too.

Later that night, Allie sat on a quiet stretch of beach near their hotel, her legs clasped to her chest as she watched the sun set into the ocean. Wriggling her toes in the warm, squishy sand soothed her after a day that had been stressful beyond belief.

Only a few hours earlier she and Jake had almost died in the ocean again. They'd ridden to shore aboard the Coast Guard cutter, the foaming wake spewing as the space widened between them and the sailboat.

She and Jake had survived the ocean again, walking away with more strength than when they'd sprawled exhausted and apart on deck before.

This time, they'd shared the blanket, silently standing side by side as they watched a second boat haul away Tonya and her crew.

Robbie had been given a blanket of his own. With the resiliency of youth, he'd bounded around the deck, peppering the crew with questions they were all too ready to answer for their pint-sized rescuee.

Lord have mercy, she loved that kid, had since the day he'd charmed her with his gap toothed grin and heart-tugging concern for his father.

And now she loved the child's father, couldn't imagine a time she wouldn't. Jake had taught her about focus and constancy.

She stared out into the ocean and waited. Seagulls swooped and called, nabbing a late day snack from the beach. She knew Jake would join her once he'd settled

Robbie in the motel for an evening of grandparent spoiling and cuddling.

As she'd hoped, Jake's uneven steps sounded behind her, growing closer until he lowered himself beside her. He draped his arm over her shoulder, and they sat quietly while the sun surrendered inch by neon inch into the horizon.

Allie watched the rippling waves that could have covered them. In fact still covered Jake's money.

The wind whipped a strand of hair across her face. Allie pulled it free from her lip gloss. "Do you think the divers will be able to find the briefcase?"

"I honestly don't care."

Surprise held her silent, only the sound of the tide rushing in and out filling the air. Finally, she said, "You've got to be kidding."

"Not at all. We're all alive. Tonya and her henchmen are in custody, where they'll stay for a damned long time. Nothing else is important. Certainly not any amount of cash." He glanced down at her. "Allie, don't you understand? The money doesn't matter. That second of time it purchased was worth every penny if it kept you and Robbie alive."

Jake's arm, warm and heavy along her shoulders, cradled her to his side. Shimmers glided up her spine. "Maybe I'll take up snorkeling and hunt around for it myself."

His chuckle rumbled through his chest against her ear. "You sure got over your fear of the water fast."

Allie linked her free hand with his and held on firmly. "With you as my compass, I know which way is up."

He leaned back, gazing straight into her eyes, his deepening from amber to that intense, near-black shade. He pulled his hand free and cradled her face gently in his broad palm. "I love you, Allie."

Her throat closed right up. Could she believe him? She

squeezed her eyes shut so she wouldn't impetuously fall into his arms.

Jake stroked her chin. "Not exactly the answer I was hoping for." He tapped her nose. "Allie? Honey? Please look at me."

Her eyes fluttered open.

"What's going on here? Where's the lady who beamed me with a pillow last night?"

A much-needed laugh slipped free.

Jake's thumb caressed along her jaw. "Where's the incredible woman who faced down a gunman today?"

Allie crinkled her nose. "That was easy compared to this. Relationships, well Jake, frankly they scare me to death. These feelings I have for you scare me. I may have a fly-by-the-seat of my pants approach to life most of the time, but with something like this... My heart just can't withstand your keep-it-simple attitude." He had always been honest with her. She couldn't offer him anything less. "You're right about me not letting go of the past. I'm scared spitless we'll start a relationship and then you'll leave me."

She waited and hoped like crazy this man of few words she'd fallen in love with would find a way to reassure her that he not only loved her, but would do so forever. More than anything, she wanted forever with Jake.

"I can say 'I love you' a hundred times. But bottom line, you're going to have to trust me. I *can* tell you this. It takes time for me to make decisions, but I don't change my mind." He rested his forehead against hers. "Allie, I'm not your father."

Everything within her quieted. "I know that."

"Do you?"

"My father would be scouring the bottom of the ocean for his money."

Jake didn't smile, just stared with those serious golden brown eyes. "So your old man and I both have hefty bank balances. And yes, I know I'm not the most romantic of guys. But look deeper than that. Look inside."

How often she'd compared being with Jake to plunging in over her head. She'd worried about him being cold, only to find his emotions for Lydia were stronger than even he'd been willing to acknowledge.

Allie looked into his eyes again and searched, only to find those same churning emotions.

Directed at her. Jake loved her. Really loved her.

"My father wouldn't have come back to anyone who pushed him away." The world suddenly felt very still. "But you came back to me even after I shoved you away."

"And I always will."

Why hadn't she realized he had much more in common with her brothers? They were men of honor. Men of constancy. Men a woman could trust. How could she have missed the obvious? "Jake, I've been so—"

He silenced her with a brief kiss. "I love you. Not second, or in comparison to anyone else. I love *you*."

She smiled at him and didn't even need to hear the words, instead *seeing* his love. Why had she thought she needed flowery phrases? The truth was there for her to rejoice in any time she bothered to look, had most likely been there for quite a while but she'd been too blinded by her anger at her father.

Jake clasped both her hands in his. "Marry me, whether you're pregnant or not, it doesn't matter. Just say yes."

Allie looked into his eyes and dove straight in without fear or hesitation. "Yes."

"Yes?" His brows raised. "No more arguing?"

"Jake, I'm sure I'll argue with you many more times, but never about this. I do love you." She brushed her lips over his and savored the knowledge that she could always return for more. "Should we go inside and tell Robbie?"

"In a minute. There's something I have to say first." He gently squeezed her hands. The sun rested half way into the horizon, bowering them with a warm glow. "I promise to be honest with you. I will cherish your smiles and give you mine, share my laughter and my children, not frown when you sing off-key. And I will be your friend, your lover, your husband. Forever."

Speechless for once, Allie gazed into his eyes and saw beyond to the man within. Even more than the first time when she'd viewed his sexy, sweat-slicked body, she liked what she saw. "Oh, Jake, it took you long enough. But I love you just the way you are. Forever."

His mouth creased into a perfect smile, and she tipped her face to his, sealing their vows with a kiss. The ceremony, she knew, would only be a formality.

Tucked in her husband's arms, Allie relaxed against the steady beat of his heart and watched the sunset's benediction. She closed her hands over his as they stared out at that thin line where the very different ocean and sky become one.

# *Epilogue*

"How much do you cost?"

"Pardon me?" Police Detective Allie Larson glanced from the open file to the male silhouetted in her office doorway.

Great! Just what she needed. A leisurely lunch with her hunkish husband. Although it appeared it would be more than lunch. Jake looked like he needed a hot shower and change of clothes after his latest overseas flight tracking money-laundering scum.

"What am I gonna have to shell out for lunch?" Jake ambled into her cluttered workspace, the glass door smacking him on the back as it closed.

"Well, that depends." Allie tossed aside the file, just missing her lopsided pile of casework. Palms flat against the edge of the desk, she pushed to her feet. "I'm not sure just how hungry the twins are."

Her hands fell to rest on top of her slightly rounded stomach.

Jake sagged against the door, his eyes wide. "Twins?"

Allie nodded.

Jake gulped.

"When I went in for my checkup yesterday, the doctor picked up a second heartbeat. An ultrasound confirmed it." Allie bit her lip and prayed Jake would be as happy as she was. "We're having twins."

"Twins."

Jake's face creased into a perfect smile that still sent her heart into overdrive even after five years of marriage. And she knew it always would.

She and Jake had married immediately after her graduation from the police academy, both having learned from the Miami kidnapping the value of second chances. A small seaside ceremony, followed by a family picnic, had set the tone they'd wanted for their family-centered life together. A family multiplying faster than they'd anticipated.

Jake circled the desk and looped his arms around her disappearing waist. He dropped a lingering, sizzling greeting on her lips before pulling back. "I missed you."

"Missed you, too."

"I love you."

Allie sighed at the rush of pleasure and security those frequently spoken words always brought. "Love you, too."

His forehead fell to rest against hers as they held each other quietly, soaking up the feel of each other after their week apart. Jake stepped back and pressed his hands to either side of her stomach as if to cradle both children nestled inside.

"Twins." A corner of his mouth tugged into an irrepressible grin. "Then you'll be doubly hungry. What'll it be today? Pizza? Burgers? I've had my heart set on a sub since half way across the Atlantic."

"Well, Jake." She twirled his tie between two fingers. "I've had this weird craving all day."

"Banana shake? Chocolate-covered pretzels?"

"Kiwi."

"Kiwi?" A laugh rumbled low in his chest. "That's a new one."

Who would have thought her junk-food addiction would fly out the window with pregnancy? Her first couple of months, Jake had flooded her with surprise ice-cream treats, actually frozen yogurt in deference to good prenatal nutrition. All the same, at the first signs of snack foods, Allie had sprinted for the bathroom.

Yet she had gobbled her body weight in mangoes, bean sprout salads, zucchini and, Allie's mouth watered, tofu burgers.

"Yes, kiwi. And lots of it." She wrapped his tie around her fingers, drawing his head down to hers. She nibbled kisses along his jaw, up to his mouth. "Followed by a welcome home, long dessert in bed with my husband."

Jake growled, slid his hands to her hips, and urged her as close as her pregnancy would allow. "Sounds great to me."

Allie sighed and sagged against his rock solid chest. Listening to the steady beat of his heart, she asked, "What do you really think about twins? I mean, I joked about it all those years ago at White Sands. And it's kind of fun thinking fate meant us to be together even then. But how do you feel about two babies at once?"

Jake lifted a curl that had escaped from her braid and twined it around his finger. "I think Murphy's Law is at work again. And I couldn't possibly be happier about it."

\* \* \* \* \*

*Watch for Catherine Mann's exciting Air Force trilogy coming in September from Silhouette Intimate Moments.*

# INTIMATE MOMENTS™
## presents:

# Romancing the Crown

*With the help of their powerful allies, the royal family of Montebello is determined to find their missing heir. But the search for the beloved prince is not without danger—or passion!*

**Available in July 2002:**
**HER LORD PROTECTOR**
**by Eileen Wilks (IM #1160)**

When Rosie Giaberti has a psychic vision about the missing prince of Montebello, she finds herself under the protection of dashing Lord Drew Harrington. But will the handsome royal keep her secrets—and her heart—safe?

### *This exciting series continues throughout the year with these fabulous titles:*

*Available only from Silhouette Intimate Moments at your favorite retail outlet.*

## Silhouette®
*Where love comes alive™*

Visit Silhouette at www.eHarlequin.com

SIMRC7

**Where royalty and romance
go hand in hand...**

The series continues in Silhouette Romance
with these unforgettable novels:

**HER ROYAL HUSBAND**
by Cara Colter
on sale July 2002 (SR #1600)

**THE PRINCESS HAS AMNESIA!**
by Patricia Thayer
on sale August 2002 (SR #1606)

**SEARCHING FOR HER PRINCE**
by Karen Rose Smith
on sale September 2002 (SR #1612)

And look for more Crown and Glory stories in
SILHOUETTE DESIRE starting in October 2002!

*Available at your favorite retail outlet.*

*Where love comes alive*™

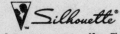

Discover the secrets of

# CODE NAME: DANGER

in

# MERLINE LOVELACE'S

thrilling duo

## DANGEROUS TO KNOW

When tricky situations need a cool head, quick wits and a touch of ruthlessness, Adam Ridgeway, director of the top secret OMEGA agency, sends in his team. Lately, though, his agents have had romantic troubles of their own....

### UNDERCOVER MAN & PERFECT DOUBLE

And don't miss
***TEXAS HERO***
(IM #1165, 8/02)
which features the newest OMEGA adventure!

*If you liked this set of stories, be sure to find*
***DANGEROUS TO HOLD.***
*Available from your local retailer*
*or at our online bookstore.*

*Where love comes alive*™

Visit Silhouette at www.eHarlequin.com                    PSDTK

# Silhouette®

# COMING NEXT MONTH

SIMCNM0602